SHADOW INVESTIGATION

CHRISTOPHER AMATO

Black Rose Writing | Texas

ISBN: 978-1-68513-194-4
PUBLISHED BY BLACK ROSE WRITING
www.blackrosewriting.com

Printed in the United States of America
Suggested Retail Price (SRP) $21.95

Shadow Investigation is printed in Gentium Book

PRAISE FOR
SHADOW
INVESTIGATION

"Move over, Jack Reacher. DEA agent Sam Dahl is coming to town. *Shadow Investigation* is a solid, seat-of-your-pants crime story, written with a legitimacy only possible from former law enforcement."
–Brooke L. French, author of *Inhuman Acts*

"Christopher Amato has written a must-read thriller with razor-sharp dialogue and richly-drawn characters. I can see this book becoming a movie based on the action, excitement, danger, and romance, coupled with the characters' use of authentic investigative methods."
–Gregory D. Lee, retired DEA Supervisory Special Agent and author of *Global Drug Enforcement: Practical Investigative Techniques*

"Amato's *Shadow Investigation* features crisp dialogue, insightful character development, and a fast-moving plot that never jumps the shark. A thoroughly-enjoyable crime thriller!"
–Brian Kaufman, author of *Sins in Blue*

"Christopher Amato relies on his years of experience working as a federal agent to walk the reader through a fascinating and harrowing story about a DEA Agent who battles with a drug cartel, and in the process, finds himself fighting for his very life."
–Ernie Dorling, author of *The Truth is Always Negotiable*

"As a favor to his sister, DEA Special Agent Sam Dahl flies his investigative skills to Florida, where he finds a little love, feels a lot of pain, and makes one awful "friend." Christopher Amato's book has the feel of a classic."
–Gillespie Lamb, author of *The Junkyard Dick*

"When a DEA agent decides to trust his gut and take a chance on another case, he unlocks the truth about a world that would rather hide in the shadows of society. In *Shadow Investigation*, author Christopher Amato mixes suspense, intrigue, and a bit of romance to keep you hooked until the very last page."
–Stephanie Letourneau, author of *The Call of Uwyn*

Dedicated to Stella, the best little buddy anyone could ever have.

SHADOW INVESTIGATION

CHAPTER ONE

Gulf of Mexico
August 1987

"Maybe it's my imagination, but that looks like the same boat that was shadowing us yesterday." Ben Jansen stood at the helm of the vintage Chris-Craft yacht, peering through binoculars across the still Gulf waters. "I think it moved even closer to us overnight," he said, drumming the tips of his fingers on the wheel.

His wife Carol stood behind him and hugged her arms around his waist. "Who's ready for breakfast?"

Ben bit into his lower lip, a decades-long habit he practiced when he was uncertain about something. "Looks like a Sunliner to me. I'm betting it's almost new, probably the 1986 model." His stare remained fixed on the distant craft. "Strange how it just seems to be hanging out there."

She poked his side. "Hey, Skipper, um, hello?"

"Forty-six-footer, if I remember correctly," Ben said, more to himself than to Carol. "It's a high-quality craft with a modified-V hull design, constructed of fiberglass, an aft cabin, and twin inboard diesels."

She squeezed his arm. "It's my turn to cook, remember? How would you like your eggs? Sunny-side up, scrambled, or hard-boiled?"

He wasn't finished yet, adjusting the thumbwheel on his binoculars for better focus. "Runs at twenty-six knots top-end speed, or maybe even twenty-seven."

"Now you're just showing off," Carol said. She stepped back and put her hands on her hips.

He whistled before clamping down on his lower lip more fiercely. "She's a beauty, but I just don't get it."

"We can rule out sunny-side up for you today," she said.

Ben lowered the binoculars to his chest and turned to look at Carol. "Sorry, I'm distracted by that boat out there. Let's see, scrambled sounds good with extra pepper. Bacon too?"

She patted his stomach. "That's more like it. Be ready soon." Her lean figure slipped away toward the galley.

Ben rested his hands on the helm, losing himself in thought, admiring the luster and richness of the wheelhouse cabinetry and woodwork. Everything was new: the refinished hull, the meticulously crafted mahogany with maple inlay decking, powerful twin diesel engines, extra-capacity fuel tanks, right down to the shiny buttons, switches, and instrumentation. Sure, it cost a pretty penny, and it had taken two years, but it had been worth it; their precious yacht had been completely refurbished.

Scanning the horizon, he was overcome by the extraordinary scene that lay before him: an endless blue sky converging with an even deeper blue sea. At that moment, he could almost taste nature's complexion of rich colors and breathe in the beauty and serenity surrounding him. He knew that miles away, Florida's coastline protruded from the Gulf, a bit too far-off to see, even with the aid of his binoculars.

Carol said, "We're close to ready, just waiting on the toast."

Roused from his thoughts, Ben took a last look at their mysterious companion to the east. "It's a big pond. I guess there's room for both of us," he said in a quiet voice.

The tantalizing aroma of sizzling bacon had beckoned, and now his mouth watered as he slid into the cushioned bench seat across from Carol.

She cleared her throat. "This is a binoculars-free zone."

Ben looked down. "Oh, yeah." He removed them from around his neck and placed them on the deck. "All right," he said, clapping his hands. "Breakfast looks terrific."

She reached to the counter behind her for the saltshaker. "You may want some; I didn't use any when I was cooking."

"Thanks, just a smidgen," Ben said as his gaze wandered through the galley. "I sure like the design and the layout of the kitchen. Don't you?"

Carol nodded in agreement. "I think it's gorgeous, and you know, I love teak, but I'm glad we went with the mahogany. Your man knew what he was doing; that's for sure."

"Tom is the *best*. At first when he said it would take him two years, I was, well, I don't know how I felt, but that's why he's in such demand. Looking back now, I realize how lucky we were to have him."

"I'm sure he also recognizes he got the best neurosurgeon in the business. He appreciates you, and I'm certain his wife does too."

Ben scooped up a forkful of egg and stopped before sliding it into his mouth. "She was a challenging case." While his eyes fixed on the polished sink and faucet behind the table, he recalled performing the risky but necessary craniotomy to remove a two-inch tumor from Shelly Houseman's brain. "They're all delicate procedures, but that one was a doozy."

Ben chased the egg with a slice of bacon and a bite of toast. "There's something about eating breakfast, or any home-cooked meal, on our boat, right?" Ben said, smiling at Carol.

"I know. It's great." She returned the smile.

He looked around, still mesmerized by the total makeover. "Now that the work is done, it was all worth it, with the stripping, sanding, staining, and sealing." He swallowed another mouthful of egg, barely chewing, before speaking again. "It's like brand new, modernized inside and out, but still packaged in its original box."

"She's your baby." Carol raised her coffee mug to clink Ben's cup.

"Hold on a second; she's *our* baby," Ben said, leaning back and gazing at the ceiling. "After one night out here, I'm thinking it may be time to hang up my scalpel and retire."

Carol sipped her coffee and nodded. "I think that's a great idea, Ben." She dabbed at her mouth. "So, when do you think we'll arrive in Sanibel?"

He used his fork to push the last strip of bacon through egg yolk. "I'm in no hurry; you tell me what you'd like to do."

"No hurry for me either; I was just curious," Carol said.

Ben rose to his feet and stretched. "You want to shoot for an easy day and enjoy the beautiful weather?"

"Sounds good to me." She raised her eyebrows. "Maybe we'll go skinny-dipping?"

"Now you're talking," he said. "We can arrive around dinnertime, if you'd like."

"Okay, that works."

He nodded toward his coffee cup. "You're coming with me." He took two steps and turned back. "I'll need these too," he said, picking up the binoculars.

After Ben reached the helm, his muscles stiffened when he noticed the boat stalking them had closed the gap and was only a few hundred yards off their port side. Tentatively, he reached into the cubbyhole under the wheel and retrieved a snub-nosed revolver, tucking it into the back of his pants. A young blonde-haired woman appeared to be staring in his direction.

Ben said, "Carol, looks like we have company with that boat I was talking about earlier."

"I'll be up in a minute. Would you like more coffee?"

"No, I'm good." He maintained his focus on the approaching boat as an uneasiness settled into his thoughts.

When Carol reached the wheelhouse, she put her arm around Ben's back. "So, what's going on with that boat?" Her hand grazed the firearm's rubber grip panel. "Do you think that's necessary?" she asked.

Red-faced, he shrugged. "I guess not." He knew the meaning of the frown on Carol's face; she didn't like guns and never had. He kissed her forehead and said, "I'm being overly cautious." While he took a long look through the binoculars, his hand instinctively hovered near the engine's push-button start.

Carol touched his arm. "Can I see?"

"Sure." He removed the strap from around his neck and handed the binoculars over.

"She's just a girl," Carol said. "Well, a young lady." She was about to hand Ben the binoculars but took a second look. "Ben ... she's pregnant."

"Looks like it. She keeps staring. Not moving at all," Ben said.

"Maybe they have a problem and need our help."

"I don't know." Ben shook his head. "The way they're moving toward us, it looks like we'll find out soon enough." He checked their coordinates and made a mental note in case he needed to make a radio call.

Carol said, "Look, there's someone else, a younger guy, maybe in his thirties."

Ben reached for the binoculars, even though they weren't necessary anymore. "I see him. They're youngsters, that's for sure."

The newcomers' boat idled about thirty feet away.

"Hey, can we talk?" The woman's voice carried across the water.

Carol and Ben left the helm and edged to the port side.

"We didn't mean to startle you," she said, hugging herself. "We've been having trouble with our boat." She wore jeans shorts, a bikini top, and despite the warmth of the morning sun, a light blue cotton jacket partially zipped up.

"What seems to be the problem?" Ben asked.

She smiled. "Sorry, that's my husband's department."

The man Ben had seen through the binoculars appeared and now stood behind his wife, his hands resting on her shoulders. "We've had problems for the past twenty-four hours with the engines. They run, then cut out, then they run again." His face clouded over as he spoke. "I can't figure it out. I guess it could be an electrical short, because our radio has been out too, but I don't know."

Ben noted he spoke English with a slight accent.

"You might have noticed," the woman said as she rubbed her belly. "I've got one in the oven."

Carol turned toward Ben and whispered, "She's adorable." Looking again toward their boat, Carol asked, "You've got water to drink and something to eat?"

Ben frowned inwardly, thinking in all his years of boating, he'd never seen a vessel approach so suddenly without signaling first. He wasn't ready to drop his defenses yet and said, "What can we do to help? We can radio the Coast Guard for you, and they could be here within an hour or two."

The woman looked toward Carol. "We're not sailors. I told Moncho, my husband, we're not ready for this, but you know men, right?" she said and laughed, then abruptly stopped. "I'm really scared because we didn't prepare for this trip the way we should've. I would, I would love something. A cup of water or a piece of fruit or crackers?" She put her hand to her abdomen. "We can't take care of ourselves, and now I'm going to be a mom." Her head sunk toward her chest.

The faintest, gray wisp of smoke drifted from inside the strangers' boat.

Carol turned toward Ben. "Can't we at least help her?"

The young woman looked up and spoke again. "I'm ... I'm not sure I'm ready for any of this." She hugged her trembling body.

Carol started to say something but stopped herself. She looked back at the lady. "Dear, you come over here on our boat, and we'll get you something to eat and drink. I promise you everything's going to be all right."

Ben said, "I'm not sure that's such a good—"

"Listen, come a little closer to us, and I'll throw a line over," Carol said.

Ben didn't like the idea, but he'd been overruled.

The strangers' boat engines revved for a second, closing the distance between them to less than ten feet.

"What's your name?" Carol said.

"I'm Beth, well, Elizabeth, actually."

"I'm Carol and this is my husband Ben. You're going to be okay; I promise."

Beth whimpered and wiped her nose with her sleeve.

Carol tossed the rope. "Secure it to your boat, honey, and we'll pull you over the rest of the way."

Ben didn't like the whole idea, not a safe maneuver to perform at sea, but he knew there was no stopping Carol now. He said, "Let's make sure we have the fenders in place before we tie together." At least he'd protect his own boat.

While Carol extended her hand to help Beth over the gunwale, Ben marched toward the closest marine fender to reposition it.

"Hey, Mister, I appreciate your help," the man said to Ben. "By the way, I'm Moncho."

Ben wasn't interested in any chitchat, especially since he saw that the smoke coming from their hold appeared to be increasing, and he was damned sure he wanted no part of a fire. He watched Carol hold the young lady's hand as they disappeared into the galley. Ben said, "Listen, uh, Moncho, you should check on that smoke; it smells like something cooking."

"I'll do that as soon as I take care of this," Moncho said as he turned to reach behind him. The spear launched with a popping sound, tearing through the skin and tissue of Ben's upper abdomen. The projectile's tip clipped his right lower lung and came to rest deep inside his liver. Ben's mouth moved, but he could only produce bloody bubbles.

Dropping the speargun, Moncho leaped in one fluid motion to the Jansens' boat.

The sudden massive shock to Ben's system made it difficult for him to process the assault or even utter a sound. He had performed countless surgeries for over thirty years and realized in a split second what only a few unfortunate patients in his care had ever experienced. Looking coolly dispassionate at the protruding spear, he knew death was calling him.

"Hey, what's this?" Moncho said, ripping the gun from Ben's beltline. "Listen, old timer, you won't need this where you're going."

Feeling a strange calm and peace with fate's decision, Ben allowed himself to be guided to the edge of his beloved boat. With his brain shutting down, his eyes strayed toward the horizon until Moncho saluted, prodding Ben's failing mind to question if he should acknowledge the gesture.

"Captain, you're relieved of command," Moncho said.

It took nothing more than a quick shove to send Ben headfirst into the seawater. His body scarcely moved, floating at the surface. The blood that had once flowed through his veins leaked into the sea, beckoning the sharks lurking nearby.

Moncho jammed Ben's pistol into his back pocket and ambled across the boat, ducking his head as he entered the galley. "Hey, babe, we're all finished up there."

Beth smiled at Moncho, then turned to Carol and said, "Thank you so much for the toast and water, but what I've got a thirst for now is vodka."

Carol eyed Beth uncertainly. "But you're ... you're pregnant."

Beth unzipped her jacket. "Look, Moncho, I just had a one-pound baby pillow."

Moncho hooted and clapped. "Cool. Let's celebrate."

Carol turned her head in the exit's direction, screaming, "Ben! Oh, God. *Ben!*" She rushed from the sink, but another man in the doorway blocked her path to go up on deck.

Moncho also turned and said, "There you are, amigo. Did you bring us some botanas to snack on?"

Well over six feet, the man had long, stringy hair and a beard that hung past his chest. He held a plate of sizzling strips of chicken, slid one into his mouth, and spoke while chewing. "Muy sabroso." Then he put the plate on the table and wiped his hands across the front of his pants before turning his dark eyes toward Carol. Speaking with a heavy accent, he said, "Hey, sweet mama, it's time me and you get to know each other."

Carol screamed, backing up against the counter filled with dishes from the morning's breakfast. She shoved glasses and plates aside to locate a weapon, then grabbed a fork and a frying pan.

The man pulled at his beard and licked his lips. "Oh, so you like to play rough, yes?"

Carol sobbed, her eyes imploring Beth. "Please don't let him hurt me."

Beth tossed the pillow on the floor and took Moncho's hand. "Let's go check out our new boat."

CHAPTER TWO

Los Angeles
September 1987

For most, people watching was a casual activity, done subconsciously without realizing they were doing it, but this wasn't the case for Drug Enforcement Administration Special Agent Sam Dahl. Not today. Not here. Not now.

It wasn't like he didn't notice the idiosyncrasies and other harmless activities of people; he did, but for Sam Dahl, there was a science to people watching, and it came with years of training and practice.

His steel-gray eyes searched for a traveler—a man who had been described as Hispanic, forty years of age, medium height, heavyset, black hair, and clean-shaven; he was supposedly wearing a wrinkled brown suit jacket and carrying a black leather briefcase.

As Sam scoured the area around Gate Eighteen in Terminal Six, he saw a young couple chasing their toddler, probably hoping the boy would tire himself out before the flight. Ten feet from where he stood, a businessman balanced an open briefcase on his lap. Sam doubted the man was aware he wore mismatched socks. In his peripheral vision to his right, a passenger was imploring an airline agent to bump him to first class, pleading his case that as a busy, important lawyer, he required the extra space.

Sam made the observations, one after the other, but dismissed them with a quick efficiency. He scanned the gate area patiently, knowing the man was somewhere close by; it would only be a matter of time as he worked the space one section at a time. Sure enough, across a sea of travelers—the anxious, the bored, and the nappers—he spotted his target standing at a bank of pay phones, his briefcase on the floor between his feet. The man unhooked a phone from its cradle, but he put no coins into the slot, nor did he use a calling card. He just stood there, looking around without speaking, while he held the phone against his ear.

Sam decided the subject was a people watcher himself, with his head moving left and right, then right and left. By Sam's count, the man had been holding the phone for three minutes when his law enforcement partner entered Gate Eighteen and joined him. Sam nodded, but he continued his watch of the phone bank area.

"I got here as fast as I could. What's happening?" Blue said.

"Got a call about a lone Hispanic male doing a quick turnaround back to Tampa. He paid cash for a one-way ticket in the name of Angel Martinez and checked a large Samsonite suitcase. Hard-sided, dark gray. He's the guy with the phone glued to his ear, acting like his head is on a swizzle stick."

Blue was tall, and he used his height to his advantage to look over clusters of people to find the subject. He was lean too and had often claimed that even at fifty-four, he could still dunk a basketball. Although Blue's claim was unproven, Sam didn't doubt it. Blue was one of those guys who had been blessed with genes that kept a person forever young.

"I see him. Damn, Angel looks like he stepped on a wrinkle bomb." Blue let loose with a deep belly laugh, the kind that carried through the wide-open airy terminal with ease, reverberating off the walls and glass. "Dude better ease up twisting his head around, or he'll strain a neck muscle. Was it Becky at ticketing who called?" Blue asked.

"Yeah, she said he was nervous and kept checking to make sure he had locked his suitcase; then he wouldn't take his eyes off it until it rolled away on the conveyor. He's been using the pay phone as a prop for the last few minutes. No coins, no card, just watching."

"Sounds like a live one to me."

"Five minutes ago, Eastern announced that the flight was delayed, so that gives us time to work him. I've seen enough; let's go talk," Sam said.

They moved purposefully but without hurry. When they had closed to within ten feet, the man hung up the phone and reached to grab his briefcase.

"Excuse me," Sam said, holding out a laminated airport ID card that identified him as a law enforcement officer. "I'm Agent Dahl, and this is Agent Baxter. Can we talk?"

"Is there a problem?" the man said.

"No, just routine stuff. We're talking to people waiting on flights. It's voluntary." At six feet, two inches tall, Sam had at least four inches on the man and stood perched like a hawk on a cliff, eyeing its prey below. "Are you on the Eastern flight to Tampa?"

"Yes."

"Like I said, we're just chatting with folks. Would you mind showing us your identification?" Sam said.

The man lowered his briefcase to the floor and reached into his jacket pocket to remove his wallet. "Here's my driver's license," he said, holding out his ID.

Sam studied the license for a moment, comparing the identification picture with the individual standing before him. "Hector Rojas. Tampa, Florida?"

"Yes, that's me."

"Thank you, Mr. Rojas." Sam noted the discrepancy in names, but he'd address that later. "Is this your current address?"

"More or less," Rojas said. "The place is my cousin's, and I just crash on the couch when I'm there."

"Gotcha." Sam returned the license to the man.

"I need to catch my flight," Rojas said, bending over to pick up his briefcase.

"You may not have heard; it's delayed. They announced a short while ago that there was a problem, which could mean a lot of things, like a minor issue or maybe not," Sam said. "You know these airlines; it seems like they never tell you what's going on."

Rojas released his grip on his briefcase and straightened. "I didn't hear anything, but I was on the phone with my business associate."

"I see." Sam nodded. "Look, Mr. Rojas, again we're just having a little voluntary chat, you understand? So, what kind of work do you do?"

"I work for an auto parts supplier in Mexico."

"That's cool. What's the name of your company?"

Sam employed a distinct practice while conducting inquiries; he often stood at a distance that most people would consider a violation of their normal personal space. He had found from experience his tactic helped in gaining an individual's willingness to continue in conversation. To that end, Sam drew even closer to the man.

"It's called A and R Distribuidora, but I'm sure you've never heard of it," Rojas said. Small beads of sweat began to form on his forehead.

"I don't know. I'm into cars, so maybe I have."

Rojas removed a handkerchief from his pocket and wiped the sweat from his brow. "It's hot in here."

"You think so? We can sit down." Sam motioned toward the empty seats nearby.

"No, I'm just a little warm."

Sam took a step to the side, allowing a wheelchair attendant to guide an elderly woman toward the gate agent.

"That's the thing about LAX," Blue said. He'd been standing near Sam but had refrained from interrupting. "A lot of folks say it looks more like a gigantic bus station instead of an airport, and that may be right, but they keep the temperature between sixty-eight and seventy-two degrees, all day and all night." Blue looked around and smiled. "I'll let you in on a little secret, Mr. Rojas; sometimes I come here in the summer just to chill out."

"Maybe I'm a little nervous about flying."

"I get that part." When Blue laughed, Rojas joined him.

Sam restarted the questioning. "So, you're on a business trip to Los Angeles?"

Rojas began nodding before answering. "Yes."

"Did you meet with anyone out here?"

"I met with a company that buys parts from us," Rojas said as his eyes searched the gate area. "I, I should catch my flight."

Sam knew Rojas was losing patience with the conversation.

"Nah," Sam said, waving his hand toward the tarmac outside. "When they say the flight's delayed, that's code for 'settle in, folks, you'll be stuck here for a long while.'" He pressed forward. "So, when did you arrive in Los Angeles?"

"Last night, late, yes, it was very late."

"A quick turnaround. Those are killers, aren't they?"

"Yes, I'm tired," Rojas said.

"I get it." Sam stretched his back. "Let me ask. Do you have any luggage?"

Rojas looked around and breathed heavily. "No, just my briefcase."

Sam could sense the man was close to shutting down the Q and A, so he quickly fired off another question. "Would you mind if I looked at your ticket real fast?"

Rojas hesitated; then he reached into his jacket pocket and removed an envelope that had a ticket receipt and boarding pass inside.

Sam studied the ticket for a few seconds. "Mr. Rojas, this is interesting because this ticket was issued to Angel Martinez. May I ask why you're flying under a different name than your ID?"

"I do a little stuff in security."

Sam stroked his chin and said, "And what does that mean?"

"I should say it's more a hobby; I like to test the system by using different names." Rojas slid his hands into his jacket pockets. "You understand?"

"Not so much, no." Sam tapped the ticket with his finger. "I see you paid cash."

"Yes, I did. Is that a problem?"

Sam ignored Rojas's question, knowing it was time to go for the jugular. "This is odd." He pointed to the back of the ticket envelope. "This is a receipt for checked luggage, so when you arrive in Tampa, you can prove the bag or suitcase is yours. I'm thinking this must be a mistake, because I thought you told us you didn't have any luggage." Sam turned to his partner. "Did I hear that right?"

Blue nodded at Sam, then turned to Rojas. "Sorry, man, but you did say you only had a briefcase."

"This heat is making me crazy." Rojas snapped his fingers. "I'm not sure what I was thinking before, but yes, I checked a suitcase."

The scratchy sound of the overhead speaker system forecast a gate announcement: *"Attention Eastern Airlines passengers waiting on Flight Eleven to Tampa. Because of an equipment problem on board the aircraft, we're looking at a ninety-minute delay. As we receive additional information, we'll pass it on."*

After the collective groans from awaiting passengers died down, Sam refocused his attention on Rojas, staring into his eyes. He thought he could read the resignation on Rojas's face and paused a moment before turning to his partner to hand him the ticket envelope. Blue slipped a pen and a small pad of paper out of his blazer pocket.

Sam looked at Rojas and said, "Agent Baxter is going to write these numbers down. I want to make sure you've got the right bag. That's okay with you, right?" Sam's eyes swept the gate area before turning back to Blue. In a low whisper, he said, "Bobby's already on standby. You want to give him a shout and tell him to bring the dog over?"

"On it," Blue said. He pulled a radio from under his jacket and walked away.

"I should call my boss to say the flight's delayed," Rojas said.

"I've got a great deal for you. You can use the phone in our office to make your call for free."

"That's kind of you, but I should call him from here."

Sam leaned forward and said, "Here's what's strange. A little while ago, I started watching you from the time before you picked up the pay phone until you hung it up. For those few minutes, you just looked around while standing here holding the phone, but you put no coins in, and you didn't use a calling card or press any numbers to make a call. And I never saw you open your mouth to speak with anyone."

"I can't explain what you think you saw," Rojas said, holding his hands out with his palms facing up.

"Not a problem. I jotted down the time, so I could check with the telephone company to see if you connected with another phone." Sam turned down the corners of his mouth. "Let me ask you a question. If we were to search your suitcase, what would we find?"

"Clothing, souvenirs, you know, gifts."

"And that would be everything?"

"Toiletries too, but yes, that's it."

Sam took a quick peek at the time on his watch; he was certain the dog handler would be on his way to where Blue was waiting with the suitcase. "Here's how this works," Sam said. "As I've said to you before, this conversation is voluntary on your part. You're traveling under a name that doesn't match your Florida ID, and I question whether you spoke to anyone on the phone. You've made inconsistent statements, including when you said you didn't have any luggage, then you admitted to having a suitcase. And—"

"Yes, but I'm tired from the trip," Rojas said.

"Fine, I understand. Look, you don't have to come with me, but we're going to have a trained dog check the suitcase for the scent of illegal drugs. You can watch, it's up to you. You're not under arrest, but I'm inviting you to walk with me to check on your luggage. Anytime you change your mind, you'll be free to go."

Rojas's shoulders slumped. "I'll go."

Roy DeLuca had decorated the budget-friendly wood-paneling in his office with an assortment of plastic framed "attaboy" certificates covering his thirty-one years of government service. Seated behind his desk, he loosened the bold paisley tie that seemed to have a stranglehold on his thick neck. "That was good work today, guys," he said with a heavy Jersey accent.

"Sam did all the talking. I just watched and learned from the master," Blue said, patting his partner on the back.

"Roy, this was a straightforward case. He didn't even resist opening his suitcase after the dog alerted," Sam said. "Maybe he's new to this money courier racket; I don't know. Now, if I were in the business of giving advice to these folks, I'd suggest they at least have a good cover story for their travels."

"How much cash are we talking about?" Roy asked.

"Five hundred fourteen thousand dollars and change," Sam said. "As usual, twenties and hundreds were the most common denominations."

Roy lifted himself from the chair. Moving around the cramped office was difficult, the problem compounded by Roy's size. A large man, years of inactivity had led to his pear-shaped body. He moved sideways around his desk toward the doorway, stopping at a chalkboard used to track a running tally, by month and year, of seized drug money.

He stood at the black slate hung on the wall, erasing the old figures, and writing the new totals. "Listen, guys," Roy said, studying the numbers, "we're ahead of the pace to break our annual record for money seized. Today's the fourth of September, so we've got twenty-six days left in fiscal year 1987." He tapped the chalkboard and turned. "Come on, we can do it," he said with encouragement. "What do you think about us getting the record? It'd be a real feather in our cap if we could."

Sam said, "Sure, Roy, we'll do our best. Listen, I'd like to follow up on leads we've developed from talking to this courier today. Plus, we made photocopies of a bunch of interesting documents from his briefcase and wallet."

Roy returned his attention to the board. "Did you hear what I said? I need you out there in the terminals."

"We've got other agents here too," Sam said.

"Yeah, but none like you and Blue. You have all the contacts, and we're so damned close. I won't be here forever, and I'd like to have the record before I retire."

Sam said, "You can still get it. I'll be around and Blue will be here too, but sometimes I'd like to do my own follow-up on the information we learn from these couriers."

Roy turned. "Look, Sam, the answer is no. Copy everything and turn it over to Group One downtown. It's their job to work the drug cases with ties to Latin America."

"What difference does it make if I do it?"

"I don't make the rules, but that's how it works."

Sam leaned forward, planting his hands on his boss's desk. "Come on, Roy, just for once, let's say screw the rules. All the confidential informants Blue and I have signed up can call on other agents. I've been here eight years. I've done my time at LAX, and I'd like to do street work again."

Roy inched his way back behind the desk. When he sat on the cushy faux leather chair, the hiss of compressed air escaping from the seat cushion sounded. "What is it, Sam? You don't feel loved? Is that it? Are you not feeling appreciated?"

Sam looked up at the dropped ceiling with the brown water stains on the tiles. "I get a paycheck every two weeks, so that covers the love and appreciation part for me. I'm just looking for a new challenge, a little change of pace—"

In a loud voice, Roy said, "Sam, this is how it's going to be. You work the terminals, find the couriers, and bring in the money, because we're getting that record this year. End of discussion."

Sam picked at the vinyl armrest of his chair, flicking pieces of the foam on the floor. "You've got it, boss." He raked his hands through his hair. "At least it's Friday, right?" He pushed against the arms of the chair to stand. "Guys, I'm getting in the wind."

•   •   •

Sam made a right turn off Ramona Avenue into the parking lot of the Villa Gardens, an aging two-story apartment complex with thirty-six units in the city of Hawthorne. Despite the overall rundown appearance, he liked the inexpensive rent, reserved parking space, and the decent sized oval-shaped pool.

He first arrived in California in 1977, hoping to live at a nice beach place, but on the government's GS-7 entry level salary of twelve thousand dollars a year, including overtime, he learned that wouldn't happen. When his limited budget pushed him east of Interstate 405, he knew he'd be settling for inland suburban living; and the beach would be relegated to a weekend thing.

He turned the key in the door to his apartment and pushed it open. The answering machine's blinking light caught his attention, and he prayed it wasn't a work-related call, because tired wasn't the right word to describe his mental and physical state. It had been a long day and all he wanted was a ballgame on TV to shepherd him to sleep. Dinner this evening, he decided, would consist of one or two cold beers.

He grabbed a can of Miller Lite from the refrigerator, then sank into the couch with his head propped against the armrest. He eyed the flashing red light, this time hoping it was a wrong number or a cold-call solicitor. Reaching over to the end table, he hit PLAY.

"Hi, Sam, it's your favorite sister. Guess you're still working. Do you ever take a vacation? Ha ha. Call me when you get in if it's not too late. I was talking with Chloe earlier, you know, Chloe Jansen. I'm sure you haven't heard, but her parents have been missing for a while. Call me and I'll explain later."

He checked the time on his watch. In Tampa, it was eleven now. *Annie called forty-five minutes ago; she'll still be up.* When the phone started ringing, he reached for his beer, popped the top, and took one long swig.

"Hello?"

"Hello, favorite and *only* sister of mine."

"Hey, Sam," his sister said. "How are you?"

"Beat. I just listened to your message."

"I knew if I mentioned Chloe's name, that would get your attention and prod you to call me back right away."

The sound of her laughter made him smile. "Sorry, Annie, my old high school crush days are over."

"Even Chloe?"

Sam laughed, then said, "You've got me there, but I would've called either way, crush, or no crush. What's going on with her parents?"

Annie sighed before speaking. "Oh, God, Sam. It's been all over the news here for a while. It was about a month ago, her parents disappeared when they were out on a cruise in their boat, an old classic they had redone, to Sanibel Island. Chloe said they were supposed to call her from there, but then she never heard from them, from Sanibel or anywhere else."

"Maybe they're having so much fun, they haven't called."

"Sam, this is Chloe's dad: super serious, by-the-book, everything's done on a schedule. Of course, they would call."

As she spoke, Sam thought back to his childhood when his big sister sometimes talked down to him. He said, "I only met him twice, maybe three times, years ago." He stifled a yawn. "Anyway, I don't know anything about boats, less than you, and you know nothing. I hate to say it, but do you think it's possible they had a mechanical—"

Annie interrupted him. "Chloe said they cruised islands close by, like Honeymoon and Caladesi the week before their trip to make sure everything was good. Ben is super careful. He's a brain surgeon. Anyway, now she's going crazy with worry."

"I'm sure." He tried to imagine what Chloe Jansen was going through. "God, that's awful. And to think *we know* what happened with Mom and Dad, and it's still incomprehensible. Damned drunk drivers."

Sam heard his sister's soft breathing during the silence—no doubt lost in sad thoughts for a moment over the loss of their parents. Finally, she said, "Listen, like I was saying, Chloe's upset, so she's going to call you."

Sam lifted his head from the armrest. "Call me? What do you mean?"

"*Hello.* She's going to pick up the phone and dial your number. What do you think I mean? Because of what you do, she thought you could help. She told me she wants someone to investigate since she's not getting anywhere with the Coast Guard and the—"

"Annie, listen," Sam said as he swung his legs off the couch and planted his feet on the floor. "I know nothing about boats or the ocean, and I've never worked or been anywhere close to a missing person case. I'm sure the agencies responsible for investigating this kind of stuff are doing what they're supposed to do."

"Sam, she thinks they've stopped looking or doing anything, the Coast Guard, I mean. She wants someone she can trust, and all she knows is you're a secret government agent and you grew up in Clearwater—"

"It's *Special Agent,* and I investigate drug-related offenses. And as far as Clearwater goes, yeah," he said, "we were kids there, but I don't think the fact that once upon a time, I was a paperboy qualifies me as anything more than someone who can fling a newspaper onto someone's porch."

"You can tell it all to Chloe when she calls. I gave her your pager number, but remember, she's upset."

"Of course, I'll be nice, and I'll let her down easy too."

"Sam, please just listen to her first." Annie drew a deep breath, as though to calm herself. "And you remember your nephew's birthday is next week, right? Trevor's turning eleven."

After the call ended, Sam's thoughts returned to Chloe. Both she and his sister were one year older than he was, and yes, Chloe had been his high school crush. If only he had understood at the time how high school girls' minds worked, he would have known they, especially the best-looking ones, never dated down a grade; it was the same age or older. "I never stood a chance," he said to himself. Sam placed the empty beer can on the floor and closed his eyes.

CHAPTER THREE

The configuration of office furnishings in the double-wide trailer was as random as the planets and stars in the sky, or trees in a forest. Over the years, investigators had pushed desks together based on friendships; others separated desks because of differences of opinion. No art hung on the walls and no posters with inspirational quotes to motivate those who labored there. The one constant was the large cluster of desks crammed together in the middle section of the trailer. Crossing the long, narrow space required walking around the blighted area.

During his eight years at LAX, Sam had worked his way out of the shabby central part to a posh corner location alongside Blue. Even so, the cacophony of conversation, laughter, and ringing phones destroyed any chance of serious concentration. Now, with Blue holding court in the center of the office, Sam knew there would be no more studying the photocopied papers and documents taken from Hector Rojas, aka Angel Martinez.

"Lemme tell you all something," Blue said, leaning over an assemblage of desks and chairs, while the faces of agents and police detectives looked upward, hanging on his every word. "The politicians in Washington are clueless, and I'll give you an example. About two years ago, Roy told me to give this congressman who was flying into LA a ride downtown to his hotel. I've never seen that in our job description, to be a taxi service, but Roy knew the man from back east and wanted to do the guy a favor."

"Did you do it?" a junior detective asked.

"Listen, if it ain't illegal or immoral, I do what the boss says, so, yeah, I did it, but the first thing the guy did to piss me off was he looked at his bag on the ground like I was supposed to put it into the car for him."

"Did you?"

"Hell no. But check this out: the dude doesn't even sit next to me. He gets in the back seat like he's in a limo and I'm his driver. There was no talk until we were about halfway to downtown, then he wants to be all friendly with me and asks how I would fix the drug problem. He says something like, 'Listen, Agent Baxter, this is off the record, feel free to speak your mind.'"

"What did you say?"

"It wasn't so much what I said as what I thought, and I thought he was an asshole." Blue's audience rewarded him with a round of laughter. "I'll speak my mind when I want, because I sure as hell don't need him or anyone else to give me fucking permission to talk." He slapped his hand on a desk. "I told him reducing demand is the real answer, like the 'Just say no' slogan, but he laughs like I'm joking. So, when I don't laugh, he says, 'Come on, Agent Baxter, we're just two guys talking; tell me what you're thinking.' I said that *is* what I think." Blue nodded at the group. "All of us here know *we* can't solve this problem alone. We've got to address the mindset of drug demand at home and school too; and I'm talking at the start of elementary school. If we wait until middle or high school, it's too late."

"What did he say?" the young detective asked.

"He laughed and said talking with young kids about that kind of stuff would be crazy, and that's when our little chat ended. When we got to the hotel, he didn't speak to me or say thank you or anything. What a prick."

Sam had heard the story at least a dozen times. He stood from his desk and walked toward Roy's office but stopped when his pager beeped.

Tampa area code. This had to be Chloe. He grimaced, thinking about the conversation to come, figuring the last time he had spoken to Chloe Jansen was close to twenty years ago in high school. In those days, he had worshipped the ground she walked on.

Sam knew he had worked hard to become a good drug agent, but he wondered how he could explain to Chloe that his narrow skill set didn't qualify him to investigate a missing person case; nor did he have the authority. Television influenced people so much, he thought, in which fictional characters could solve a mystery in an hour, including commercials.

He returned to his desk, looked at his pager again, pressed the numbers on his phone, but with zero privacy in the office bullpen, he turned his chair to face the wall.

"Hello?"

Her voice hasn't changed. "Chloe?" he said. "It's Sam, Annie's brother."

"Hey, Sam," Chloe said. "Thank you for calling me back. I hope I'm not bothering you."

"Not at all. I'm sorry about your parents. Annie filled me in a little. Has there been more news?" He thought it best to go right to the point.

"No, nothing," Chloe said. "Mom and Dad went missing over a month ago. At first, everyone was helping: the Coast Guard, different police departments, various volunteer groups, and people I had never heard of before. After the second week, things got quiet, and now there's nothing."

"I'm sorry." He knew his thought was lame, but he hoped to focus the conversation on something positive. "Annie told me your folks have a new boat."

"They refurbished an old cabin cruiser, or I should say someone did the work for them, and they just got it back two weeks before their trip. They were taking it out for three days to skirt along the coast to Sanibel Island."

Sam leaned forward, resting his forehead against the wall. "That's a beautiful place."

"It's gorgeous," Chloe said. "Anyway, they said they would call me from there, but after the fourth day, I started worrying and called the Coast Guard. They said something about starting an inquiry, and after the fifth day, I told them my father was a careful planner, and that he left a document with me called a float plan that covers all the details of their boating excursion. Plus, he had a checklist for his safety preparedness kit and checks everything off every time, even if he's only going out for an hour."

"That sounds good." Sam was uncertain what to say next.

"After a week, I started hearing these know-it-all people suggesting my dad was inexperienced or careless. One guy said they might've changed their minds and were taking a longer trip." Chloe's voice trailed off, followed by a sniffle, then a quick cry.

Sam sat up straight. "That's terrible. People can be so insensitive."

"They sure can," Chloe said. "That same guy said maybe my parents just didn't bother to say anything, but those aren't my parents, so I know that's not true."

"Of course not," he said, recalling his sister's words to be a good listener.

"I don't know what to do." Her voice was at the level of a whisper. He had to turn in his chair to shush two agents who had gathered close by his desk to have a conversation. Chloe said, "I mean, I'm not sure what else to do. My mom, my dad, they've got to be somewhere, but I can't find them, and I need to know they're okay."

"I understand, Chloe."

"Please help me. Will you?"

Sam closed his eyes and pinched the bridge of his nose. "Listen, Chloe. If I could—"

"You don't understand, Sam. Everything has stopped, and no one is doing anything anymore. I understand they can't search forever, but these are my parents."

"Chloe, I don't know—"

"Annie told me what you do," she said. "I know this isn't the work you're used to doing, but I need someone I can trust."

"I appreciate the trust, but—"

"About two weeks ago, after all the other help stopped, I hired this guy, a private detective, who's supposed to be a specialist in missing person cases. He's like an expert with boats and ships too and knows everything about things that can go wrong in the water, the sea, the ocean."

Sam was relieved. "That sounds good," he said, trying to sound encouraging.

"It wasn't, but I didn't care about the money—what it cost—even though he charged a ridiculous amount, but that didn't matter. These are my parents," she said again.

Chloe's crying had begun in full force. Sam had never been adept at helping people who cried, whether at a funeral or because of a relationship that ended. It was a skill one was born with, Sam thought, and he had missed out. "Chloe, I know this is awful, but please don't get—"

"I've got to tell you this," Chloe said between sniffles.

He felt helpless. *Just listen*, he reminded himself.

"The second or third day after I hired this detective, he asked me to meet him at some beach restaurant. I thought it was strange and wondered why he couldn't tell me on the phone, but I went, and this Mr. Wonderful super-duper investigator that everybody recommended just wanted me to come back to his house. He turned out to be a real pig."

Sam drew in his breath. "Jesus, Chloe."

"I fired him on the spot and walked out of the restaurant. Please, don't say no, Sam, because I can't give up on my parents."

"Chloe," he said, then paused, looking toward the ceiling before continuing, "you have to understand—"

"Think it over," she said, "just a little. Annie said this wasn't your specialty, and I understand, but will you at least give it some thought?"

"Chloe, I don't think my answer will be any different because this isn't something—"

"I'm a basket case now, Sam," she said. "Did you know I have a son?"

Sam moved the handset to his other ear. "I think Annie told me."

"Ryan is the same age as Trevor, your nephew. Their birthdays are two weeks apart. I raise Ryan alone, but I'm not doing so great as a mom right now."

"Your son understands, Chloe. He's upset too, I'm sure."

She sniffled again. "Sam, thank you for listening. I won't bother you any more today."

"You're never bothering me."

"I understand how you feel, but something might change your mind," Chloe said. "Is it okay if I call you again?"

"Sure, of course you can." He scratched his head. "It's still good to hear your voice and talk to you, even under the circumstances."

"You too, Sam. Goodbye."

He held the phone against the side of his head for several seconds, recounting her words, then he spun in his chair and hung up.

Blue was still at it. "And look at the conditions we work in; it's not even an office," he said, stroking his pencil-thin mustache. "Think about it; we toil all day in a trailer on concrete blocks at one of the busiest airports in the whole damned world." His voice became louder the longer he spoke. "This is one pitiful, saggy-ass double-wide trailer literally sitting on blocks of concrete."

Sam knew that story too and resumed his walk toward Roy's office. He tapped on the door frame. "You got a minute?"

Roy sat hunched over his desk, and when he looked up, the oversized reading glasses dominated his appearance, making him appear like a tree-hugging lemur with the trademark large brown eyes. "What the hell is going on out there?" Roy asked.

"It's story time with Blue."

Roy tossed his readers on the desk. "Oh, great, so, what's up?"

"On Friday, I asked you about following up on leads we developed on the courier we lifted the five hundred—"

"Come on, now," Roy said. "Not this again."

"Roy, please give me a second. The courier we nabbed, Rojas, had a bunch of business cards and papers with phone numbers and addresses, and you know Group One will sit on this for months and maybe do nothing with it. I can run with this and make something happen."

Roy leaned back in his chair. "Look, Sam, I understand your frustration and I appreciate the dogged determination, but you know the drill; it's out of my control. Besides, you're my cleanup hitter here, finding the money couriers in the terminals."

At that moment, a seed germinated inside Sam's mind. "I know what my problem is," he said. "I'm burned out." He took a sharp breath and rubbed his chest. "I need time off. Look, I haven't taken a vacation in a long time, but I'm talking about a real vacation, Roy. I promise I'll be back in time to help you get the record."

"Jesus, if you need a break that bad, then I won't stop you."

"I'll head downtown tomorrow first thing to drop off the Rojas stuff at Group One, then start my vacation Wednesday, if that's okay?"

"Sure. Do you have any plans?"

He had a plan, a crazy plan he wouldn't share, but he said, "Nothing specific, except rest up some, I guess."

The next morning, darkness surrendered to daylight moments before Sam slid the key into the car's ignition. The engine came to life with its unique Scandinavian sound, somewhere between a pleasant hum and a low rumble. A convicted drug dealer once owned the low-mileage, almost-new 1986 silver Volvo 240 DL, and Sam had requested the vehicle when it became available for government use through the asset forfeiture program.

Appreciative of the light traffic, he raced eastward toward the 110 Freeway that would take him into downtown LA. Twenty-five minutes later, he walked off the elevator at the World Trade Center and stepped out onto the building's seventh floor. Group One's office was to the left, but he continued straight ahead and pushed open the door to the Intelligence division. Behind every flashy front-page drug bust, it was here that the intel analysts toiled anonymously to support the drug investigations. Sam was quite familiar with the work accomplished by the unsung heroes, as they were the specialists who took in field agents' raw data, the subjects' names and aliases, the addresses, the phone numbers, the licenses, and registrations for various conveyances, then made sense of it all, connecting dots no one else could see.

Sam hoped his friend Bill Dunkirk would already be at work, and when he heard the squeaking of the wheelchair's movement from several feet away, he was certain Bill was at his desk. Sure enough, standing at the entrance to his friend's cubicle, he peered down at the thinning gray hair on the back of Bill's head. Twenty-odd years ago, Bill had been one of the Federal Bureau of Narcotics' finest street agents; then an undercover drug deal went awry.

Sometimes a .22 caliber round can ricochet off a bone and exit the body cleanly, without causing much damage, but in Bill's case, the light, fast-moving bullet that struck his rib cage took a bad turn and lodged at his spine. Robbed of the use of his legs, the agency gave Bill the unique job title of Agent Analyst.

That was one thing Bill and Sam had in common; both had been involved in shootings related to undercover activities. Sam had come out on top, with no permanent physical injury; however, the incident had left him, all tough talk aside, shaken. It was Bill, through the experiences of his own misfortune, who had helped his new protégé navigate the emotional trauma and its aftermath. Sam had welcomed the reassignment to the airport detail; but after eight years, he was more than ready to return to traditional drug investigations.

"Are you going to stand there staring at me, or are you coming in to visit?" Bill asked without turning.

"How did you know I was here?" Sam said.

"When my legs were paralyzed, it enhanced my senses, in particular, my hearing."

"Really?"

Bill spun his wheelchair around. "No, dummy. I have a mirror hanging on the cubicle wall and I saw you walk in." He pointed behind him, then asked, "What brings you here? The news is you've been on fire at the airport. You got another seizure Friday, right?"

"Yeah, we're getting good tips from informants," Sam said. "In fact, I came by to see if I could bug you to look at the documents we copied from the courier on Friday. He might be new to the business; it was pretty easy."

"No match for you, huh?" His crooked smile curled his lips up farther on the right side than on the left.

"I'm not so sure about that, but we caught some lucky breaks." He shook his head, thinking about his friend. Even though a cruel turn had resulted in a life sentence confining Bill to a wheelchair, he had somehow maintained a positive demeanor. He recollected Bill, telling him one day that a counselor had given him sage advice, and in his words, she had 'saved a drowning man.' The counselor said the focus in Bill's life shouldn't be on what had been taken from him, but on making the best of what was left. The story had etched a mark in Sam's mind, and he had never forgotten Bill's words.

"Can I ask you something?" Bill said. "Is there anything I need to be aware of with this request coming from you instead of Group One?"

Sam lowered his head without saying a word.

"Want to have a seat and talk?"

Sam looked around the office first to see if anyone was nearby, then he pulled an empty chair away from an unoccupied desk and sat. In a subdued tone, he said, "Look, I've been asking Roy for a while if I could follow up on the leads we've been getting from these money couriers. Dammit, Bill, I've been at LAX for eight years, and now I want to do something different."

Bill drummed his fingers on the armrest of the wheelchair. "Be careful what you wish for."

"Come on, you know what I mean. Right now, I'm supposed to be in Group One talking to them."

"Look, Sam, it makes no difference to me who I do the intel work for. Leave it all with me, plus your DEA-6 report documenting the money seizure, and I'll see what I can do."

"Thanks, and there's something else."

"Talk to me."

"I'm headed to Tampa tomorrow on vacation."

"Do these records you're leaving with me have anything to do with your travel to Tampa?" Bill's eyes narrowed as he gazed at Sam. "Was this courier you mentioned from Tampa?"

Sam shrugged. "Yes, why?"

"I just wanted to make sure I knew how to reach you when I finish with this stuff."

"We'll have to talk by phone, if that's all right?" Sam said.

Bill nodded. "I guess I better put a rush on this if you're going to work on your unauthorized investigation starting tomorrow—and while on vacation too."

"Look, Bill, I don't want you to get in trouble doing this for me."

"What are they going to do to me?" he said, gripping the arms of his wheelchair. "Take away my mobile throne? You let me worry about my end, and you just make sure you cover your own ass. In the meantime, let's go through what you have, then you can buy me a bagel."

Sam winked. "You got it. There's one more thing too."

Bill raised an eyebrow, as though shocked by Sam's brashness. "More? Where does it ever end with you?" He stared at Sam for a few moments, but he couldn't maintain his poker face. "Just kidding, so what's up?"

"I have another reason for going to Tampa."

"Oh? Not for love, is it?" His smile matched the sparkle in his bluish-green eyes.

"Bill, this is not to be repeated."

"I love a mystery. Do tell."

"I'll give you the short version now, then we can talk about it more later." Sam drew in his breath and held it for a second. "My sister lives in Tampa, and her best friend's parents went out on their boat a little over a month ago, but they never came back. The Coast Guard and the locals investigated, but nothing. The daughter even hired a private eye after the official help dried up. Bottom line, she got nowhere, so now she's asking me to investigate their whereabouts."

"And all this time you've been holding back on your secret talents?"

"No, not at all; in fact, I told her I didn't know anything about missing person cases. Plus, I hate boating, and I have no authority to do anything related to this. Besides, I live on the opposite side of the country, and—"

Bill held up his hand. "You've convinced me. You'll be perfect for the job." His head fell back as he laughed. "But it doesn't sound like much of a vacation."

"I suppose you're right, at least not in the traditional sense. I'll do a little digging, whatever that means. We'll see."

"Tell you what, Columbo," Bill said. "First, let's go through what you got from your courier friend, then later, while you're paying for my coffee and a hot bagel that I'm going to slather with an excessive amount of butter and cream cheese, I'll tell you how I can assist you on your missing person case. My job here puts me in contact with lots of people in the intel communities around the world, so I might be able to help." He leaned in close to Sam. "Now let's get started, because I'm getting hungry."

• • •

An hour later, Sam walked next to Bill's wheelchair as they passed over the sky bridge connecting the Bonaventure Hotel and the World Trade Center. Stopping in the lobby, Sam extended his hand. "Bill, take care of yourself while I'm gone." He watched his friend roll into the open elevator. Before the doors closed, Bill pivoted the wheelchair around and nodded to Sam. "You do the same in Tampa and thanks for the bagel."

CHAPTER FOUR

Sam's preferences were aisle seat first, window seat next, and middle seat never. One perk of the job was the airlines liked to keep armed law enforcement officers happy, and sometimes he got bumped to first class. Even though carrying a gun prohibited the consumption of booze, the legroom for a tall guy was hard to beat.

No first-class seat today, and the plane was almost full, but the gate agent had moved him to the aisle with the center seat open. After takeoff and within seconds of the pilot turning off the NO SMOKING light, the party began. He had read about a nationwide smoking ban on airplanes in the near future; until then, he had to suffer through it. *At least in the double-wide, I can walk outside to escape the smoke.*

The cross-country flight gave him five hours to read through a book he had just purchased about boating for beginners. After the first chapter, he knew he should never refer to the front and back or left and right of a boat; using those words would mark him as a rookie. It was *bow* and *stern, port* and *starboard,* and he repeated the terms in his head, hoping he would sound natural if he were ever pressed to use them.

His recollection of the conversation with Chloe from the previous evening interrupted his focus on the book. She sounded happy that he had agreed to make inquiries into her parents' situation, but how that would happen was a mystery. His *vacation* plans also included following up on all leads concerning the cash he and Blue had nabbed from Rojas on Friday.

When the wheels touched down on the runway at Tampa International Airport, Sam realized he had done as much thinking as reading. The situation involving Chloe's parents was confounding and the work relative to the money courier was problematic, especially since Roy had specifically denied his request. He shrugged off those worries and slipped the book into a carry-on bag, satisfied that at least he knew more about boats now than he had at the start of the day.

After retrieving his checked luggage, he stopped at the rental car desk to pick up the Ford Escort he had reserved. It was the kind of car he liked to drive because it wasn't flashy, and he wanted the work he would do to go unnoticed, however, the clerk said they were out of Escorts, but at no cost he could upgrade to a Dodge Shadow. Sam wondered if he had a choice and asked the clerk, "Is a Shadow considered an upgrade from an Escort?"

The man leaned in and said, "That's what we're supposed to say to make customers feel better. Some new 1987 Shadows come with the turbocharged engines, but we don't have any."

Sam inched forward too. "That's fine, because I'm not looking to go anywhere fast."

"Good, then this car will be perfect for you," the clerk said with a smile.

An unattractive automobile, the Shadow was shapeless and forgettable, the color an ugly brown, like an old catcher's mitt. Sam started the engine, and as he drove away, he realized the vehicle was even less exciting than its mundane name. The underpowered three-speed automatic wasn't fast, and it wasn't pretty; it was precisely the car he needed for the job.

• • • •

Sam turned onto a quiet cul-de-sac in an upper middle-class Clearwater neighborhood to find a single-story stucco house at the corner on the right. He rolled up to about six feet behind a white BMW parked in the drive.

As he walked toward the front door, he recognized the fierce battle raging in the lawn, where the Bermuda grass was losing badly to the dollar weeds. Sam grimaced, recalling the weekends he had spent with his dad fighting the never-ending war against the invasive weed. His father's wise words echoed in his head: *The best neighbors keep weeds out of our yard by keeping them out of their own yards first.*

Sam pressed the doorbell and waited for a minute. His finger hovered over the doorbell again until he opted to knock on the pale green door. He noted the galvanized steel nameplate on the attached mailbox had been covered over by a plastic stick-on version. Her maiden name, JANSEN, handwritten in blue ink, signified the apparent return to her life before marriage.

When the door opened, Chloe said, "Sam, I'm sorry if you've been waiting long. The doorbell needs to be fixed. My list of things to do keeps growing. Please, come on in."

He stepped onto the tiled entrance. "It's good to see you, Chloe. You haven't changed a bit." She was still devastatingly beautiful, but she had cut her long blonde hair short, and he could see a combination of worry, doubt, and fret in her eyes and smile.

She said, "Yes, I have. These dark circles are from a lack of sleep; plus raising a preteen takes a toll."

Sam bowed his head. "I'm sorry again about everything you're going through."

"These last several weeks have been, I don't know, wretched," Chloe said. "Thank goodness for Annie; she's been such a great friend since this happened. Of course, she's always been a wonderful friend, the best in fact, but you know that already." Her blue eyes softened for a moment. "I'd be lost for sure without her."

"Annie's a good person."

"My son Ryan is at his dad's house," Chloe said. "I thought it would be easier for us to talk because even though he loves his grandparents, I'm sure he's tired of hearing about this nonstop."

"I understand."

"What am I thinking, making you stand here in the hall? Would you like something to drink?" She walked into the kitchen.

"No, thanks," Sam said, following behind her.

"Oh, come on. Have something," she said as she looked up from the open refrigerator door and brushed away the hair from her eyes. "You have a choice of water, iced tea, let's see, grape or apple juice, or if you'd like, I can add something stronger to it."

"No, I'm—"

Her head had ducked behind the door again. "I've got three bottles of beer I didn't know I had."

"On second thought, iced tea sounds great. Thanks." He wanted nothing but sensed she would continue searching until he agreed to something.

She looked up and stared without blinking. "Tea?"

"Sure. That sounds good."

Chloe nodded. "Me too. Have a seat in the den and I'll be there in a minute." She smiled weakly, but her eyes diverted elsewhere. For a moment, Sam wondered where she went.

Seated on the couch, he looked at the surrounding space while listening to the sound of the ice maker dispenser in the kitchen. Thick wooden shelves, overloaded with books, wrapped around a muted twenty-five-inch console television set. The books were stacked with no apparent order, and those at the edge appeared ready to jump or be pushed by the others to the floor. A pile of magazines covered most of the coffee table, while others spilled onto the variegated wall-to-wall white carpet. Silverware, a plate, and a balled-up paper napkin from an earlier meal took up the rest of the table's cluttered surface.

Chloe's voice called out from the kitchen. "Sam, do you want any lemon?"

"No, thank you." He leaned over to leaf through a magazine.

Moments later, Chloe carried two glasses into the den. "Glad you said no to the lemon." She crinkled her nose. "Turns out it had gone bad."

She handed him a glass and sat across the room in a large leather recliner crowded with light blue cotton throw pillows crushed between the armrests and seat.

"This is perfect; thank you. I was admiring your work on *The Pelican*," Sam said, holding up the magazine.

"Oh, thanks. I'm sorry about the mess in here." She rolled her eyes. "I hope I'm a better editor than a housekeeper."

"What mess? It's fine, Chloe."

While they each took sips of iced tea, a silence smothered the room until Chloe said, "Um, Sam, I very much appreciate you coming here because I know how busy you are."

"I want to help you. I'm not sure what I can do or what I will do, but I'm here in Tampa for a while, and I'm also working on something else from my job."

"Please tell me I'm not interfering with your work schedule."

"Not at all. Like I said, I'm happy to lend a hand in any way I can, so you can put your mind at ease about that." He paused, wondering if Chloe was up for a discussion about her parents, but forged ahead anyway. "Please start from the beginning and tell me about your parents' plans and anything that other investigative agencies have already done. If you have any reports from them, they would be good for me to read over, and if you could give me pictures of your parents' boat, and if you don't mind, a recent photo of them as well? I know I'm throwing a lot at you," he said, "but I can't be sure what I might need, so it's best to get this stuff up front."

Chloe gripped her glass with both hands and stared at the floor. "All the things you're saying are logical, and I've got most of that stuff you're asking for in a box in the kitchen."

"Great, and also, I'd like to take notes while we talk, if that's okay with you."

"Yes, of course," she said, "whatever you need to do."

He removed a small notebook from his jacket pocket and held it up. "It's something I carry around with me with a list of things to talk about, so I don't forget to ask you anything."

She leaned her head back against the chair. "Everything's so different, isn't it? Twenty years ago, we were kids and now look at us." She exhaled deeply. "Life sure takes some weird turns. I never thought I'd be divorced, living in a house four blocks from where I grew up, and I sure never imagined I would go to sleep every night—when I can sleep—not knowing where my parents are."

She looked at the TV for a moment and as the tears gathered, she leaned over to set the near empty glass onto the carpeted floor. When she sat back up and focused on Sam, a small fire was lit in her bloodshot eyes. "No, dammit, I swore I wouldn't start crying." She wiped a tear away. "I just want to find Mom and Dad." She clenched her fists and took a deep breath. "My mother first told me about their plans a week before they left...."

Chloe talked for twenty minutes nonstop. While she spoke, Sam studied the melancholy that had taken up residence on her face. He jotted keywords to serve as reminders for things that might prove helpful later. When their conversation concluded, Sam promised to be back in touch soon.

After backing out of the driveway, he headed toward the beach and wondered what the hell he was going to do. Besides checking into the motel and getting a good night's sleep, his next step was hazy.

CHAPTER FIVE

It was nine when he arrived at the Bywater Motor Court Inn, a modest one-story building with a brick exterior painted white and rooms that ran parallel along the water. A warm and starry night, he was happy to find a parking space in front of his door. After unpacking his suitcase, he went straight to work spreading photocopies of the various documents taken from Rojas—identification cards and business cards, receipts, miscellaneous notes—on the small desk. It was too late to catch Bill at the office, but he wanted to have everything organized for the next morning.

Lying back on the bed, he turned his attention to Chloe's parents and sorted through the documents and various papers she had given him. Ben Jansen's float plan was the logical starting point, but he didn't stop until he had read and made notes about everything. But when he tried to think of the initial step he might take, he hit a wall.

• • •

A sliver of morning light made its way through the folds of the curtains. Sam had been awake for over an hour, reading in bed, thinking, and rereading. Looking at a photograph of the Jansens standing beside their boat, he decided the best place to start his investigation would be by contacting the Coast Guard.

The work he planned regarding Rojas was familiar ground, requiring basic investigative steps. He had organized the copies of the items in the courier's possession geographically, and would knock out the St. Petersburg addresses first, then come back north through Clearwater, before working his way to the Tampa side of the bay where most of the places of interest were located. He wanted to put an eyeball on each location, then let Bill work his magic by checking and analyzing telephone, utility, and real estate records. The driving to and through the cities for data collection purposes would take a good part of the day, but since LA was three hours behind Tampa, Bill would still have plenty of time to do his searches.

By the time he rolled out of bed, it was half past eight; and a wonderful way to begin a vacation, he thought. Coffee was the most immediate priority, even if brewed in a machine sitting on a motel bathroom countertop. While waiting for Los Angeles to wake up, he changed into his running gear and took a long jog by the beach.

• • •

Back at the motel and working on a second cup of coffee after his shower, Sam sat on the bed in his room with the phone resting on his lap.

"Bill Dunkirk speaking."

"Hey, Bill, I'm here in Tampa and ready to roll."

"I'm fine. Thanks for asking."

"Sorry, I'm anxious, I guess. How are you?"

"Forget it; it's too late now," Bill said, then addressed Sam's unasked question. "I've done basic checks and your courier doesn't have much in his background. Could be a novice, as you suspected."

Sam thought for a moment. "Yes, it's strange though, because that was a chunk of change to entrust to a newbie."

"I agree; regardless, I did NADDIS queries," Bill said, then without pausing, he asked, "Agent Dahl, do you remember how

NADDIS, the Narcotics and Dangerous Drugs Information System works?"

"Come on, Bill, why are you giving me a hard time already?"

"I know you airport guys don't use NADDIS much."

"Are you kidding me? I use it every day, and besides, you may recall I was on a plane yesterday," Sam said.

"Then you're the exception, not the rule. Anyway," he said, "Hector Rojas, aka Angel Martinez, had one hit, but it was a tenuous connection, so I'm always a little suspect about stuff like that. Too much garbage put in NADDIS results in too much garbage out, but before I say more and start opining, Sam, I think it would be helpful for you to swing by each of the places you have addresses for, copy down business names, license plates, and anything else you think is pertinent. The more you get, the more I'll be able to process and feed back to you."

"We're on the same page because that's my plan for today," Sam said.

"By the way, where are you now?"

"At my motel."

In his mind, Sam could picture the frown on the intel analyst's face during the ensuing silence until the smooth voice sounded. "Sam, call me paranoid, but you know I don't like to talk specifics to anyone using a phone at a hotel or motel."

"Good thing the motor inn where I'm staying has a secure state-of-the-art communication system in place."

"All right, smart guy," Bill said, "I'll make an exception in this case."

"No, you're right. I'll be stopping at the DEA office later today or tomorrow to say hello to an old friend, so I can use the phone there. I went through basic training with an agent assigned to Tampa, and he would kill me if I didn't visit. Rafael Guerrero, do you know him?"

"No," Bill said, "but I've seen the name."

"And I'd like to visit my old buddies at the police department too, that I went through the academy with, including a good friend all the way back from high school who's a lieutenant now. So, I've got places I can call you from, including pay phones."

"Let me do more digging, then we'll talk about this later. And tell me," Bill said, "what's going on with your missing persons deal?"

Sam turned toward the desk and shuffled papers. "Last night I went to see the daughter and go over all the details about her parents' boating trip. I'm kind of shooting in the dark on this."

"Sounds like you had a date."

"It wasn't and isn't like that at all," Sam said.

"Whatever you say, but if you need any help, give me a shout. I think the Coast Guard office will be a good place to start."

"That's my next phone call."

After saying goodbye to Bill, Sam found Chloe's point of contact at the Guard and secured an appointment for the following day.

• • •

A light rain began falling before he left the motel, but when he reached St. Petersburg, the sun was punching through the clouds. Being in Florida again, Sam was sure he hadn't seen the last rain shower for the day. Driving south on Ward Avenue, Sam looked for the house matching the home address Rojas had provided to the hotel where he stayed in LA. No surprise, the house number didn't exist.

He drove over to Fourth Street South, scoping out an address for a pet grooming shop in St. Petersburg that was taken from a business card in Rojas's wallet. He entered to find an unenthusiastic twenty-something white female wearing a tag with the name Sheila pinned to her shirt. Maybe business was slow, or maybe Sheila didn't care; either way, she was using her time on the clock to apply a fresh coat of nail polish. After a quick chat with her, Sam reasoned any connection between the shop and Rojas was innocent. But before he exited the parking lot, he recorded the license plate from an old beater parked in front.

He finished checking two addresses in Clearwater, a women's clothing store and a discount furniture outlet, then drove over the Courtney Campbell Causeway and descended into Tampa. He knew the area well from his work as a police officer, and quickly located the address listed on Rojas's Florida driver's license. It was a modest one-story bungalow in a neighborhood with a significant Mexican American population, but with no activity around the house and no cars on the property, Sam made a U-turn and scooted away.

Next, he drove by an address that had been scribbled on a folded-up sheet of paper in Rojas's wallet. The ragged apartment building in a depressed part of Tampa complemented the surrounding neighborhood perfectly. There were several cars in the parking lot, but which apartment belonged to each of the cars was anyone's guess. He copied the name from the mail slot inside the building and planned to ask Bill to do utility checks and cross-reference the data in NADDIS.

Sam fished through his folder, finding a photocopy of a business card for a running shoe store in Apollo Beach, a suburban area south of Tampa. He recalled his promise to Annie that he would come by her house early to help set up for Trevor's birthday bash. Dropping the paper back into the folder, he turned the car in the causeway's direction to take him to his motel first.

Given the short notice, he knew he'd been fortunate to secure an appointment with the Coast Guard the next day. Since their office was only a ten-minute drive from his sister's house in the Allendale neighborhood north of downtown St. Petersburg, he packed a bag for an overnight stay at Annie's.

•   •   •

The following morning, it took Sam a second to realize he was in the lower bunk bed in his nephew's bedroom. He scooped up his watch from the floor. It was twenty minutes after six, and he hoped to slip out of the bedroom without disturbing anyone and make a pot of coffee.

The house was still dark when he pulled the door closed behind him and crept through the hallway. Rounding the corner into the kitchen, the tile floor cooled his bare feet while the soft light above the stove provided enough illumination to avoid bumping into counters.

The quiet voice surprised him. "Somehow, I knew you'd be stumbling in here first thing this morning." Annie, wrapped in a large blue flannel robe that had once belonged to their father, sat at a pub-style table pushed into a cozy kitchen nook.

"The bad habits of being an early riser are hard to break," Sam said.

"Did you sleep okay?"

"Oh, sure, I may wake up early but sleep and I have an excellent relationship."

"There's coffee in the pot," Annie said.

"You're an angel." He opened the cabinet. "Coffee is all I need to jump-start my day."

"That's a clean mug on the countertop right in front of you."

"Whoa! Glad it wasn't a snake."

"Fake and real sugar are there too."

Smiling, he said, "Now why would I go messing up a perfectly good cup of coffee with sweeteners, natural or otherwise?"

"That's what Dad would have said."

Sam tilted the carafe of coffee to fill his cup. "By the way, good morning to you, Annie. Where's that husband of yours?"

"David has always been a sleeper; he won't get out of bed until he has to, and not one moment sooner." When she paused, Sam sensed what was coming. "You think you can help Chloe?" she asked.

He opened his mouth without speaking at first, then said, "Listen, I hope I can. I've got an appointment this morning at the Coast Guard office with their Deputy Sector Commander."

Annie held her coffee mug with both hands, taking slow sips. "Chloe's overwhelmed with worry, and it's understandable. The bubbly, happy, positive person isn't there anymore. Even when she went through her divorce two years ago, it didn't wreck her like this."

Sam leaned back against the sink. "I'm sure this is a tough thing to go through."

"You want a seat?" Annie asked.

"Thanks, but I'm going to jump in the shower before Trevor wakes up. I've got a bunch of things to do today; I just wish I knew what they were."

"You'll figure it out. I can see the wheels turning."

"That's the coffee waking me up."

"Now tell me why you couldn't stay here the whole time you're in town?" Annie said. "We're offering the family discount rate, you know?"

"Yes, I do, and thank you, but you know it's nothing personal. You have to understand, with my schedule, coming and going, maybe working late nights, I might be a nuisance."

Annie grinned. "All right, I understand, but thanks for coming to Trevor's birthday. It meant so much to him because he looks up to you. He watches police shows on TV and always says, 'That's what my Uncle Sam does.'"

Sam tilted his head and gave a quick shake. "If he could come out to Los Angeles with me, we could do the take-your-kid-to-work thing; then he wouldn't be as impressed. In fact, he'd be bored, I'm afraid."

"I'm sure you have a little excitement in your job."

"Yes, but it's no television show with nonstop action where the good guys always win," Sam said.

"How's your arm doing? Any problems?"

He stretched. "Like it never happened."

"Do you think about it much?"

"Much? No. Sometimes? Sure. It was so many years ago, it's like the shooting happened to someone else." Sam took another sip of coffee. "We got a new agent assigned to our office a few months ago. He reminds me of me in some ways from when I first started. He's roughly the same age as I was when I went to LA, except he's married. I heard the other day he and his wife have a baby, a boy, on the way. I feel sorry for him."

Annie eyed him curiously. "Why would you say that?"

"Because of what the job does, or we allow it to do. It takes over and there's not enough time in the day to do both justice. And family too often comes in second place."

"And you base this on all the years you've been married?"

"No," he said, "and I'm sure I sound like a cynic, and I hope I'm wrong, but I've seen it too many times with the ones that are married. It's the irregular nature of the work, the hours, the broken promises, the ruined weekends, the missed dinner dates. The job takes a toll, and the divorce rate is high, higher than normal."

"So that's why you're not married."

"I'm not married because no one will have me." He smiled and put his cup into the sink. "I've got a date with the Coast Guard. Thanks for the coffee, sis."

CHAPTER SIX

Sam turned the volume of the classic rock and roll station down on the radio and inched the Shadow toward the security gate at Coast Guard Station, District 7, St. Petersburg Sector. One of five branches of the U.S. military, the Guard had always struck him as an efficient, well-oiled organization.

Their motto was *Semper Paratus* or Always Ready, and Sam believed it. He had worked with them in Los Angeles, including the single occasion he'd been required to go out on a Coast Guard cutter; the ride was a wild and bumpy five-hour cruise on choppy seas, and the crew's professionalism and "can-do" attitude was impressive. To his hosts for the day, he had tried to appear at ease with the experience, but the truth was quite the opposite.

The night before, he had applied an anti-nausea transdermal patch behind his ear to prevent motion sickness, and although the patch was small, he was certain it was obvious to those around him and that they had understood what it meant. But the Coasties had treated their landlubber guest well, and when he finished the outing, he looked forward to focusing on the drug trafficker types who worked on land.

Sam pulled forward and displayed his badge and credentials to the gate guard, knowing the use of his agency identification for anything other than official government business was prohibited. The activities regarding Chloe's parents fell outside his authority to conduct drug investigations, but he also knew agents sometimes ignored agency policy.

"I have an appointment with Deputy Sector Commander Champlain," Sam said.

The guard raised the gate. "Have a good day, sir."

He drove straight to the building housing the command staff, parked his car, grabbed the folder with the notes and documents about the Jansens, and entered the one-story concrete building through glass doors. Everything inside was uncluttered and tidy, including the shiny tile floor.

He felt a little underdressed in his usual attire: jeans, a blue blazer, and comfortable loafers. After greeting the officer on duty at the reception area, he said, "I'm here to meet with the deputy commander at eight-thirty."

The officer said, "Sir, please have a seat and the commander will be with you soon."

He took in the surroundings. The officers walking past him wore sharp-looking uniforms and spit-shined shoes. There was no chitchat. It seemed everyone spoke only when there was a requirement to do so; even then, they spoke in normal, everyday tones, no shouting or wild laughter. He chuckled to himself, thinking the office couldn't have been more different from his own.

The next moment, a thought hit him; the air was fresh with no trace of cigarette smoke, and he wondered if the Coast Guard was ahead of the curve and had already banned indoor smoking. When he was called back to the front desk, he looked down at his well-worn jeans and loafers again and thought, *At least I don't smoke.*

"Deputy Commander Champlain will see you now," the uniformed officer said.

Sam followed his escort down the hallway. "I've never seen floors as clean as this."

The officer gave a quick nod. "The commander says if you can't see your reflection, the floors haven't been cleaned properly."

"In my office, the indoor-outdoor carpet gets vacuumed on a weekly basis, whether it needs it or not."

The officer remained outside the entrance to the last door on the right to announce Sam. "Sir, Mr. Dahl is here."

"Agent Dahl," the man said, standing from behind his desk, "I'm Deputy Commander Harold Champlain and this is Lieutenant Timmons."

Sam had expected the deputy commander to be older; he wasn't certain why. DC Champlain was in his early forties, he figured, but there wasn't a gray hair to be found on the man's head. He was short, lean, and quite fit, dressed in a perfectly pressed uniform. Lieutenant Timmons was younger, maybe thirty, and exuded confidence and ability. Sam nodded toward the lieutenant, thinking she could have been a model from any small town in America. She had short, auburn-colored hair, large brown eyes, and the cutest dimples he'd ever seen, even without a smile.

Champlain came around his desk and waved Sam to one of six empty chairs positioned neatly at a government-issued, rectangular conference table with steel-tubed legs and a faux-wood surface.

"Thank you for seeing me on such short notice." He took a chair that kept his back to the wall, a habit he'd fallen into years before and persisted to the present day.

"We're always happy to accommodate law enforcement," Champlain said.

The deputy commander sat across from Sam, while Timmons took the seat next to her boss. The commander clasped his hands and rested them on the table. "How may we be of assistance, Agent Dahl?"

As a kid, Sam had always thought of the Coast Guard as the uniformed boaters who rescued people in trouble somewhere off the coast of west Florida. He had learned the Coast Guard was a military service only after joining the DEA, and although the Guard wasn't part of the Defense Department, it had broad operational missions relative to national defense, marine safety, drug trafficking, and migrant interdiction.

Sam rested his elbows on the table. "Let me try to explain my purpose for being here."

Champlain tilted his head; his piercing blue eyes bore into Sam.

"I'm a DEA agent assigned to the airport in Los Angeles, and I've done work with your counterparts out there, so I have some appreciation for the fine work you do."

Champlain remained motionless and after an awkward silence, Sam said, "I'll be the first to admit I'm not a fan of boating or putting myself in any bodies of water bigger than a bathtub or a small swimming pool."

While Champlain maintained his stare, Sam sensed Timmons wanted to smile but followed her supervisor's lead. He decided to dispense with any further lame attempts at humor. "Although I work in Los Angeles now, I grew up in Clearwater and was a police officer here in Tampa before joining the DEA—"

"Agent Dahl, my time is short," Champlain said flatly.

Sam frowned, knowing the conversation wasn't going as planned, whatever that meant. "Sorry, I don't mean to take up your time needlessly," he said. "My sister's friend is Chloe Jansen, who's the daughter of Ben and Carol Jansen, the couple who disappeared off the coast at the beginning of August while boating—"

Champlain interrupted again. "In their refurbished Chris-Craft vessel, and yes, I've met Ms. Jansen on a few occasions."

Sam pursed his lips. "Right. I'll cut to the chase."

"Please do."

"Chloe, Chloe Jansen, that is, asked me to look into her parents' disappearance, and by the way, she has expressed no complaints about the Coast Guard or the local police—"

"Agent Dahl, how is the Jansens' disappearance of any official concern to the Drug Enforcement Administration?"

"It isn't, and I don't mean to mislead you. Chloe asked for my help because of concerns the search efforts, after several weeks, seemed to have waned and—"

"Sir, while active efforts on the water have ceased, we continue to do what we can through announcements to the public at large and proactive efforts through other organizations, public and private." Champlain lowered his head, but maintained his focus on Sam. "We won't stop looking for the Jansens."

"I didn't mean to imply you had or would; it's just Chloe thinks that because of what I do, I might somehow be—"

"Agent Dahl, I think you should stick to your job and allow the professionals to do theirs."

The comment referencing professionals struck a nerve, and he hoped his facial expression didn't give away his feelings, but he also knew there was no stopping his mouth. "Excuse me, Commander Champlain, if I may finish? She was just hoping that I could help. Look, this is your turf, and I'm out of my element. I'm crystal clear on that, but the one thing I *know* is this lady is suffering beyond all imagination because her parents have disappeared without a trace. I didn't ask to do this. I'm more comfortable dealing with the scum of the earth in LA, and clearly, I'm out of my league here," he said. "So, I was just seeking a little help, answers from the experts, you, on what's been done and if there was anything I could do on the side to help solve this mystery and somehow comfort their daughter. It seems I was mistaken. I'm sorry to have taken up your time this morning, and I'll see myself out."

He stood, tucked the folder under his arm, and left. In the two minutes it took to reach the parking lot, his anger had dissipated, and his mind flashed to what he might do next. He didn't know. Champlain was right in that he didn't belong here; he had no authority to do what he was doing, and it was damned frustrating. What he wanted to do at the moment was punch something. He rested the folder on top of his car while he searched for his keys.

"Agent Dahl?"

Sam turned to find the lieutenant facing him.

"I doubt Chloe would remember me, but I met her once," the lieutenant said. "She seems like a nice person."

Sam stared for a moment, unsure what to say, if anything, then he relaxed. "You better be careful being seen with me. I don't think your boss likes me much."

"Sorry about that," she said.

"Listen, I can understand where he's coming from. It's cool," Sam said and smiled.

"Agent Dahl—"

"Please, call me Sam, and I'm sorry, but I forgot your name. Normally, I'm good at remembering all kinds of things."

She extended her hand. "I'm Lieutenant Natalie Timmons, and my boss is not a bad guy."

Sam gripped Natalie's hand. "I'm sure he's not, and thanks for coming all the way out here to say that, but I don't want you to get into any trouble."

"Not a problem. He knew I was leaving for a meeting. Listen, there's a dive in the building where I'm going that sells stale doughnuts and hot coffee. I've got a few minutes, and I thought maybe I could help you."

Inside the canteen, the yellow walls matched the yellow-tiled floor. Steel housing supporting a single glass-enclosed cabinet filled with a variety of breakfast sweets was the only break in the color pattern. A sightless older man with dark sunglasses sat at one end of the serving line, holding a cash box in his lap.

"Good morning. How are you, Natalie?" the man said.

"Hi, Wayne. I'm fine, and you?"

"You mean other than being blind?"

Natalie laughed. "Wayne, you're something. Where's Betsy today?"

Wayne said, "Can you believe my wife left me for a little while to run the place all by myself?" His belly laugh was infectious. "Who've you got with you today?"

"Oh, this is Sam, who came all the way here from California to try out a doughnut and coffee."

Wayne's face angled toward the floor, although he directed his conversation to Natalie. "I've told you before, young lady, telling tales won't get you into heaven."

Natalie laughed again, then said, "I know he wants a doughnut—that part's the truth."

Wayne turned his head. "Young man, my advice to you is if you're stuck here and can't go to a real doughnut shop, then take a bear claw."

"All right, I will," Sam said.

"Full disclosure, I make an extra quarter on each one I sell, so that's why I'm pushing them today."

Sam chortled. "I appreciate your candor." He turned to Natalie. "What would you like?"

Still looking at Wayne, she said, "You're a natural-born salesperson. I'll have a bear claw too, and a cup of coffee."

"Make it two coffees, please," Sam said.

"That'll be two bear claws and two coffees. How does six dollars sound?"

"Like a great deal."

"Lord, we've got another one here who's never getting into heaven," Wayne said.

Sam placed a five and a one on the plate in front of Wayne. "That's six dollars. Thank you, sir."

"You're welcome and thank *you*, and if you don't mind when you're done, please put your dishes in the plastic tub here." He nodded toward a red container on a small stand in the corner close to where he sat. "Makes it easier for an old blind man to clean up."

"Will do," Sam said.

"Listen, young feller," Wayne said before Sam turned away. "Your loafers sound like they're getting worn thin on the bottom. The advice is free, but it could be time for a new pair."

"That's amazing," Sam said, looking at Wayne first, then at Natalie. "I had plans to buy new shoes before I flew here this week, but I ran out of time."

They took a seat in the far corner of the room next to a window overlooking the parking lot. "How could he know about my shoes?"

"He's got incredible hearing," Natalie said. "If you came in here tomorrow, he'd know your voice and your walk, and he'd chastise you if you hadn't bought new shoes too."

He looked at Wayne with his hands folded on his lap, waiting for the next customer, then he turned back to Natalie. "I suppose I can trust you."

"You think so?" she said.

"Yes, since you were up front with me when you said the doughnuts were bad, I think I can."

"What I said was the doughnuts were stale, and the coffee was hot."

Sam wagged his finger at Natalie. "I'm thinking you'd make an excellent agent."

"If I became an agent, I'd want to do undercover work in lots of foreign countries, and I bet I'd be good at it."

"I'm thinking the same thing." Sam sipped his coffee and wiped his mouth with a napkin. "The age cutoff is thirty-six for hiring on, so I'm guessing that gives you ten years."

"Very kind of you to say, but wrong. That would give me four years. I'm thirty-two. How about you?"

"I've already got a job as an agent."

Natalie flicked his hand with her finger. "No, *Agent* Dahl, I mean, how old are you?"

"I'm thirty-five."

Their eyes met, sizing up the moment, and each other.

"So, what are your plans for looking into this?" Natalie asked.

"My plans were to visit the U.S. Coast Guard today and see where that took me."

"I have an idea about what you might do to start; mind you, we, the Coast Guard along with the police departments, do a good job searching for boaters."

"I'm sure."

"Listen, Sam, I'm not trying to be a Debbie Downer, but it's not looking good for the Jansens after so much time." She held her hands up. "With that said, there are things you could explore, but I've got to run soon."

"Oh, sure, I don't mean to keep you," Sam said.

"But I'd like to help you. I don't know, maybe we could talk later."

The laughter from Wayne sounded like a clap of thunder from across the room. "You're not real swift, are you, Sam? Don't make her do all the work. She's trying to see if you want to get together later."

Sam turned in his chair. "Thanks, Wayne. I was getting ready to make my big move."

"The advice is free, but the day's not getting any younger." As Wayne spoke, every part of his face smiled.

Sam turned to face Natalie and shook his head. "Sorry, I was thinking that, but I'm still nursing my ego from the earlier beatdown in your office."

"Forget about what happened with DC Champlain—he's just a serious guy."

Sam nodded and said, "Natalie, I know we just met, but would you be interested in doing something later? Maybe have dinner with me tonight?"

"Shucks, I'm busy." She paused for a moment. "Just kidding. Do you have a pen in your folder somewhere?"

"Sure."

She wrote her number on a napkin and slid it across the table. "That's my direct line; it doesn't go through anybody at the front desk."

Sam nodded again. "All right, I'll call you later today."

"I'm counting on it," Natalie said.

Sam stacked the plates and cups in the tub. "Wayne, it was nice meeting you."

"Bye-bye, Wayne," Natalie said.

"Bye, now," Wayne said. "You folks have a great weekend."

Once outside the canteen, Natalie turned to Sam, extending her hand. "Thanks for the stale bear claw. Catch you later?"

Sam took her hand, feeling the softness of her skin. "Definitely. And you're welcome."

CHAPTER SEVEN

Sam walked to his rental car, unlocked it, and sat. He looked at Natalie's phone number, thinking of the unexpected turn of events; dinner with a pretty lady and someone who could give advice on what to do about Chloe's parents, no less.

He drove out of the Coast Guard station parking lot and came to a stop at the first traffic light but had to remind himself he didn't have a plan for where he was going next. The gas station at the corner seemed like a good idea to organize his thoughts, and he took a quick right into the lot.

Since Natalie had said she had an idea to share, he thought he would put the Jansens' situation on the back burner. He searched his mind to recall where he had left off the day before, regarding following up on the Rojas leads. Maybe he should visit his friend at the DEA office in Tampa, and although he had little to share yet, he could make use of the free phone service and call Bill for any updates he might have. He looked at his watch; Bill should be at work and would have already finished his first cup of coffee.

He scanned the front and side of the service station building for a pay phone, thinking he'd better check to see if his friend Rafael were in the office before going to the trouble of driving into downtown Tampa.

"Drug Enforcement Administration," a flat, mechanical female voice said.

Sam said, "Good Morning, I'm looking for Rafael Guerrero." He heard no response other than a cold voice that said, "Hold," then a series of clicks, leading him to conclude he'd been sent to phone purgatory before he even had a chance to identify himself.

A male voice, sounding more annoyed than anything else, assaulted him. "Who's looking for Rafa?"

Sam started to identify himself again but was cut off.

"Rafa's not available," the gruff voice said.

"Yeah, listen, I'm visiting from the LA office, working here for a while and need to make some phone calls."

The voice turned hurried and uncaring. "You can talk to the duty agent."

"Hang on a second; I'm not Joe Shit the rag man calling. I'm a DEA agent too, and I just need an empty desk to make a few phone calls. That's not too much to ask, is it?"

The voice softened. "Hey, sorry, it's a little crazy here right now. Sure, come on over and ask for me, Joe Barber in Group Two, and I'll set you up."

"Thanks, Joe. I'll be there in about thirty."

• • •

Sam took out his ID and showed it to the receptionist. "Good morning. Can you call Joe in Group Two and let him know he has a visitor?"

She put the phone to her ear and started working hard on the gum in her mouth. "Got a guy up here waiting for you." She hung up, saying nothing and making no further eye contact with Sam.

He turned around, chalking up her disposition to an employee having a hard day. A minute later, a balding white guy around forty years of age walked in. "Sam?"

"Yes, that's me."

"Hey, I'm Joe Barber—sorry about before." He turned to the receptionist. "Rita, can we get a 'no escort' pass for Sam, please?"

Rita looked from Joe to Sam, then back to Joe, and huffed. She pushed a logbook across the desk toward Sam.

Joe said, "That's Rita's way of saying you have to sign in."

Sam scribbled his name in the book, then entered the date and time.

She frowned, looking down at the spot where Sam had signed; then she slid a red laminated tag toward him that read LEO—LAW ENFORCEMENT OFFICER.

Joe said, "Come with me. Things are nuts here now because we're up on a Title III and stretched thin, covering the wiretap, and keeping a surveillance team on the street."

"Sorry, I'm here at a bad time," Sam said. "I just need to make a few calls to my office."

"Not a problem at all, and where do you know Rafa from?"

"We went through basic training together, and we were roommates there."

Joe stopped walking and placed his hand on Sam's arm. "Rafa's talked about you. Do you work at the LAX airport?"

"Yes, that's me."

"Right, right, Rafa has been very complimentary of you. He's sitting in our Title III room now; being a Spanish speaker, he always gets stuck on the Español wiretaps." They resumed walking. "Listen, while you're making your call, I'll duck in there and let him know you're here because I'm sure he'd love to see you. There's another agent in there too, just not a fluent Spanish speaker; but if a call comes in, he can come out here and grab Rafa."

"Thanks," Sam said. "In that case, I'll wait to make my call."

After passing a small conference room, Joe led Sam into a large office space with a dozen unoccupied desks, the majority butted against the windows. "As you can see, everyone's out on the street on surveillance. Hang here, and I'll drag Rafa out unless he's monitoring a call now."

Sam watched Joe pass through a door with an affixed placard reading TITLE III IN PROGRESS. A minute later, a handsome man about the same age as Sam stepped out of the corner office, wearing a matching black tracksuit. In a loud voice, he said, "We've got to do something about security around here ... are they letting any pinche vato in here now?" He strolled into the main office.

Sam extended a hand toward Rafa.

"Man, that's not good enough," he said and wrapped his arms around Sam and squeezed. When he released his grip and took a step back, he said, "When did you get here, and why didn't you call?"

"This trip came up at the last-minute. I'm on leave, but I'm doing a little work too."

Rafa sported jet-black hair and a mustache and had straight, white teeth that complemented his huge smile. "You know you're crazy, right? Only you'd be on vacation and still be working. I guess Joe told you we have a wire going; of course, I'm always stuck, if it's a Spanish Title III."

"Right, he told me. So, is it Cubans, Colombians, or who?" Sam asked, taking a seat.

"It's a Mexican-affiliated group, but I listen to this garbage all day. Tell me what you're up to."

"I'll give you the short story; it may turn into a good case for you." He lowered his voice and said, "I'm here on what you would call an unofficial capacity. My boss doesn't even know I'm looking into this."

Rafa raised his eyebrows. "I bet this is good."

"Look, I've grown tired of working airport cases."

"I'm sure you have." Rafa nodded. "Man, you need to escape the left coast and come home. I'm sure you've made your office of preference choice known and Tampa's on your wish list. Come on, you've done your time in one of the dirty dozen cities." He laughed, then smacked his hand on the desk twice. "That's assuming DEA still considers LA to be on the dirty dozen list."

"Oh, yeah, Los Angeles still makes that list," Sam said.

"So why not try to come back here? Man, we could work together."

"I'm thinking about it. I've asked my boss before about letting me follow up on leads we develop from our courier cases, but he won't, or he says, he can't."

Rafa leaned back and laughed even more loudly. "But you're doing it, anyway. I love it. You've become a rebellious motherfucker."

"Not really, but this stuff I'm following up on relates to a seizure we made last Friday, in the neighborhood of five hundred thousand on a Tampa-bound flight."

Rafa whistled. "Nice work."

"And I'll feed you all the leads I develop on this."

"I'm not worried about it," Rafa said.

"And the other thing I'm doing is something on the side, involving my friend's parents who disappeared when they were out on their boat a month ago—"

"The husband and wife—I heard about it. He's that type of doctor that does surgeries on the brain—what do you call them?"

"A neurosurgeon," Sam said. "So, the friend I'm talking about is my sister's best friend from high school, and she asked me to see what I could find out. She's desperate to learn what happened to her parents."

"I didn't know you did that kind of work." Rafa pointed at Sam. "You're a sly one."

"Hey, I know nothing about this stuff, and I tried to tell her that. Anyway, both issues came up at the same time, so I thought I'll use my vacation time instead of losing it, like I do every year."

"Man, you're something else. You're like, what's that cat's name on TV—the detective. What's his name?" He snapped his fingers several times.

"Beats me, but I'm stumbling around a bit on this thing because I know nothing about this kind of stuff."

Rafa said, "I'm scheduled to work the wire today through Wednesday, then I'll be ready for my two days off, and we can hang out like the old days."

"Sounds good."

"So, what are you up to with these missing boaters?" Rafa asked.

"I met someone from the Coast Guard this morning right before I came over here, and she's going to help me with ideas."

"Man, you're a dog." Rafa smiled. "I knew it wouldn't take you any time at all before you found someone to cuddle up with. Ever since I met you, it's always been that way." He pointed at Sam. "Women just love you."

"It's not like that," Sam said.

Rafa shook his head. "I followed the news on that story every day, but after a couple of weeks, things got quiet. I guess because they didn't find anything."

A shout from the wiretap room interrupted their conversation. "Rafa, we have an outgoing call in Spanish."

The speaker, a young guy with fiery red hair, stood in the open doorway looking hurried and flustered. Sam thought he didn't appear to be much more than twelve years old.

"I'll be right there." Rafa turned back to Sam and held his hands out, palms up.

He watched Rafa jog back into the corner room. "Take it easy," Sam said as the door closed.

•   •   •

Alone in the empty office, Sam opened the folder with the Rojas documents and retrieved his notebook. He lifted the receiver and dialed Bill's number in Los Angeles.

"I was wondering when you would call in," Bill said, after exchanging quick hellos with Sam. "I started thinking you were enjoying the Florida sunshine too much and forgot about me."

"Not a chance. What do you have for me?"

"Not as much as I'd like," Bill said. "Your boy, Hector, was carrying lots of documents on him, but I'm hitting dry holes. That could be good. He could be more schooled than we thought and is part of a top-tier organization. I'll keep digging." He cleared his throat. "In the meantime, here goes. The home address on his license is his cousin's place. The pet grooming shop, furniture store, and clothing store are what they appear to be, places he's frequented. I could find no connections to any drug-related persons or organizations from any of them."

"Then a big strike out on the first day for this?" Sam asked.

"Not so fast, because I found one report in NADDIS, concerning a routine traffic stop by the Bradenton, Florida, Police Department in July 1985, involving the seizure of a baggie of cocaine in a car with a license plate registered to the apartment you went by yesterday in Tampa."

"That's a little something, at least enough for me to go to the Bradenton PD and read their report." Sam tapped his pen on the folder. "Thanks for checking those places out, and for coming up with that little nugget in Bradenton. By the way," Sam said, "I spoke with Rafael Guerrero earlier and told him what I'm up to."

When Bill didn't respond, Sam could sense the tension in the silence until his friend spoke. "That's all well and good; but if your boss finds out what you're doing, you'll find your hind tit in a ringer and good. Roy *won't* be happy."

Sam frowned. "Yeah, I'm sure he won't be."

"All right, enough on that. How's it going on your other unauthorized investigation?"

"I got lucky and found someone from the Coast Guard who's going to help with an idea on what I might do."

"What's her name?" Bill laughed.

"If you must know, it's Natalie Timmons. Lieutenant Natalie Timmons," Sam said. "But listen, from the start, my meeting didn't go well. The deputy commander wasn't friendly, sort of the all-business type. But in fairness to him, he questioned right away why the DEA would have any interest in two missing boaters. I left in a quiet huff, but when I reached the parking lot, the lieutenant who was in the meeting caught up to me. I'm sure it was out of pity, but she offered to help."

"Sometimes pity can be a good thing," Bill said.

It was Sam's turn to laugh. "Well, we'll see, so back to Hector Rojas. Thanks again for your help. I've got one other place to check out. He had a business card in his wallet for a running shoe store, and I got to thinking about this while I was driving around. Assuming Hector stays at his cousin's house in Tampa, why would he drive thirty minutes just to go to a store that sells running shoes in Apollo Beach? There are plenty of stores much closer where he could buy shoes."

"Sounds thin," Bill said.

"You're right. It's a stretch, but this lead is the last one on my list to look over. I was going to do it yesterday, but I ran out of time. A little support and encouragement would motivate me because it wouldn't take much convincing for me to blow this off."

"On second thought," Bill said without hesitating, "I think you should check the store out. I bet you'll break the entire case wide open with the stuff you learn."

Sam said, "That's the Bill I know and love."

"Are you heading out there now?"

"Yes, but first I'll swing by the Bradenton PD to look over the traffic stop report with the ounce of coke."

"Good man," Bill said.

"I'll call you later if that works for you."

"Hey, in for a penny, in for a pound."

Before Sam hung up, he had Bill give him the police case number and date for the NADDIS hit on the coke seizure from the vehicle.

CHAPTER EIGHT

Sam took a long look around the office after saying goodbye to Bill, wondering if Tampa could be his next assignment. It wasn't a trailer with worn-out carpet, and there was abundant light passing through actual windows, tinted to keep the office cooler while the sun lazed in the sky. Most of the agents' workstations had plants sitting on top of their desks or next to them on the floor. Emotions he hadn't experienced for years crept into his soul, as thoughts of family—his flesh and blood family—not even thirty minutes away, dominated his mind.

Then he imagined himself in a house with his own family, planting a garden with his wife, kids running under a water sprinkler in the yard, or riding bikes to the neighborhood park. On warm Saturday evenings, they'd sit on the front porch swing counting fireflies. *Why not? The years are racing by and what do I have to show for it?*

Sam stood with a renewed vigor and when he passed the reception area, he said, "Have a great rest of your day, Rita."

• • •

In all the time Sam lived and worked in Tampa, he'd never been to the Bradenton Police Department, yet, he knew where it was, and as he fought his way through heavy traffic heading south on

Highway 41, the burnished glow he'd been enjoying began to fade. He wanted to hold on to the high as long as he could, but the traffic, not as bad as LA, but a pain in the ass all the same, chipped away at his good mood. Upon his arrival at the Bradenton PD, the glow was gone, and he stood facing a youngish female police officer sitting behind the clear bullet-resistant barrier. He held out his badge and credentials and said, "Good morning, ma'am. I'd like to review a report from July 1985, concerning a traffic stop that resulted in the confiscation of cocaine."

The officer said, "Turn to your right to go down this hallway, and the office will also be on your right. You can't miss it; there's a sign on the wall beside the door that says RECORDS."

Sam went to the office, completed a form to request the specific report and was told to wait while the document was located. About ten minutes later, a woman in plain clothes behind a window summoned him inside and gave him a visitor pass to clip to his jacket. She pushed the document through an open slot with a cover sheet on top marked BRADENTON POLICE DEPARTMENT. "Sir, you can sit at the table behind you and when you're finished, please return it here."

The report detailed what began as a routine traffic stop of a 1982 Mercury Marquis for a broken taillight. A uniformed officer on scene detected the smell of marijuana, and, upon request, the driver, Ronaldo Gomez, exited the vehicle and gave permission to search the car. The officer, with the help of another patrolman, discovered an ounce of cocaine in the glove box. Despite Gomez's denial of any knowledge of the cocaine's presence in his car, he was arrested and booked at Bradenton PD. The next day, he posted bail and disappeared.

Sam made notes about Gomez, including his identifying information and address, then returned to the window and asked, "Excuse me, ma'am, is this the entire file?"

"Yes, sir."

"Would it be too much trouble to print a copy of Gomez's driver's license photo?"

The clerk eyed Sam for a moment, then asked, "You're with the DEA, right?"

"Yes, ma'am."

"All right, I can do that," she said. "Have a seat. It won't take long to make you a hard copy."

Less than five minutes later, Sam took the document in his hand, studying the photograph and details of the suspect. While the woman sat on the other side of the glass, he pointed to the man's face in the picture and said, "I'm not sure he's human; it's hard to see where the hair on his head stops and his beard picks up. This Gomez is a tall guy too: six feet, five inches."

The clerk's jaw tightened. "I don't think he's anyone you'd be likely to forget meeting, that's for sure."

• • •

Sam drove north on Highway 41, looking for a pay phone to call Bill, so he could get background on Gomez. He started pulling into the gas station but at the last second, veered away. Since it was only midday in LA, he figured he had plenty of time to catch Bill before the end of his workday. He'd drive by the running shoe store first, then call and have all the queries done at the same time.

Apollo Beach Boulevard was straight ahead and when he reached it, he took a left and drove two traffic lights to the west. On his left, he saw The Runner's Choice, the corner store in a line of six small merchandisers and a sandwich shop. Sam parked his rental car away from the other vehicles in the small lot outside the string of stores. It was mid-afternoon on a Friday, but the shoe store didn't appear to be open. Sam approached the front, gazed through the window, and saw a large empty space except for a display stand with six pairs of shoes, but no signs or prices. He looked right, then left, and not seeing anyone near the shop front's facade or any lights inside the store, he gave the door a good push and pull, but it was locked.

Next door, in a baby furniture store, a middle-aged woman stood on a ladder, hanging a carousel crib mobile in the window. Sam walked over and leaned in through the open doorway. "Would you happen to know when your shoe store neighbor might open?"

The woman's laugh echoed off the glass. "You and a whole slew of people ask the same thing. Did you catch their shoe display—if that's what they're calling it?" Her laugh was more of a snort this time. "Strange way to sell something when the place is always closed. Every week, this man unlocks the door and goes inside, then waits on a truck that shows up and drops off boxes. But I don't think I've ever seen any customers in there from day one."

As Sam listened, he nodded. He had met this type before and knew he wouldn't need to ask questions to keep the woman talking. "That's too bad," he said, "because I'm here in town for a while, and I left my runners at home. Guess I'll hit the mall instead."

"Something's not right about the place," the woman said, "and I'll tell you why it bugs me." She grabbed her tools off the pail shelf and began backing down.

"Can I help you?" Sam said, stepping toward the ladder.

The woman produced a quick hiss of a laugh. "I can handle it. Thanks all the same."

He retreated to the entrance and waited. The woman was broad-shouldered and seemed like someone who didn't tolerate any nonsense. As soon as she made her way down to the floor, she gave the ladder's two spreaders a shot from her forearm, popping them upward; then she delivered a swift kick to the side rail and front feet, and with one hand, she propped the closed ladder against the wall.

"I do this all the time." With a hint of a smile, she looked at the various carousels hanging in the display window. "Looks nice, right?"

"Yes, you have a knack for—"

She cut him off. "That store bugs me because I want a place next door that brings in its own customers, and I'm talking about the kind who buy things with money, then maybe they'll stop in here to buy something too. But no, they're never open." She bit down on her lip. "Mind you, I'm watching too, and whenever the owner comes around, he just disappears inside. You'd think after the truck drops off their merchandise, the display might change, but it never does."

"That's strange," Sam said.

"Strange, you say? Well, thank you, Captain Obvious. I'd say it's damn peculiar, is what it is."

Sam smiled to himself. *Dang, she's feisty.* He'd better be careful—she might turn on him next. He slowed his speech and tried not to make any sudden movements as he spoke. "You're right; it's like you say, peculiar."

"I went in there one time and the owner said he was still getting the shop together. I told him, you've been working here for over a year—how long will it take you to get your store going?"

Sam noticed the more the woman talked, the more agitated she became. "That's a fair question," he said, using his calm voice.

"I got lots of fair questions. He was nice enough and a handsome fella too. You want to hear what he said to me?" She didn't wait for an answer. "He spoke with an accent and said, 'Yes, you are right madam, and it is taking much too long.'"

Sam laughed at the way the woman had mimicked the man's accent. "I guess I can come back over the weekend. What's the hurry to go running anyway?"

"Mister, it won't matter when you come back here. I'll bet you my last dollar it'll be closed. Now if you're asking me where to get your running shoes, I'd tell you to go to Dixie's Shoe World on Highway 301, at most a ten-minute drive from here, and they have the best prices too."

"Thanks, I appreciate the advice," Sam said. "Maybe I'll do that."

"Well, think about it. Why would you want to pay mall prices? All you're doing is just paying for their fancy store and their swanky shoes with all those bright colors, and *only* if you're ready to shell out a hundred bucks. They always have that little routine they do where they make you run around the store for them, then they use all those complicated words to describe what your problem is and tell you they've got the perfect shoes to fix whatever's wrong with you. No wonder the poor customer gets all bumfuzzled about what to buy."

"Yeah, no wonder." Sam questioned if he would be able to escape. She was lonely and seemed to like the company, but he could tell, she also had a mean streak.

"That's what they want, for you to purchase the most expensive shoes in the place. It makes no sense to me why people throw away good money. Let me show you what I'm talking about."

Oh, Lord, he thought.

"Look here; I have a baby crib for sale at forty-nine dollars." She smacked her hand on the crib's headboard. "Now that's quality, but you go to a big department store, I guarantee you'll pay double for the same crib."

"You're right. That's no good." His mind raced for an escape plan while he reached for his pager.

She said, "No good? Let me tell you about no good—"

"Sorry, excuse me. That's the hospital paging me because my wife must have gone into labor early."

"Your wife's in labor? Here? Now? While you're out shopping for shoes?" She practically spit at him. "What sort of husband leaves his pregnant wife at the hospital?"

Sam began backing his way out of the store, retreating from the woman's assault. "Yeah, I can't imagine what I was thinking. I need to go, but thanks for the help." He turned to leave and trotted toward his car.

She shouted, "You seem like a nice man, so if you want a good deal on baby products, I can ship them. Tell me where you live."

"Anchorage. I'll be in touch, thanks." Happy to reach the Shadow, he hurried to unlock the door before it was too late.

"Anchorage?" the woman shouted again, only louder. "Mister, we don't ship to foreign countries."

Sam started the car, waved, and breathed a sigh of relief. He could be back at the motel in forty-five minutes. First, he'd call Natalie to set a time for dinner, hoping she hadn't changed her mind, then he'd talk to Bill and ask him to check both the name Ronaldo Gomez from the police report and the shoe store in NADDIS.

He tore out of the parking lot, taking one last look at the woman, who was still talking while her arms flailed about. She could make a great witness, and she could also be an agent's worst nightmare. He was certain that she didn't know the shoe store was likely being used to consolidate deliveries of drug money for shipment overseas. Sam thought, that's the thing; everyone focused on the difficulties of smuggling drugs into the U.S., but the bigger challenge was getting all the cash out of the country. It weighed more and took up more space than the drugs.

Rafa flashed through his mind. Poor Rafa, he mused. After he briefed him on the suspicious activity at the store, his friend would be interested in talking to the baby store owner about her next-door business neighbor that had no legitimate business. He would also be pleased with getting a case handed to him on a silver platter. Pleased at least until he interviewed the baby store lady; then his eyes would darken, and he would curse his friend. Sam couldn't help but smile at the thought.

• •

Back in his motel room, Sam dropped everything on the table, lay down on the bed, and used three of the skinniest pillows he'd ever seen to make one normal-sized pillow for a cushion behind his head.

He held the telephone receiver to his ear.

"Lieutenant Timmons."

"Hello, Natalie, it's Sam."

"I was beginning to wonder if you were going to call."

"It's been a long day, but one thing for sure, there was never any doubt about me calling. Would you want to get together later, maybe dinner?"

"Sure. You like seafood?"

"I'm a native Floridian. I love seafood," Sam said.

"I know a wonderful place that's walking distance from where I live. Maybe you'd like to come over and watch a gorgeous sunset with me before dinner?"

"I know the perfect wine for the occasion."

"You read my mind. Do you still have your trusty folder and pen with you?"

"I always keep it close at hand."

"I'm at the Isola Bella condos, unit 4A, Gulf Boulevard in Madeira Beach."

He repeated it back to her.

"Do you think you can find it?" she said.

"I carry an excellent compass with me at all times, so I think so."

"That's funny. Is seven good with you?"

"Sounds perfect."

Sam hung up, thinking he should do more of these working vacations.

He dialed a second number and listened to the phone ring. A voice, not Bill Dunkirk's, answered, "Intel."

"Judy, it's Sam," he said. "I'm looking for Bill."

"Hey, Sam!" Judy always seemed especially cheerful to him. "Bill left early. He wasn't feeling well."

Not what Sam was hoping to hear. "Nothing serious, I hope."

"No, I think it's a little stomach thing," Judy said. "I'm sure he'll be back on Monday, but is there anything I can help you with in the meantime?"

He thought about his answer. "No, it can keep until Monday," he said, signing off. "Have a great weekend."

CHAPTER NINE

It was seven on the dot when he walked up to the entrance gate of the Isola Bella condos. The metal fencing surrounding the property blended seamlessly with the simple yet abundant broad leafy foliage and the smattering of vibrant flowers. Sam commended the effort to achieve security without falling victim to the prison effect.

He pushed the call button next to the name TIMMONS.

Natalie's voice sounded from the tiny speaker box. "Very prompt, Sam."

"I've been told it's one of my strengths."

He heard a cheerful laugh, making him smile.

Natalie said, "Use the elevator or come straight up the stairs to the building's seaside, unit 4A."

"I can use the exercise."

The buzzer sounded, releasing the lock on the gate. When he reached Natalie's door, he tapped twice.

"Hey," she said. "Come in." Her appearance differed from the uniformed Lieutenant Timmons. Civilian Natalie wore a mid-thigh beige sweater dress with a tie around her waist. The zipper down the front bodice hugged her body smoothly. Simple brown ankle boots and gold hoop earrings completed the ensemble. Hair curled around her ears, accentuated a lovely face with flawless skin.

"You look wonderful."

She bowed her head. "Thank you."

"And how does this look?" He held out a bottle of wine.

"I had been hoping for a German Riesling, and here it is. This is perfect. Please, follow me."

She led him to the kitchen. "Let me throw it in the fridge for a sec, and I'll give you the grand tour."

They entered an open space with a combined living and dining room. "It's small, but this is what sold me." She turned to face the large sliding glass door, revealing a wide balcony with an unobstructed view of the Gulf.

Sam practically whistled. "This is breathtaking and fitting for a Coast Guard lieutenant who's always on the job, right?"

"I take time off every once in a while," Natalie said.

"I bet this is a nice place to sit, read, think, or maybe do nothing at all."

They stood at the railing for a few moments. She said, "We have a reservation at eight, only a three-minute walk from here. Do you want to open the wine?"

Sam held up his index finger. "I have to confess I bought it based on the advice from the guy at the liquor store."

"I can't wait to see if he knows what he's talking about," Natalie said.

They sat on the balcony with a small table and the bottle of wine between them.

"Is this a typical vacation for a DEA agent?"

"I wouldn't think so," Sam said. "This is the result of several events coming together that brought me here. Work drove me to take time off, and since I was going to be here, I promised I would try to explore the circumstances of Ben and Carol Jansen's disappearance."

"Tell me something. How did you meet Chloe Jansen?"

"She was, and still is, my sister's best friend."

"That's right, you said she's a friend of your sister's earlier today."

"They were a grade ahead of me in school," Sam said. "When my sister called, then Chloe called, I tried every way I knew how to explain to them this is not what I do. I know nothing about this kind of thing or boating activities, but like I said, work sometimes intervenes, so, I came here to follow up on an investigation from LA, and to not be a total bad guy, I said I would check out the Jansens' situation."

Natalie's eyes sparkled. "That's nice of you to give up vacation time."

"In all honesty, I tried to get out of it. But when you said you had an idea for me, it intrigued me. Chloe's in rough shape, so if I can help her a little, it's good for her and good for my sister."

He could see Natalie studying him while he spoke. "And that's it in a nutshell," Sam said.

"I suppose you've noticed Chloe is quite attractive."

"She is, yes, and yes, she was. Half the boys in high school had crushes on Chloe Jansen."

"Including you?"

"Yes, including me."

Natalie smiled. "Okay, you passed the test." Changing tack, she said, "Listen, Sam, I'll give you my unvarnished and unofficial opinion on the Jansens. Anything is possible, but I'm afraid they're gone." She stopped and looked over the balcony's railing at the vast stretch of water. "Chloe will need to come to grips with that."

"I'm guessing she knows they're gone now," Sam said. "Maybe she's just hoping—in a situation that makes no sense at all—that she can find out what happened."

"I'm sure this is a difficult time, and I feel so horrible for her." Natalie opened her mouth to say something more; instead, she exhaled and shook her head. "What do you say to another splash of wine? Then I'll tell you about my idea for what you might do regarding their disappearance."

"I appreciate your help," Sam said. "I'm hoping over dinner we'll have time to talk about you."

Natalie batted her eyelashes. "I think we can work that in."

•   •   •

After dinner, they walked barefoot along the beachfront. Natalie said, "As busy as it is on the boulevard side, I've always marveled at how this one stretch here can be so quiet."

"I know, right?" Sam said, looking at the nighttime sky. "I was just thinking about how peaceful it is."

Natalie smiled when she turned to face Sam. "Would you like to come up for a cup of coffee?"

"Sure, that would be nice." He couldn't resist a quick gaze into her eyes as he extended a hand to help her step up on the walkway leading to the street. They returned to Natalie's balcony and pushed aside the small table that had sat between them before.

Natalie said, "One thing I love about the sea is looking at the stars above."

"You've got a beautiful place here. It's so quiet, and the view of the water and sky is fantastic." He took a sip of coffee and faced Natalie. "I think the view right here on your balcony is amazing too."

When she turned toward him, her fiery brown eyes lit the night air like two torches.

Sam placed his coffee cup on the floor against the railing. "Can you lean this way for a second?"

"I think I can, sure."

His hand stroked her cheek while his lips grazed hers. She returned the kiss forcefully, then moving from her chair, she sat on his lap. Their faces were inches apart until their lips touched cautiously at first, then they kissed more urgently. She undid the top button of his shirt and ran her hand across his chest. Taking a break for a moment, they breathed heavily before resuming their intimacies.

She slipped her hand from underneath his shirt and stood. Loosening the tie around her waist, she unzipped her dress in front, allowing it to fall to the floor. The wondrous beauty and stirring sight before him took his breath away. When he stood, she took his hand and led him to her bedroom.

• • •

Later, while they lay in bed, Natalie traced the tips of her fingers over Sam's chest up to his arms.

"I guess you work out a little," she said.

"When I can."

"What's this?" Her hand had found a ridge of skin on the biceps muscle of his left arm.

He stared at the ceiling. "That would be a by-product of the job."

"What does that mean?"

"It was a drug deal gone bad, and a bullet passed through here," he said, pointing to his biceps, "and went out the back of my arm. It left a scar, but everything still works."

He pulled her closer. "I could ask the same about this tiny little scar under your chin. We have matching ones, see?" He leaned his head back to show a half-inch line that ran underneath his jaw. "Mine was from playing football, but I want to know how you got yours."

She said, "It wasn't from football, and I can promise you, Special Agent Dahl, it didn't come from a drug deal. The real story is I was five and fell running at the beach. Miles and miles of nothing but sand, but my chin found the one broken seashell."

"If it makes you feel any better, it's almost not even noticeable, and I had to be looking from underneath you to see it."

"So, that's what you were looking at?"

"And other things. It's cute." With his arm under her back, he rolled her on top. "You think I can have another look?"

• • •

Early the following morning, Sam was sitting on the balcony with a cup of coffee when he heard the sliding door open behind him and felt a warm hand caress his neck.

"I hope you're Natalie," he said.

"I am." She bit his ear. "How's the coffee?"

"Wonderful. I hope you don't mind—I took notes last night on your coffee-making operation."

"No, it's nice to wake up to hot coffee waiting for me." She took a seat next to him. "Early start to the day for you?"

"I wanted to get going on your idea. I thought I'd better grab a fresh set of clothes from the motel, especially if I'm going to make the rounds along the coast. The list of small seaside satellite police offices you made isn't long, but it'll take time today to visit all of them."

"Our normal business practice is to reach out to the larger police departments in missing person cases, and I know it's a long shot," she said, "but you might learn something from one of those that fell through the cracks."

"Tell me if this makes sense. I'm thinking of going south because the float plan Ben Jansen left Chloe showed they planned to travel to Sanibel Island."

"If they followed their plan, it makes total sense for you to focus your attention in that direction."

"I've been thinking more about what you said last night," Sam said. "Take into account I know nothing about the boating world; I want to run something past you."

"Let me get a cup of coffee, and we can talk it over."

After Natalie went inside, Sam leaned back in the chair, basking in the warmth of the morning seaside air and the afterglow of a marvelous evening. "

Once she returned and settled in, Sam ran through a mental list of his observations regarding the Jansens. "I've looked over the reports Chloe gave me from the Coast Guard and various police departments. It said you found no wreckage anywhere."

"Correct."

"And there were no emergency radio calls reported."

"Right."

"The weather on the day the Jansens left, and for the entire week, was great with no storms, no high winds, and I think one report even addressed the possibility of a rogue wave as being almost mathematically impossible."

"That's true."

"The Jansens, by all accounts, don't fit the profile of an unhappy couple. According to Chloe, my sister, and others, they are happily married, meaning it rules out any sort of, and I hate to say this, murder-suicide."

Natalie kept her eyes trained on him. "Okay."

"They're both experienced boaters. In fact, I remember when I was a teenager, Ben Jansen's passion, other than his professional career as a medical doctor, was boating. Carol's life too. That would tend to indicate they didn't screw up out there. Anything's possible, but he fits the definition of super meticulous."

"Yes, that's consistent with what we heard too."

Sam shifted in his chair. "It's been far too long to think they went boating happy and haven't bothered to call in; that's crazy at this point."

"Agreed," Natalie said.

"So, where does that leave us?"

"Tell me what you're thinking."

"Logic dictates if we can eliminate the other possibilities, that leaves us with the conclusion something sudden and unexpected happened: not weather or being unprepared, not marital strife, no wreckage and no flotation devices found anywhere, an event so unexpected and so sudden, it prevented either of them from making a simple SOS call on the radio."

Sam looked at Natalie for a long five seconds without speaking.

"What are you saying?" she said.

"Could folks from another boat have surprised them? I'm sure I sound like I'm twelve years old, but are there still, you know, pirates out there? I'm not talking about the kind with a patch over their eyes, but just bad guys who attacked them, for any number of reasons. Does that happen here in these waters?"

Natalie sat back and considered. "It's rare in the Gulf," she said. "There have been a handful of isolated cases where armed assailants attack an oil platform and hold the workers captive and take anything of value." She shook her head. "Other boaters—we almost never hear of that."

Sam nodded. "I'm trying to approach this like a detective and find a scenario fitting all of those circumstances. Something happened, and all the other things we talked about don't fit, so where does that leave us?"

"Sam, it's possible something like that happened. We don't encounter it, well, almost never."

"It's an idea I'm playing with in my head." He gazed at her steadily. "I'm going to keep an open mind while I work my way south and ask questions today."

"Will I see you later?"

He took her hand and pulled her onto his lap.

"I thought you'd never ask." He kissed her. "I'd love to pick up where we left off this morning."

"How does a home cooked meal sound tonight?"

He kissed her again. "Like a dream come true."

CHAPTER TEN

Sam took the Sunshine Skyway Bridge over Tampa Bay, then dropped onto surface streets leading to the Marine Unit of the Bradenton Police Department. He knew using the term long shot to describe the police and marina checks was overly optimistic, because as Natalie and others had told him, the Coast Guard worked with the local and state police, so the chances of learning something new were almost nil.

He'd already decided he would allow anyone he spoke with to assume incorrectly that the DEA had an interest in the Jansens' disappearance, otherwise he feared being rebuffed and redirected to the Coast Guard.

After entering the Marine Unit, he flashed his badge and introduced himself. "I'm looking for any information your department might have regarding the two boaters, Ben and Carol Jansen, who went missing a month or so ago."

The man behind the Marine Unit window, a studious-looking type with thick-rimmed glasses and a squarish face, looked up with an expression in his eyes of equal parts surprise and curiosity. "Troubling how they vanished." He pursed his lips. "Um, we had a couple of boats help on the search. I must say, I don't envy the Coast Guard's job with all their other responsibilities." His expression changed into a frown. "You don't realize how big an area there is to cover until you're out in the middle of it with a three-hundred-and-sixty-degree view of that vast and intimidating body of water, you know?"

Sam didn't, but he nodded in agreement, saying, "Yes, I'm sure it can be."

"And what specifically are you looking for, if I can ask?"

Sam thought it was an appropriate question, one for which he had no answer. He said, "Just any information about these boaters, or other boaters, who were found in similar circumstances, you know, anything that might be helpful to tie this instance together with others." He knew he was babbling, hoping if he threw something, anything, into the conversation, it would cover his own ineptitude and jog something of interest from the man.

"The DEA is looking into this—do I want to know why?" the man asked.

"No, sir, you don't. We're just trying to cover as much as we can and as fast as we can, you understand?"

"Sure, sure. I do." The man nodded. "I can say I don't have anything to add to this, but I have no problem giving you a report of what we did in conjunction with the Coast Guard. We were at it hard for days, then between the elapsed time when they disappeared and the approach of a major storm, we had to end our efforts. We're still open to hearing anything from anyone about it."

"I understand," Sam said. In reality, he didn't understand at all. He was flying blind, but he made a well-practiced knowing nod and a disconcerted look to express his agreement.

"Would you like a copy of the report?" the man asked.

Sam knew he had struck out, plus he already had a copy from Chloe. "No, but thanks for your time. We appreciate your efforts on the matter."

Who's this we I threw out there? There's no we; it's just me alone, stumbling around in the dark.

He nodded again and said, "Sir, you have a good day." On the walk to the parking lot, he said to himself, "One down, many to go." By the time he lowered himself into his car, he felt like a slow, burning cauldron of foolishness and ineptness, with a sprig of hopelessness added in to enhance the flavor. He sat, looking at himself in the mirror. "Sam, you're wasting your effing time." Then he thought about Chloe for a moment, imagining she was sitting alone in her kitchen, waiting for the phone to ring, hoping for news. He told her he would give the inquiry a shot and figured what was the worst that could happen; he'd see some pretty coastline and later, he'd treat himself to a pleasant lunch somewhere.

Looking at the next police department on his list, he tossed the notebook on the seat beside him and started the car, repeating the same scenario at various police departments and sheriff's offices along the coast, with every stop analogous to three months of his life passing by. The carrot tugging him forward was the lunch pledge he made to himself, and in a small town called Nokomis farther south on Highway 41, he delivered on that promise.

It wasn't much more than a shanty with a two-by-twelve piece of lumber for a table in front. Sam figured the man behind the counter, with the gray, shoulder-length hair and skin that resembled a twice-baked potato, had been there forever. His neck was nothing more than stringy tendons connecting collar bones to his chin and his mouth had only a half a dozen more teeth than a newborn baby.

When he spoke, it sounded like English, but damned if Sam was sure. On the third try, he grasped that the man was asking him what he wanted to eat. His new friend liked to talk, and he was funny, Sam gathered, based in part on how he punctuated every sentence or two with laughter coming from deep in his belly.

Sam concluded there were three choices for lunch: fried fish or fried fish or more fried fish. From what he could decipher from the ragged menu and the man who multi-tasked as cook, server, and afternoon entertainment, a sandwich consisted of two sesame seed buns doing their best to corral a huge fish patty made up of grouper, Greek seasonings, cornmeal, beer, egg, tartar sauce, and a big, juicy slice of tomato and leafy lettuce to top it off. The eight-dollar meal included a pile of hush puppies, savory, deep-fried round balls of cornmeal-based batter, on the side, and sweet tea to wash it all down. When he finished lunch, Sam felt well rewarded for all his morning's activities.

But he knew fun time was over, and he had to get back to work. As he motored down the highway, Sam thought life sure seemed simpler along this part of the coast. Each little city had a quaint downtown area of a block or two where townsfolk conducted all manner of business in a single afternoon. He was certain by five or six in the evening, the town rolled up the sidewalk and shut down until the following morning.

His next stop was the small police department in Venice, yet they had both a marine and a bike patrol. Once again, Sam showed his credentials and introduced himself.

The officer, a portly middle-aged man sporting a dandy handle-bar mustache, spoke with a deep baritone voice. "Forrester Tuttle," he said, pointing to the metal name tag pinned to his uniform shirt pocket. "Nice to make your acquaintance." He pushed aside a pimento-cheese sandwich and said, "Most people just call me Tuttle or Tut, but the fact is, I don't care what they call me, as long as they don't call me late for dinner." His rich voice matched the booming laughter. "How may I be of service to you, Agent Dahl?"

"Please, call me Sam." He started right in. "I'm conducting routine checks with the various departments along the coast here, trying to collect any information I can relative to the missing boaters, Mr. and Mrs. Jansen, from a month ago."

Tut leaned forward and said, "That's interesting you'd be looking into that, Sam. There's not much I could tell you, other than we knew about it, but we weren't involved in the search; sure, we kept a look-out, because a boater in trouble—there's nothing worse. I'm sorry I can't help you."

With another defeat under his belt, Sam said, "Yeah, I've been hearing that today and not for the second or even third time, but thanks, I appreciate your time." Sam paused, then said, "It sure is pretty here."

"In my opinion, there's nowhere better." Tut swung his arms upward and said, "I can't imagine living or working elsewhere. My older brother, Winston, worked here at the station too, but he's retired now. Holds it over my head every chance he can get."

"I imagine so."

"I think he likes the feel of retirement, the freedom it gives him, but he still misses the work." Tut stared off into the quiet, empty office space for a second. "We have a volunteer policing thing going on here, like some smaller fire departments, and Winston can come and go when he wants."

"That's nice."

"Yeah, he's one of the good guys. If he's not boating, he's sitting over at the wharf in this little closet he likes to call his office. He enjoys talking to people and helping where he can. I'll call and see if he's around; you might speak to him."

"Um, thanks, but I better get—"

But Tut wasn't finished speaking, and his voice drowned out Sam's. "The whole time he worked here, he kept this little box, like a recipe box, with index cards—his own little system—where he'd maintain notes about complaints on different things. Like I said, Winston talks to a lot of people, so he's got a bunch of records." Tut let loose with another rumble of laughter. "I'll call over and tell him you're on your way. He'll get a kick out of a federal agent wanting his help."

Sam said, "Like I was saying—"

"No, sir. No need to thank me." Tut held up the palm of his hand to Sam. "I have to give Winston a shout to make sure he's there, but it could be worth your time."

While he waited, Sam felt captive to his present circumstance and reminisced about lunch, wishing he had another hush puppy to eat.

"Hey, Winston, wake up!" Tut said into the phone. "I guess you answering means they're still letting you hang around the wharf. Listen, I'm sending a federal agent your way to talk, so tidy up your office."

There was a pause in the conversation on Tut's end, then he said, "Hell, I'd say so; it's a big dang deal anytime D.C. sends a narcotics man all the way down here to little old Venice, Florida." After another pause, he said, "Just straighten up your tie, Winston, he'll be there soon enough."

Tut hung up the phone. "My big brother—now he's a character, that one. Listen, he's easy to find. Drive over to this building at the wharf, it's gray and has a roof with red tiles—it's not a big place—and look for a room that makes you think this is where I'd stick the mops, brooms, and whatnot. That's where you'll find my brother Winston."

"Okay," Sam said, "I will." He couldn't help but smile. "It was a pleasure meeting you, Tut, and thanks again for your help today."

Officer Tuttle cracked his knuckles and reached for his sandwich. "You're welcome. Take her easy."

As Sam walked toward his car, he debated skipping the visit with Winston Tuttle, but his brother had gone to trouble to set up the meeting. To make himself feel better, Sam decided this would be his last stop for the day.

• • •

It was a three-minute drive to the wharf. He pulled into a parking space next to the building Tut had described and went inside. He looked around until he saw a man standing outside a doorway, waving him over.

Sam presented his identification. "Your brother suggested I should come talk to you."

"Yes, sir, I'm Winston Tuttle, retired. Make no mistake about that."

"It sounds like you still volunteer your time to something worthwhile. Good for you."

Winston said, "I do what I can, because when you get right down to it, I believe that's what policing's all about, helping people."

"That's a nice way to look at it. Can I call you Winston?"

"I've been called worse," he said.

"And please, call me Sam."

"Okay, Sam," Winston said, gesturing behind him. "Let's have a seat in my office."

The "office" was a six-by-six-foot closet, with a small wood kitchen table and two chairs with protective plastic material stretched over floral-printed seat cushions. Sam guessed the table and chair collection must have been a spare set from Winston's home or possibly his grandmother's house in the 1950s. The only art decorating the wall was a 1983 calendar with bikini-clad women promoting a line of oil filters for automobiles.

After they took their respective seats, Winston folded one hand into the other and rested them on the table. "I never imagined I'd be meeting up with a big shot narcotics officer all the way from Washington, D.C., today."

"Yeah, I think there might have been a little misunderstanding; I'm from Los Angeles." Sam waved his hand to the side. "I haven't been to D.C. in years, and I'm doing fine without it."

Winston said, "A snake pit if ever I saw one. The trouble is, they get themselves elected, promising the sun, the moon, and the stars, then they won't go home. They're good at squabbling, but they never accomplish much of anything."

"That's a fair assessment." Sam nodded. "I grew up close to here, in Clearwater."

"Oh, my goodness, I can remember when she was a lovely little town," Winston said. "I'm sorry, but Clearwater's too grown up and out for me now."

"I know what you mean."

"All right, so what are you hoping to accomplish here in Venice?" Winston asked.

"I'm looking into the disappearance of those boaters from a month ago, Ben and Carol Jansen."

"Oh, yes, I remember; so troubling." He paused for a moment before eyeing Sam. "If I may ask, what's a federal drug agent doing investigating the circumstances of those missing boaters?"

Sam thought about the same pitch he'd been making all day and decided against it. "Winston, I'm going to give it to you straight. Me looking into this thing has nothing at all to do with my job, and everything to do with the Jansens' daughter, Chloe, who's a friend of mine from back in high school in Clearwater. She doesn't understand the differences between our jobs, from the local police to the Coast Guard to drug agents, and so on. She thinks because I work in law enforcement, I can help."

"You might, you never know, you might just help. Listen, Sam," Winston said, "I appreciate your honesty. There's too little of that these days, and if you can't help a friend, then what good are you?"

"Agreed, but I don't see what I can do that hasn't already been done." Sam shrugged. "But a promise is a promise."

Winston scratched at the whiskers on his chin. "I'm sorry to say I don't have any idea at all about what happened to them."

"Forrester suggested I come to speak with you, so I thought I would follow through, but I understand." And with another loss, Sam rose from his chair.

Winston patted his hand on the table. "I'm old school." He leaned over and picked up a small gray box from the floor, just like the one Tut had described, and set it on the table between them.

Sam sat down again.

"I keep this box," Winston said, "with notes from anybody who makes a complaint, and unless it's criminal, then I send them to the real police. My brother thinks I'm doing this, so I can collect a bunch of stories to write a book, but it doesn't matter what he thinks. Anyway, if I'm not spending time on my boat, then I'm walking the docks or sitting in here, so people tell me things." He opened the box. "You're welcome to look through these index cards. This is the 1987 box, and they're related to just about everything under the sun: the town, the waterfront, and a good deal about boating stuff. And these cards are in chronological order, so take your time, and I'll step away to give you breathing space. I'm sure Forrester told you I like to talk, and if I stay put, that's what I'll do." Winston stood and took a step toward the door. "I'll be back in a while."

Sam watched Winston walk away, then he directed his attention back to the task at hand, curious about information an eccentric man like Winston would collect. There were dozens of cards inside the box, and he removed one at a time to start his review. He noted Winston had an organized system with notes written in a legible, handsome print: the top left corner of each card had the date of contact, followed by the name or names of whomever he spoke with, then a sentence or two or even a brief paragraph about the subject matter.

Some cards were comical, such as a fisherman who complained that the noise from the airport was scaring away the fish, while another reported that tourists were feeding junk food to the seagulls. Others were more serious; the most frequent complaint dealt with boaters speeding through the no wake zones.

One card toward the back of the box caught his eye. Earlier in the year, a middle-aged husband and wife reported being approached by another boat several nautical miles off the coast. The complainants suspected a young couple may have been falsely claiming engine trouble for reasons that were not clear. They didn't allow the young couple's boat to draw too close, and after talking for a few minutes, the young couple got underway with no apparent problem.

Sam wondered what happened when a boat broke down at sea. Being immobilized on water wasn't like being stuck on the highway, he reasoned, where the worst-case scenario meant walking a few miles to the nearest gas station for help.

Winston leaned against the door and said, "Now you see why Forrester is always after me about why I keep going with this silly box; says it's a lot of hooey."

Sam looked up, still deep in thought over the card he had just read. He caught up to Winston's words after a few moments. "No, no, I think you've got a nice program here," he said. "Sure, some of them are a little odd." He held up the index card. "But this one might be something worth following up on."

"Oh?" Winston said. "What do you got?"

Sam refocused on the card. "It says here that on the twenty-first of June, according to this card, two people, Steve and Cindy Ardman, told you about an encounter they had with another boat off the coast. They think those people might have been faking mechanical or engine trouble."

Winston took the card from Sam and held his reading glasses to his face. "Yes, I remember them now. I had been out on the water for about three hours that day and was cleaning up my boat before heading home. These two, the Ardmans, came up to me at the dock, and like it says, this young couple approached them, claiming a mechanical problem. They talked for a short time and the Ardmans became suspicious."

"Is that a common thing to happen out there—where people stop to talk?" Sam asked.

"We come up on each other sometimes out on the sea. It's not that unusual to stop and talk, especially if you know one another. Less so if you're strangers, but you can learn a great deal from fellow boaters."

Winston flipped the card over. "I made a note on the back here; the Ardmans are from St. Pete, and I wrote a telephone number for them too."

"Oh, I hadn't gotten that far yet. If you don't mind, I might follow up with them."

"Not at all," he said, and handed the card back to Sam, who made a note of their names and phone number.

"What's this written here on the back at the bottom?" Sam said.

Winston put his reading glasses back on. "Hmm, I take pride in my penmanship and can usually read my handwriting. Oh, this word here is *blonde* and the other, dang it, I can't make out, but you say you're going to call them?"

"I'm planning to," Sam said.

"They may be able to decipher what I wrote. If you'd like, I can make a copy of both sides of the card at my friend's office two doors down. If she's in, I'm sure she won't mind."

"That would be great, thanks."

Winston returned a minute later with a photocopy in hand. "It's not much to go on, but I wish you luck helping your friend."

Sam thanked Winston, saying it had been a pleasure to speak with him; then he got back into his car. As he drove north, he thought about Winston's notes and the new lead to follow. He knew it was unfair to think the information provided hope for the Jansens. It didn't. It was an event fitting a story line that he'd created in his own mind.

Natalie had said to come over at seven. He was looking at a ninety-minute drive straight through to Clearwater. That gave him enough time for a nap and a shower. He also needed to call Chloe to let her know he had nothing so far.

CHAPTER ELEVEN

Sam hadn't expected to be so tired, but the one-hour nap was the right prescription. The driving wasn't bad; it was the talking throughout the day that had worked him over.

When he called Chloe, he found her in a fragile state. He was careful with how he spoke, avoiding anything that amounted to wild speculation on his part. He told her he had followed up with various coastal police departments to check if they had any new information the Coast Guard didn't already possess. That part was the truth, and he was comfortable sharing it, but he was careful to avoid mentioning his own theory of what might have happened, and he also left out his next step, but promised to stay in touch.

• • •

Standing at the entrance to the Isola Bella complex, Sam pressed the button next to Natalie's name. He had made two quick stops along the way and was carrying his purchases in his arms.

"Right on time. You know the way," Natalie said. "Come on up."

When he heard the gate release, Sam eased up the stairs, thinking about the previous evening. It was more than a slice of heaven; it had been the whole damned pie. He found the front door ajar and pushed it open another foot. "Hello, Natalie?"

"Come in." She was standing at the counter in the kitchen, arranging bagel chips on a plate. "I hope you came hungry."

When she turned, they kissed for a long moment, until she pulled away and placed her hands on his chest. "I need to focus. Dinner, dinner, dinner," she said. They kissed again before she slid back into the kitchen. "You stay on your side, because I've got to finish up in here."

Sam eyed a large pot on the stove. "What's going on there?"

"It's a surprise. What about you? You came bearing gifts."

"I visited with my old friend at the liquor store and asked for a recommendation, but all I could tell him was you said dinner was something seafood and something soupy." He removed the bottle from the bag. "He told me it was important not to overwhelm all the flavors in a seafood stew, so I accepted his advice and went with a dry Pinot Grigio."

"Of course, you did," she said. "You've known him for twenty-four hours."

"Hey, we go way back, like bucket seats."

"I think you two have made an excellent choice. This will go well, and what's that?"

He opened the other bag. "I had to rely on my own instincts at the supermarket, but I applied the liquor store guy's principles for selecting the proper ice cream and ended up going with a simple Butter Pecan."

"You're the best shopper." Natalie gave Sam a thumb's up and winked. "I have to meet your wine guy."

"If it hadn't been for his lessons in the last twenty-four hours," Sam said, "I might have gone with Butter Pecan's crazy uncle, Pecan Turtle Fudge."

"You made the right choice, but we'll have the crazy uncle over for dinner another time."

She opened the pot and stirred. "Dinner will be five more minutes, so you should start with the appetizer," Natalie said.

"Don't be shy, it's a shrimp dip, one of my favorites with cream cheese, green onions, chili sauce, and a couple of other things."

She reached for the ice cream and turned to place it in the freezer. When she turned back, Sam was smiling at her.

Natalie blushed. "What is it? Did I do something funny?"

"No, I was just admiring you from across the counter. I like your blouse. I like your style too."

She looked down and smoothed over her blouse with her hands. "It's soft, breathable, and great for summer."

Sam said, "Besides preparing a wonderful dinner, what else kept you busy today?"

"I might have fallen back to sleep after you left, then I did a little shopping for dinner and relaxed. Tell me about your day." Instead of waiting for an answer, she leaned over the counter. "Come a little closer for a sec." She wiped a smudge of dip from the corner of his mouth. "That's all better."

"Thank you. I went straight down the list you gave me, one after another. Everyone was receptive to talking about the Jansens, even when they had nothing new to add to the investigation."

"Yes, I'm sure," Natalie said, turning back to the pot of stew.

"But then after I stopped for lunch—"

"Oh, where'd you go?"

"I stopped off at a place along Highway 41 called Nokomis."

Natalie looked at Sam. "Nokomis is a cute little town."

"We should go there sometime. I stumbled on a guy who has a kind of shack along the coast, and he fixes great fish sandwiches right in front of you. He was quite the character with tasty food, but not so easy to understand."

"A local, huh?"

"Yeah, I bet he's been there forever," Sam said. "Long hair, great tan, like he's spent his entire life in the sun, and very few teeth left, but he knows his way around a frying pan. The lunch alone was worth the drive, then I made my last stop in Venice, and a long story short, I got information that could be worth checking out. I met these two brothers, one active and one retired police officer, but the strangest thing was the retired cop does a one-man volunteer police thing like a volunteer fire house. He keeps this box of index cards where he documents complaints from people; that's the best way to describe it, I guess."

Natalie gazed at Sam. "He's retired, so where does he work?"

"That's the cool part for him. He loves boating, but when he's not on his boat, he sits in this building at the wharf, at their waterfront. Neat for him because he likes being there anyway, and he enjoys talking with folks. Anyway, he keeps a record of people reporting something that doesn't measure up to a criminal complaint at the police department."

Natalie narrowed her eyes. "Interesting."

"A lot of the cards are about nothing, even funny, but it gets better, you'll see, because he let me look through these cards, and I found one dealing with this couple who went boating about three months ago. He made a photocopy for me." Sam fished the paper out of his back pocket and handed it to Natalie. "You'll see where this couple encountered a boat, and the people were acting strange or faking like they needed help with a mechanical issue, I guess. The couple became concerned and didn't get too close, but after they parted ways, the suspicious boat seemed to get underway as if they weren't having any problems."

Natalie's focus remained on the paper, then she asked, "What's this say down here?"

Sam walked around the counter to look over Natalie's shoulder.

"This part," she said, pointing at the card.

"The retired officer said that word is *blonde*, but he couldn't read this other word."

"It looks like Hispanic to me," Natalie said.

Sam leaned in closer, resting his chin on Natalie's shoulder while he looked at the card. "You'd make a good detective."

"I'm used to reading people's terrible handwriting at work," Natalie said. "It comes with lots of practice, believe me."

"Before I drove over here, I called the number on the card and spoke with the husband who invited me to come to their house to talk with him and his wife tomorrow morning."

"What did you say—did you tell him why you want to meet?"

"Yes, I told him about my conversation with Winston, the retired police officer they spoke with in Venice," Sam said. "I told him I wanted to follow up and would explain more tomorrow."

"Could be something, right?"

"Yeah, it could be. They live in St. Petersburg, so I'll head over in the morning."

Natalie looked up into Sam's eyes. "I guess you'll need your sleep tonight."

He put his arms around Natalie's waist. Their bodies pressed together when they kissed. "I don't think I'll need much, just a little catnap."

Natalie patted Sam on his belly. "Good. How about dinner?"

"I can't wait to see the surprise," Sam said.

"Would you grab the plates and bowls off the table? It's my version of Brazilian fish stew with grouper, coconut milk, onion, tomatoes, carrots, chili peppers, garlic, lime, and fish stock." She removed the cover from the pot and stirred while Sam brought the dishes into the kitchen and leaned over to take in the aroma. "Fantastic."

Natalie ladled the stew into the bowls. "We've got brown rice here too," she said, pointing to a smaller pot. "And I'll get the salad."

"You've been busy today," Sam said.

"Not really—this stew is simple to make."

"I'm impressed all the same."

Natalie brought the salad to the table while Sam carried the two bowls of stew; then retrieved the wine and poured two glasses. They ate for a moment in silence, until Natalie said, "Sam, you said something about your arm and a shooting, and I was curious what happened—if you're okay talking about it, but if not, that's fine too."

"No, I don't mind. I don't talk about it much, but it's not anything I'm keeping secret."

Natalie put down her spoon, picked up her glass of wine, and held it close to her lips.

Sam took another spoonful of stew. "Delicious," he said before wiping his mouth with his napkin. "I had been on the job for two years and was doing an undercover deal where I was supposed to buy a couple of kilograms of coke from two dealers. We were in a car, my car, an undercover vehicle, where the plates come back to a fictitious name and address." He took a quick sip of wine before restarting. "The long and short is these guys had no real plans to deliver the cocaine to me. As I was to learn later, they thought I had the money in the car."

"Money for the cocaine, right?" Natalie asked.

"Right, but I've thought it over so many times in my head, and there's no reason they should have thought the cash was with me, because I made it clear over and over; the money would arrive in a separate car, but only after I saw the powder. I guess they thought I was lying and had it with me in the trunk or something."

"Why do you want them to think you don't have the money with you?"

"It's a safety issue. If someone is predisposed to ripping you off, and they believe you have the money with you, they'll try to do that, so that's why we're taught to emphasize the money is elsewhere, then if you run into rip-off artists, what would be the point of trying to rob someone if there's no money? Does that make sense?"

"Yes, and the whole thing sounds dangerous."

"It can be, but the typical scenario is the bad guys show the dope, then the undercover agent gives the bust signal, and we arrest the bad guys."

Natalie took a sip of wine. "It still sounds dangerous to me."

"In this case, instead of showing me the coke, they demanded the money, but I said I didn't have it with me. They told me to open the trunk, so I tossed the key to the one guy sitting next to me in the front seat and said, 'Here, you open it.' He did, but like I told them, there was nothing in the trunk."

She took another sip of wine. "So, what happened?"

"The man in the back seat had a gun pointed at me, but he got distracted when his partner said there was no money in the trunk. As he started turning his head back to me, I grabbed at his gun, and we struggled, until I managed to turn it toward him." Sam held out his hands and shrugged. "The gun discharged, and he died instantly."

Natalie was holding her breath, her complexion a pale gray.

"We can stop, if you'd like."

She swallowed first, then said, "No, I want to hear the rest."

"After that happened—the shooting in the car—I had to get out because I was a sitting duck in there. I half fell and half jumped from the car, but I had dropped the other guy's gun on the floor in between the seats by accident. In the time it took for me to get to my knees and draw my pistol from a holster hidden inside the back of my pants, the guy at the trunk had come around the car and fired off one shot. Took one round right here," he said, holding up his left arm, "but I could still use my right hand ... and he died too."

Natalie shook her head. "Jesus, Sam, that's awful."

"Yeah, it was. The thing is, I wasn't supposed to be alone, but my partner, another DEA agent, called in sick that morning. When the informant called later in the day and said we could do the deal, a group of us agents talked it over with the boss. Because I had already met these two jokers before, we thought it would be better not to introduce someone new into the picture." Sam swallowed another spoonful of soup. "By the way, this is great soup! Anyway, we should have put the deal off to another day, but I was willing to go through with it, because I was a young hotshot and didn't want to miss out on getting the thing done."

"My God, that's an unbelievable story, I mean, believable that it happened, but you must have been scared." She reached over and placed her hand on Sam's arm.

"It all happened in an instant, but after it was over, I was shook-up. It caught up with me, and anybody who says different, is not telling the whole truth. The stuff on TV isn't how it works in real life. In the make-believe world, someone gets in a shooting, and after the commercial break, he or she is right back on the job."

Natalie nodded. "I guess that's TV for you."

"In the real world, there's an aftermath: the internal investigation, the second guessing, the armchair quarterbacks. I agreed with what they, the review board, had to say, and I'm okay. Things have a way of getting—I don't know—compartmentalized, I guess, and I've dealt with it."

"What did the review board and internal investigation people say?"

"That we should have delayed the deal until my partner came back, and they were right, but they were complimentary of my actions, something like my response was 'commensurate with the threat level.'"

Natalie stared into her glass of wine, breathing in and out.

"Hey, this stew is terrific. You should try some."

"Thank you. I will." Natalie looked up, then said with a gentle tenderness, "That's quite a story." She stood and stepped behind Sam. "I've got a better idea." She kissed his neck and whispered into his ear, "Leave everything here and come with me."

•   •   •

Later, they lounged in bed with the sheet draped over them. Natalie leaned back against Sam's chest; his legs straddling hers while he caressed her arms. "I bet you'll find this entertaining, but I read a book about boating for beginners on my plane trip over here; sort of technical, but still interesting, with explanations on basic terminology and stuff for newbies like me. I think I learned a fair bit."

Natalie turned her head back toward Sam. "Hmm, I suppose you're feeling confident about your boating knowledge?"

"Yeah, I suppose I am." He tickled her side.

"I've got a little idea," she said.

"Great, I like little ideas."

"Okay, smarty-pants, let's see how good you are. We visit elementary schools as part of our outreach program and for fun we give short quizzes to the students. Why don't we put your knowledge to the test?"

He kissed her shoulder. "Bring it on, Lieutenant Timmons."

"Let me find copies; they're around here somewhere." She leaned over to the edge of the bed but turned back to look at Sam. "You have to close your eyes while I go to the kitchen."

"I've already seen you—"

She held the sheet in front of her. "Close them or you forfeit the game."

"Closed. See?" He pointed to his eyes.

After Natalie dashed away, Sam heard kitchen drawers opening and objects inside being jostled. A minute later, the pattering of footsteps came back toward the bedroom. "I'm coming in. Your eyes are still closed, right?"

"Of course."

She crawled into bed, facing Sam, and covered herself. "You can open them now."

"You're sure?"

"Yes. I have two separate quizzes; one we gave to a sixth-grade class and the other we gave to fifth graders. Or was it the other way? It doesn't matter; let's see how you do."

"Is it multiple choice or—"

"You'll find out in a second. We'll do five questions. Are you ready?"

He stroked her arm. "I was born ready."

"We'll see about that. Number one. This is super easy. What is the front of the boat called?"

"You're right," Sam said. "Way too easy; it's the bow."

She held up her hand. "Very good, but they get harder. Number two is a multiple choice, so listen up. If the boat you're on capsizes, what should you do? Should you abandon the boat or use the boat for flotation or swim as far away as possible?"

"I didn't read about this," Sam said, crossing his hands behind his head. "Common sense tells me to stay with the boat, so I'll go with the flotation option."

Natalie patted his leg. "You're on a roll; someone has been a good student." She studied the other quiz for a moment. "Okay, the third question is what is the purpose of a lazarette on a boat?"

"A lazarette?" Sam said. "I don't remember reading about this either, so do I get any hints?"

Natalie said, "Fine, I'll give you three choices: one, a lazarette is used to help steer a boat in rough waters, or two, a lazarette is another name for a bucket when someone becomes sick on a boat, or three, it's another term for storage."

"A lazarette," Sam said, mimicking a foreign accent.

"If you were trying for French, that was terrible."

"Yeah, accents aren't my thing, but the word does sound French, right?"

"And how does that apply to the quiz you're taking at the moment?" Natalie asked.

He rubbed her thigh. "I was hoping for bonus points."

She brushed his hand away. "Nice try, but no bonus points. Answer, please."

"This is the hardest one so far," Sam said. "Steering in rough water sounds important, so I'll go with that."

She poked out her lower lip. "Sir, that's incorrect. A lazarette is positioned near or aft of the cockpit and used as a storage locker for gear and equipment."

He slapped the palm of his hand on his forehead. "That was my next guess."

"Uh huh, sure it was," she said. "The fourth question is what's anemophobia?"

Sam said, "This has something to do with boating?"

"Yes, sir, it does."

"It's a fear of something, and no choices are necessary this time because I think I've got it. I'll go with a fear of water."

"Oh, no, I'm so sorry." She frowned. "That would be incorrect. Anemophobia is a fear of wind."

"A fear of what? Wind? That could apply to lots of jobs besides boating, like pilots, truckers, and, let's see, kite testers."

"There's no such thing as a kite tester."

"Yes, there is because I almost became one," Sam said with a straight face. "The pay and benefits are great."

"Now I know you're full of it." She flicked her finger at his leg. "You've got two right and two wrong, and this is the last one; and as they say, this one is for all the marbles. So, how can you tell when a boat feels affectionate?"

"A boat can feel affectionate?" He stared at her. "This was a question for elementary school kids?"

"Yep," Natalie said.

"I don't have the slightest. Ha, just a second, I've got something; it's feeling affectionate because the boat wants to wave at people. Get it? *Wave* at people, like waves in the ocean." He moved his hand to demonstrate.

Natalie laughed.

"I don't know," Sam said. "I can't believe this was on the quiz."

"Everyone knows the answer to this oldie but goody." She tilted her head and looked at Sam. "You can tell a boat is feeling affectionate when it hugs the shore."

"You made that up."

"I didn't make it up, but someone did, I'm sure. We're talking Coast Guard Humor 101 here."

"Hilarious," Sam said. "I guess this means I failed."

"You came close, but, yes, you failed; so, your punishment is after we finish our dinner, you have to do the dishes."

"Fair enough, but you ought to know I cheated earlier when you ran out of the room; I peeked."

She grabbed his sides to tickle him.

"If it's any consolation, you have a nice butt."

She laid her head on his chest. "Are you up for going for a walk along the shore with me later?"

He kissed her on the top of the head. "Yes, I'd love to."

CHAPTER TWELVE

With the window rolled down in his car, the noise from an occasional vehicle passing by was the only interruption to a quiet Sunday morning drive. As Sam passed over the Snell Isle Bridge in the historic area of St. Petersburg, he recollected Natalie's urging to enjoy the splendid scenery. The old-world charm of the sculpted balusters lining each side of the two-hundred-plus-foot bridge provided a fitting introduction to the magic of the grand Mediterranean-influenced homes awaiting him. It stood a world apart from the other neighborhoods, one that he couldn't ever remember seeing as a child growing up in Clearwater. Tree-lined streets framed large waterfront homes, some dating back to the early twentieth century.

Once Sam located the Ardmans' address, he parked several feet away from the gated entry, taking a minute to admire the Italian-inspired architecture of the graceful manor. He grabbed the folder with notes about Chloe's parents, then walked over to the gate and reached to press the call button.

"I've been looking for you," said a middle-aged man with a touch of gray in his hair and dressed in comfortable light-green slacks and a polo shirt. He stood on the drive inside the gate, his gloved hands holding a pair of garden clippers.

"Steve Ardman?" Sam asked.

"That's me."

"Good morning, I'm Sam Dahl. We spoke yesterday."

Ardman placed the clippers in his back pocket, removed his work gloves, then walked toward the gated entrance. "I thought since I was out here waiting, I may as well put myself to good use because the real challenge is Mother Nature never rests." He pressed a button, releasing the gate latch, and extended a hand as Sam approached.

"Pleased to meet you." Sam held out his DEA credentials for Ardman's inspection.

Steve waved it away and said, "I'm sure you're who you say you are."

"I was admiring your place from the street for a minute."

"Thank you, we love it here," he said as he kicked the yard waste off the graveled walkway. "Queen's Wreath produces spectacular clusters of star-shaped purple flowers in the spring, but like most vines, it takes over and results in the classic man versus nature battle."

"I'm sure."

"Let's walk over there," he said, pointing to the edge of the porch at the back of the house. "I can show you why my wife and I were so desperate to buy this place."

They stopped by the porch with a stone foundation, admiring the bay of Tampa. "This was the big draw," Steve said.

The uninterrupted view of the water from the back side of the house could have been from a magazine cover. So spectacular, it almost made the neighboring estate homes disappear. "You must spend all your free time out here," Sam said.

"When we're not working or out on our boat, this is our life right here." He pointed toward the water and said, "The view remains the same, but the scenery changes constantly. You know what I mean?"

"I think so, yeah."

Steve turned to him. "Can I offer you something to drink?"

"I'm fine, no thanks."

"Let's grab a seat," he said, gesturing to the peacock wicker chairs sitting on the porch next to large and small clay-potted flowering plants. They settled in without speaking for a minute, simply admiring the beautiful bayfront view. The house felt comfortable, and Sam knew if this were his home, sitting and napping on the wide and welcoming porch would become a common ritual to his day.

"You said you wanted to talk about those boaters we encountered, right?" Steve said.

"Yes, that's correct, and thanks again for agreeing to meet with me."

"I told my wife you were coming, so I'm sure she'll cut her after-church socializing short and be here soon."

"I hope I'm not causing an inconvenience to her."

"Not at all. Believe me, she puts in plenty of time with the good Lord on Sunday mornings," he said. "I like to put my time in from right here on the porch."

"This is not such an awful place to attend worship," Sam said.

"A little secret between you and me: I prefer my church over hers. I figure God can bless me here all the same."

They were both laughing when the back door opened and a tall, graceful forty-something-year-old woman stepped onto the porch. "It sounds like I'm missing all the fun," she said.

"I didn't hear the gate out front open, but we just sat down." Steve said, "This is Agent Sam Dahl, and Sam, this is my wife, Cindy."

Both Sam and Steve stood.

"Good morning, Mr. Dahl," she said with a faint Southern accent.

"Pleased to meet you, but please call me Sam."

"It's part of my upbringing, so it's a hard habit for me to break. Did you want to talk with both of us together, Sam?"

"Yes, if it would be convenient for you?" She had a way of holding her head high when she spoke, making her appear elegant and confident, Sam thought.

"Of course, it's fine," she said.

"Thanks for taking the time out on a Sunday morning to meet with me. I was hoping to get your impression and any details you can remember about the encounter you had with boaters from a few months ago."

Steve turned a third chair to make it more of a circle and said, "Hon, please sit here."

Sam nodded to both. "I'm sure you're wondering what all the fuss is about after I spoke with Steve yesterday. I work for the Drug Enforcement Administration and was doing routine visits with the local police along the coast yesterday, when I learned you met with a retired police officer in Venice by the name of Winston Tuttle."

"Yes, we did," Cindy said. "Mr. Tuttle was an interesting character, like someone out of a movie."

"I agree with you. I must tell you I can't go into the details about my inquiry, you understand, but I have a professional interest in those individuals on that boat you met."

Sam had already decided before the meeting he wouldn't disclose the true purpose of his inquiry, figuring the boating community would be close-knit, and he didn't want to start any unfounded rumors connecting the Ardmans' encounter with the Jansens' disappearance. His reasoning was also selfish; he knew the scuttlebutt that arose from his questioning might lead back to him conducting an unauthorized investigation. This would create at least two problems. First, Coast Guard Deputy Commander Harold Champlain would be unhappy, and once he notified the DEA about Sam's activities, and there was little doubt in Sam's mind that DC Champlain would do so, his employer would be even less happy.

"By the way," Sam said, removing a piece of paper from his folder, "Officer Tuttle gave me a photocopy of the index card he prepared based on your experience that day."

"What a curious habit. He took great care to write what we talked about," Cindy said.

"It's interesting, for sure, and, as you say, it's curious, but his practice might prove helpful."

"We went into the Venice Yacht Club to meet with friends," Steve said. "While we were there, our friends suggested we talk to Mr. Tuttle about our earlier experience out on the water."

"Please start at the beginning and tell me anything you think is pertinent, and please dumb it down for a non-boater like me."

Cindy leaned forward and smiled. "We saw a boat approaching us; now, Sam, I'm a cautious individual, and Steve is too, though not as much as me." She turned to look at her husband. "As they approached, I remember you slowed down a bit, but you said you were keeping the engine running, and I agreed with you." She looked back at Sam. "We had no idea who these people were, after all."

"In my book, there's a protocol," Steve said, "and they violated it by coming up on us too fast and too close."

Cindy frowned for a moment, then said, "This young gal was waving at us, and once they got close enough, she said they were having trouble with their engine. Now, I know so little about boats, but I could tell, for someone with an engine problem, they sure came up on us in a big hurry."

Sam nodded, thinking it sounded like a provocative action to him.

Cindy said, "Then this younger man came out to the side of their boat and right away, he started in on the problems they were having and asked Steve if he knew anything about boat engines. I saw the young lady crying a little, and I could be wrong, but her tears struck me as phony, and I whispered that to Steve too."

Sam held Cindy's gaze as he considered her words. "Interesting."

Steve said, "I told them I didn't know much about engines. Besides, I found their behavior suspicious, and I didn't want to get caught up in something—"

Cindy interrupted her husband. "We didn't know what to make of them. Steve told them in a kind way that he couldn't help with their engine problem, but he said we could travel alongside them to the closest port to get assistance, if necessary." She turned to her husband. "Where were we at the time?"

"We were off the coast of Sarasota, and they would have been able to find mechanical help if they needed it."

Cindy said, "Sam, as quick as you can snap your fingers, they lost complete interest. It was like night and day with them. They turned and took off, and we didn't think that much about it and continued going south on our way to visit with friends in Venice."

After a moment, Sam said, "That sounds suspicious."

"We mentioned it to our friends, Hank and Becky Corcoran," Cindy said. "They were the ones who said we should talk to Mr. Tuttle. He was still working on his boat, and we had to walk right by him on our way out, so we stopped and chatted."

"Could you describe the man and the woman for me?" Sam asked.

"The woman was in her twenties," Cindy said. "She was pretty, with blonde hair and an adorable figure. The man was a little older, either late twenties or early thirties, tall, dark hair, good-looking man, and he spoke with a slight Hispanic accent."

"If I'm being honest," Steve said, "their behavior seemed more odd than threatening, but it was something I sensed, and Cindy did too, that didn't feel right to us, especially when they just took off."

"Could you describe their boat to me?"

Cindy turned in her chair. "Steve, that question is for you."

"It was an Ocean Yachts Sunliner, and if I'm not mistaken, it was new, or near new, and I'm thinking it was forty-something feet."

Sam asked, "Do you remember what color it was?"

"It was white just like our boat. Yachts and cabin cruisers don't have to be white, but most are, and there are reasons for that. A white color has the natural attribute of looking shiny and clean and boaters like that. Another reason has to do with the manufacturing process, where the pigmentation mixed in with the epoxy is typically white. A boat can have another color, but that makes it more complex and therefore more expensive. Another plus is the white color also helps to hide defects. That's more than you wanted to hear, I'm sure."

"Not at all; I appreciate the explanation. Anything else I should know?"

"I can't think of anything."

"Steve, yes there is," Cindy said. "Don't you remember I told you I saw the young lady from the boat again?"

When Steve shrugged, Cindy turned back to Sam and shook her head. "Excuse me for saying, but I think it's a male thing. He never listens."

Steve said, "I listen, but I suppose I also forget."

"Maybe that's it." Cindy put her hand on Steve's arm and said, "Anyway, I saw her waiting in front of a bar restaurant near the Gandy area where the bridge crosses over into Tampa. It's a young person's hangout. What's that restaurant's name? Oh, shoot, I can't remember, but I noticed her because she was standing with a court reporter I know from the circuit courts. I'm a lawyer, so I run in to this young lady from time to time at the courthouse. We've never spoken other than a good morning or hello."

"Do you know the reporter's name?" Sam said.

"If you give me a minute, it'll come to me. If I try to think of it, it won't. Anyway, I just caught a quick glance of them while I was driving by the restaurant—oh, her name is Melissa, no, that's not right, it's Melanie, that's it, Melanie Tunnenton. T-u-n-n-e-n-t-o-n. I only remember because it's an unusual last name and spelling."

"Yes, it is," Sam said and nodded.

"Melanie seems nice enough," Cindy said. "I see her every so often when I go to court, but it never crossed my mind to ask about her friend."

"That's okay; I might like to talk to her. Could I ask you not to approach Ms. Tunnenton about your run-in with the couple out at sea, or our conversation?"

Cindy shook her head. "I won't do that."

"That would be great," Sam said. "I'll get out of here and leave you to enjoy your Sunday. You've been quite helpful. Thank you."

"Maybe one day we'll see something on the news that will give us a hint of what's going on," Steve said.

Sam slipped the folder between his arm and his side. "Sometimes it works out that way, but for now, I would appreciate this conversation being kept between us."

"You can count on it," Steve said. "I'll walk you back to the gate."

•   •   •

After leaving the Ardmans, Sam drove to the nearest phone booth he could find that still had a book intact, wondering where this latest information might take him. He couldn't stop his inquiry now; he felt compelled to look up Melanie Tunnenton.

A small chain attached the phone book to a metal shelf. Holding a pen between his teeth, he leafed through the white pages, thinking how lucky it would be to find her. He reached the names starting with the letter T and began scanning the page using his index finger as a guide, only stopping when he saw an M. Tunnenton in Pinellas Park.

He wrote the number and address down and closed the book, allowing it to hang from its chain, then dropped coins into the slot and dialed a number.

"Hello?"

"Hello, Natalie. How are you?"

"Are you having fun?" she asked.

"A blast, yes. Listen, I'm going to be another hour. I've got one other thing to check, then I'll come over, if that's okay. You still want to go to the beach?"

"Yes, it's shaping up to be a nice day, and I'll start getting stuff together for us." After a momentary pause, she asked, "Did you have any luck with your meeting?"

"I did, and I'll catch you up later."

He parked on the street in front of a three-story, older brick building. The address in the phone book hadn't revealed the address for Melanie was an apartment house, so he knew he'd have to go inside and check the directory or the mailboxes, hoping to find her name listed. He kept his focus on the building's front door. Within minutes, a man entered with a simple yank on the entrance door. *No key. That's good.*

He had decided while he was at the Ardmans' house that he wouldn't try to talk to Melanie today. First, he wanted to run queries on her, so he could be armed with as much information as possible when he approached.

He got out of his car and walked into the building. A single vintage Otis elevator stood next to a stairwell in the lobby, and on the opposite side, he found four rows of individual mail slots attached to the wall. Scanning from right to left, he studied the names until a ding sounded from the elevator door behind him. Sam turned to see a young couple. "Hey, how's it going?" he said. He tapped his foot, shrugged, and looked at his watch. After they left the building, he began checking names again. At the far end on the right of the first row, he spotted *M. Tunnenton apt 102.*

Sam examined the lobby. A double door framed with wood and glass separated the building entrance area from the first-floor apartments. He pushed his way through and started checking numbers on doors, then turned to the right. Apartment 102 was on the back side of the building at the end of the hallway; meaning the side of her place would be visible from the street.

Sam returned to the entrance and walked outside to the side of the building. Each apartment had an attached porch with solid walls extending about two feet from the exterior of the building, providing minimal visual privacy for their outdoor space. He took a quick look at the ground-level porch that belonged to Melanie and noted chew toys and a ball on the decking. *Melanie must have a dog.* A gate from her porch led to a common green area.

He'd seen enough; nothing more required his attention. He was happy with the thought of spending the day with Natalie, but tomorrow, he'd be back, knowing better where he stood with Melanie Tunnenton.

CHAPTER THIRTEEN

On his way to Natalie's condo, Sam stopped at a store to pick up a swimsuit. He pawed through a limited selection of suits bunched together in a pile marked for clearance. Since it was late in the season, he felt lucky to find one reasonably close to his size. He detested the idea of being stuck inside shopping, so he rolled it up into a ball and went to the closest checkout line.

Ten minutes later, he stood waiting at Natalie's entrance gate.

"Hiya," she said, her voice sounding scratchy over the intercom.

He passed through, then took the steps two at a time to the fourth floor, where Natalie met him at the door in a semi-sheer cover up over a pink one-piece. He put his hand to his chest. "Be still my heart. Wow! You look terrific."

She turned in a circle. "Thank you."

"I wish I could say the same for me. I picked up a suit on the way over, but I'm telling you right now, there wasn't much to choose from."

"Come on; I'm sure it's fine." Natalie peered at the bag.

At the same time, Sam grimaced. "All right, but don't judge," he said as he reached for the new suit.

"Oh, no. I want to see it on you. And while you're changing, I'll finish packing the beach bag."

He went into the bathroom and pulled on his new trunks, tying them tight at the waist. A ridiculous image stared back at him in the mirror. Leaning into the hallway, he said, "It's worse than it looked at the store, so you may want to bring two blankets, then you won't have to sit with me."

"It can't be that bad. Come on out."

"Bet she won't say that in a minute," Sam said quietly to himself.

He stood in the living room like a little boy, trying on clothes at a department store, waiting for his mother's approval. When Natalie turned to him, she put her hand to her mouth and laughed. "You were right," she said.

"There was a reason this suit was on clearance. Who else would want it? Besides, it was the only one close to my size."

Natalie pointed to the pattern on the swim trunks. "Are those little birds' eggs in nests or polka-dotted Easter egg candies?"

"I'm not sure," Sam said. "I wish I had brought my suit from home, but I thought it was too late in the season and I wouldn't be going to the beach." He poked out his lower lip and asked, "Do you want me to wait in the car while you're at the beach?"

"My goodness," she said, staring at the suit. "It's fine, well, I guess the legs are a little short on you too, like they're preshrunk or something, or were you striving for the European look?"

Sam hung his head.

"Yes, I'll still go with you." Natalie moved directly in front of Sam and pinched his stomach. "Besides, I like this kind of Easter candy, and listen, if it's any consolation, the body wearing them looks great. Come on, we'll have fun." She kissed him. "And when we get back here, you won't need to wear it anymore."

"My kind of beach day."

"Okay," she said, reaching over to retrieve a large beach bag from the kitchen counter. "I've got towels, snacks, and water in here, but we'll need to make a quick detour to pick up sunblock, then it's only a five-minute walk from there." She brushed her hand over the side of one leg of his suit. "Thank goodness."

• • •

With light foot traffic on St. John's Boardwalk, Sam and Natalie made quick work of their walk to the beach, passing along typical touristy outlets promoting snorkeling expeditions near the islands, sailing excursions to waters rich with dolphins, and sunset dinner cruises along the shore.

The early September sun hung lower in the sky, bowing in recognition of the approaching autumn. The brilliant light reflected off the pillow-soft sand as if it were a blanket of snow. Small seashells of every color decorated the beach as clear, warm water more akin to a gentle bath than to a broad, seemingly endless sea lapped the shoreline.

Sam lay propped up on one elbow, facing Natalie lying on her back, her face angled toward the sun.

"What are the beaches like in California?" she asked.

Sam considered her question for a moment. "The sand isn't as inviting; it's a lot darker than here," he said. "There are big waves, and the surfers love those. The coastline is rocky in places; but other beaches are like this one, except they're more crowded. In Redondo or Manhattan Beach, and especially Santa Monica, they are packed with people. There are differences, that's for sure."

"A sea of humanity by a sea of water," Natalie said.

"You got it." He rolled onto his back, shielding his eyes with his hand.

"What are your plans for tomorrow?" Natalie asked.

"I'm going into the DEA office in the morning to do follow-up on names and addresses, so I can gather all the information I can on the court reporter. It was an incredible stroke of luck that the lady I spoke with earlier, Cindy Ardman, saw the court reporter and recognized her right away. Anyway, I'll talk with the reporter, and with luck, she'll be able to identify the couple on the boat. It may be a wild goose chase," Sam said, "but it's my one lead."

"Have you been keeping in contact with Chloe?"

"I've spoken with her a couple of times, including yesterday," he said, "but I'm not going into any detail because there's not much to tell her, and I wouldn't want to upset her with speculation."

Natalie shook her head. "Your job is kind of all-consuming."

"I know, and I'm sorry, and this isn't even my job, but you're right, it can be hard to separate myself from it." He ran his hand over her arm. "Being with you is great, because I can forget about everything."

"Me too." She held his hand. "Sam, can I ask you a question?"

"Sure, of course."

"Have you ever been married?"

"Me? No, never married." He ran a hand through his hair. "I was engaged once upon a time."

Natalie sat up. "You were? I want details, please."

"Uh-oh, you've become Agent Natalie again."

"That's right, and you *will* tell me everything."

"There's not much to say." Sam closed his eyes. "I was still living in Clearwater, working for the Tampa PD, right after I got out of college. This girl and I dated for a year. I was young, like twenty-three. We got engaged, then we got unengaged."

"You're not getting off that easy." She ran her finger across his chest. "Who was she?"

"Her name was Kendra." Sam reopened his eyes. "She was my age and worked at a bank." He flicked sand off his towel. "Things were great, but after some time, it was clear we were both too young, and we drifted apart." He looked her in the eye. "I could ask the same of you; were you ever married or are you secretly married?"

"Yes, I'm married to three men. I'm what you call a serial marrier, now, back to your relationship. Do you keep in contact?"

"No, not at all. When it ended, it just ended, and it wasn't like this terrible breakup either. Thank God we were mature enough to work our way through that part. I had so much on my mind." He sat up and crossed his legs. "I told you about my parents being killed in a car accident. It was an awful time, and it may have led me in some ways to seek a big change in my life, because that was when I made the jump to the DEA." Sam watched a sailboat tacking into the wind during the ensuing silence, before turning back to Natalie. "It was a dark period for my sister and me."

Natalie stroked his arm. "I'm sorry about your parents. I can't imagine." She kissed his cheek. "I'm lucky mine are both doing well. If you want to meet them while you're here, we could get together for dinner or something." She shaded her face, looking into Sam's eyes.

"Sure, I'd like that," Sam said. "And you're not getting off the hook yet either, young lady. You were saying you were married several times, so what's the story on all your relationships?"

"I've been married four, no, five times, if you count my current marriage to an Elvis impersonator in Vegas. No, I've just dated some, and I had what you would call a serious boyfriend until a year ago, but we broke up because he was an asshole."

"Sounds like you're still kind of riding the fence on this guy."

"Ha. Not at all. He didn't believe in a monogamous relationship if you follow my meaning. He cheated on me, and trust is a big issue with me," Natalie said.

"Trust is as important as anything else in a relationship; I agree with you." Sam squeezed her hand. "I'm sorry that happened to you."

"Thank you, but I'm doing fine now; besides, I like a man who's not afraid to wear a ridiculous swimsuit to the beach."

He grabbed at her sides, tickling while her laughter carried across the sand.

Natalie squealed. "I won't say anything else; I promise."

When he stopped, she said, "Except for one other thing."

"Somehow ... I knew you weren't finished."

"I was just going to ask about the possibility of seagulls mistaking these things on your shorts as eggs and wanting to nest with you here at the beach."

Sam fell back onto his towel, laughing.

"I only say that because I wouldn't want to interfere with nature." She rolled onto her side next to him and rested her hand on his stomach. "I've got grapes and apple slices in a little cooler. Do you want something to eat before we go for a swim?"

"Sure, if you're eating, I will."

She reached into the beach bag but stopped. "Then once we're back at my place, I can throw your suit away."

"You know, I'm starting to like my new trunks. You'll have to wrestle them away from me."

"I'm feeling good about my chances."

CHAPTER FOURTEEN

Sam passed through the first-floor atrium of the commercial building housing the DEA. The door to the elevator started to close as he approached, but at the last moment, a hand shot through from the inside, forcing the door to reopen.

"Thanks," Sam said.

One of the two men already in the elevator said, "You're welcome. What floor?"

"Fourth. Thanks again."

The man who spoke nodded once. The light for the fourth floor was already lit. He could feel the two sets of eyes tunneling into him as the car moved up.

When the doors reopened, Sam held out his arm to allow them to pass first.

He watched as they went in one direction, resuming a conversation that he must have interrupted. When Sam stopped at the reception area, Rita said, "Hi, I know you," and slid a no escort LEO badge across the counter to him. When he turned left to enter Group Two, he bumped into Joe Barber.

"Hey, Sam. Back again, huh?"

"Yes, I need to make queries, a driver's license check and work on NADDIS too."

"Which do you want to do first?"

Sam told him the DL query was his priority.

Joe said, "Let me run something over to the boss, then I'll log you into the Florida system." He gestured across the office bay area. "It's the cubicle in the corner over there by that potted mini palm tree; be back in a flash."

Sam looked at his watch. Bill should be at work in another hour, which gave him enough time to conduct basic checks on his own before he turned his research over to the expert to analyze the data and help tie it all together. He opened his notebook to the page with the name *Melanie Tunnenton* underlined.

A minute later, he heard footsteps approaching. "All right; I'll slide in here and log you in," Joe said. "Are you working on anything interesting?"

"Yeah, I told Rafa about it the other day. I guess he's back on duty in the wiretap room, right?"

"Yup, his shift started at eight, but if you want to talk to him, you can knock on the door. Now, it'll just take a second to log in." He tapped his fingernails on the table while waiting for the computer to go through the vehicle and driver database start-up. Once the home screen popped up, he said, "All right, you're all set. The system is user-friendly, but if you have any problems, give me a holler. Also, I'm sure you saw the NADDIS terminal is right here, so make yourself at home."

After Joe left, Sam entered Melanie's full name and a rough guess for her date of birth. The search took scant seconds, then the relevant data popped up: Melanie Catherine Tunnenton, twenty-eight years of age, five feet, six inches tall, a hundred and thirty pounds, at the same address he visited the previous day. He pressed a button on the keyboard, and several seconds later, the printer beside the computer terminal came to life, producing a copy of her driver's license. Not long after, Sam completed the registration check, revealing a 1982 blue Datsun 210 registered to Melanie.

Sam scooted his chair over beside the NADDIS terminal and input Melanie's information into the system. As he suspected, there was no record of her. He didn't know what the requirements or prohibitions were for a court reporter, but he was certain drug dealing was off limits.

His next query focused on The Runner's Choice shoe store, a place he suspected was a front for illicit activity, namely, a collection point for drug money. After he entered the company name, he waited for what he expected would be an extensive list, but to his surprise, the NADDIS query produced a blank screen.

Sam knew something was wrong with that store. He opened his folder and took the photocopies of documents out pertaining to Rojas. His recollection was that there were no people's names identified on the shoe store business card, but he wanted to make sure. He thumbed through the papers until he came to the photocopy of the card. His memory had been correct; the card only showed the name of the company, an address, and a phone number.

He checked the phone number from the business card in NADDIS but got a blank screen again. Perplexing, he thought, because while NADDIS had a few issues with a bit of *junk* information, it was widely respected in law enforcement as one of the world's most powerful tools in the fight against drug traffickers. Glancing at his watch, he guessed Bill would be at work in thirty minutes.

Sam looked out into the bay of the office, noting it was empty except for Joe Barber, who served as the conduit between the wire room and the surveillance agents in the field. The wiretap operations had decimated the group's workforce.

A Title III wiretap represented perhaps the government's single biggest legal intrusion into an individual's reasonable expectation of privacy, and for that reason, persuading a federal judge to authorize the massive incursion into people's private lives was difficult; this was true even though the investigations were allowed by the 1968 omnibus crime law that established the rules for obtaining them. And, once a judge approved a wiretap, the problems for those in charge of such operations began. They were difficult to manage, challenging to operate, and demanding on agent resources.

An ongoing Title III wiretap affected every agent and their cases, because if investigators weren't in the wire room, their butt was sitting in a car somewhere on surveillance. And the DEA was no different from any other law enforcement agency, in that the complex investigations affected all agents in the group, which meant even greater pressure would be applied to ensure the enormous effort resulted in bucketloads of arrests, drug seizures, and forfeiture of ill-gotten money and property. Statistics made the world go round; every agent, including Sam, knew that. And the success of the DEA's operations was always a key factor when it came time to request increased funding from Congress each year.

Sam walked to a bookshelf jammed full of phone directories, and grabbed the most recent white pages, then returned to his cubicle. He scooped up the phone, hoping a nice person could help him.

While he waited for someone to answer, he thought again of the agents stuck in their cars for hours on end. The worst part was the waiting for something exciting to happen or to hear the police code *ten twenty-two* called out on the radio. At the DEA, a ten twenty-two was often an agent's favorite thing to hear, especially after a long day because it was used to advise agents to disregard, to stop their activity, to pack it in, or if it was late at night, to go home.

"Better Business Bureau. Mrs. Davenport speaking."

Sam introduced himself, saying he was on temporary assignment with the Department of Justice in Tampa. "I was hoping you could help me with identifying who might own a particular business in the Apollo Beach area," he told Mrs. Davenport.

"Yes, sir," she said. "I can help you with that."

Sam thanked the universe for his good luck. "I appreciate it. The name of the business is The Runner's Choice."

"The Runner's Choice in Apollo Beach. Let me see what I can find." While she was checking, she said, "We publish a book every year with business listings, but I swear it's out of date as soon as it's printed."

"Nothing stays the same, does it?" Sam said.

"No, sir, it doesn't. I'm not showing a listing. Is it new?"

"No, ma'am, the limited information I have is the store has been open for over a year."

"Then there should be an entry for the business here."

A silent dammit passed through Sam's mind.

"Oh, hold on, I should have looked under the letter *T*. I was looking under *Runner's* instead of *The*." Mrs. Davenport cleared her throat and said, "The name we have as the proprietor of The Runner's Choice is a Mr. Victor Alderete Perez."

Sam thanked Mrs. Davenport for her help and turned back to face the NADDIS terminal, inputting Perez's full name from Apollo Beach. He waited. And waited more. The screen flickered before the words flashed across the screen: ACCESS DENIED.

He stared at the screen in disbelief. "What the hell?" Then he thumbed through his folder to locate the name of the suspect involved in the traffic stop in Bradenton. *Ronaldo Gomez. Here he is.* He typed in the name to see what trouble Ronaldo might have gotten himself into. The same message as before appeared: ACCESS DENIED.

He wondered if the system was down and looked for Joe, but he wasn't at his desk any longer. Sam had seen the denied access message only once before in his entire career. He believed it meant the information he was seeking was sensitive, so sensitive that only a limited number of DEA personnel could access it. He would have to go through Bill, after all.

Finding himself at a standstill, he looked around the room, wondering what to do while he waited for Bill to get into the office. He went to the lobby on the first floor in search of coffee. On his return to the fourth floor, the cup was so hot he had to transfer it from hand to hand until he reached his desk. He was careful to set it away from the keyboard, then scooped up the telephone handset next to the NADDIS terminal.

"Bill Dunkirk speaking."

"Hey, Bill. How are you? Judy told me you left work early on Friday."

"I did," Bill said. "A new medicine I'm taking gave me an adverse reaction, but I'm fine now. Tell me what's going on in Florida."

Sam ran through his weekend's work and the help he needed. He said, "I ended up calling the BBB, the Better Business Bureau."

"I love it when criminal investigators do quaint things." He heard Bill huff. "I guess it's time for me to send out another gentle reminder to field agents."

"Why?"

"Because there are other ways to access that information. Why am I ever surprised that agents only ever think of using the phone book or calling the operator for information?"

Sam said, "Is this a trick question?"

"No," Bill said flatly.

"For most agents, I would say it's because they're old-fashioned dinosaurs, but not in my case. I do it because I like to listen to your sweet voice first thing in the morning."

"I'm so glad my voice brings you joy."

"Look, Bill, I tried to run the name I got from the BBB in NADDIS, but I received an access denied message."

"That can happen when the subject being queried is in a protected mode in the NADDIS system."

"Can I give you the information so you can cut through all the red tape?"

Bill said, "Sure. Because you've got several irons in the fire right now and due to our time difference, I'm going to make an exception, and, if you need to, you can call me at home in case you're working late at night, or I have to leave work early again. I'll bring this stuff with me, but if you breathe a word of this to anyone—"

"I promise—"

"Slow down, Slick. I want you to hear me out. If you breathe one word of this to anyone, you'll go to the end of the line and no more favors from me. I don't want everyone thinking Bill Dunkirk is available twenty-four seven. I've seen that movie, and I know how it ends."

"My lips are sealed," Sam said. "I have two people's names and one company. You ready?"

"Shoot."

• • •

It was after twelve when he finished talking to Bill. He had a couple of hours to kill and wondered if Carl Schneider, his old high school buddy, was in the office. They had worked together as patrol officers with the Tampa PD, but Carl had advanced rapidly up the chain of command and was now a lieutenant.

Sam's plan for later in the afternoon was to act just like the agents working the wiretap; his butt planted in his car, parked close to the apartment building where Melanie lived. He didn't know the typical work schedule of a court reporter, but he intended to be waiting for Melanie when she arrived home.

He dialed Carl's number. After four rings, his friend's voice sounded firm and cool. "Schneider."

"That's not a very enthusiastic way for a public servant to answer the phone."

After a momentary silence, Carl said, "Agent Sam Dahl from Los Angeles? To what do I owe the privilege?"

"I'm in town, working. I know this is last minute, but I wanted to see if you'd be interested in lunch."

"You're here in Tampa?"

"Yeah, I'm at the DEA office, not too far from you right now."

"Son of a gun," Carl said. "Listen, let me make one call, then if you can, swing by and pick me up out front. My rust bucket of a car is in the shop. You remember how to get here, right?"

"Yeah, I think I can manage. See you in ten."

CHAPTER FIFTEEN

It had been great to catch up with Carl over lunch. A strange but wonderful feeling: hanging out with his old high school friend always made worries more distant and laughter much easier.

After he dropped Carl off at the police department, Sam drove around residential neighborhoods, cruising past Melanie's building every twenty minutes. When a parking place opened on the street—one protected by the shade from a magnificent Live Oak—he squeezed his rental into the desirable spot. From Sam's vantage point, he could keep his eye on three critical areas: the building parking lot, the front door entrance, and a window on the side of Melanie's apartment. He felt he had done this a million times; in reality, it was probably only a thousand. No matter, this was the job: watching, waiting, and reacting.

It was twenty minutes after four. A courtroom might close at five, maybe earlier, and he hoped Melanie wouldn't be going out after work, but if she did, he still planned to be waiting for her. He had told Natalie he wasn't sure what time he would come by; it was the nature of the job, even investigations that weren't agency sanctioned.

Cars entered the lot. Cars left. He watched, but no 1982 blue Datsun 210 showed itself.

Fifteen minutes before six, a white three-door Civic entered the lot with two occupants. He recognized Melanie's pretty face from her license photo, but her dark hair was shorter now. When she got out of the passenger side of the car, she leaned in through the open window, but Sam wasn't close enough to hear the conversation. Then Melanie straightened up and took a step back while the driver backed into a parking space. This was unexpected.

Sam wondered whether he should break up the party and ask to speak to her alone or wait. He opted to wait, watching the driver—another woman—lock her car. Now Sam could hear the conversation and laughter as Melanie was trying to convince her friend to hang out. When the friend agreed to ten minutes, Sam figured he'd made the right choice—as long as the friend stuck to the plan.

Through the window of Melanie's apartment, he saw a light come on in what he guessed was the kitchen or living room area, or both. As the minutes passed, he saw shadows go by the window inside the apartment. Sam had marked the time when they entered the building, and after ten minutes had passed, he thought, *Come on, friend of Melanie, stay true to your plan and leave.*

She did. He watched her open the door to the Honda and get in, then listened as the car refused to start on the first, second, and third attempt. Sam figured the Honda had a clutch, so, if necessary, he would play the Good Samaritan by pushing the car to start it. It wasn't necessary. Friend of Melanie was used to her car's peculiarities; the engine cranked on the fourth try. She pulled out of the parking lot and whizzed past him down the road.

He waited a minute, watching and listening. A small mutt nosed around the grassy area by the building. He heard a voice matching Melanie's from the parking lot earlier: "Jiminy, come over here."

It was time. *Forget the front entrance. Walk to the back porch.* Surprise could sometimes be a positive thing; Sam knew from experience.

He reached the point in the side yard where he could see Melanie sitting on the porch, having a one-way conversation with her dog.

He took another step and watched her leaning over the table, rolling a joint. "Hi, how are you?" Sam asked.

She jumped. "You scared the shit out of me. Who ... who are you?"

"I'm just passing through. By the way, you're doing it all wrong." He pointed toward the joint on the table. "Too much air. You're wasting a little weed every time you roll it like that."

"Oh, yeah?" She glared at Sam. "I didn't know I was in the presence of an expert."

"Hey, everybody has to be good at something." Sam stood with his hands on his hips. "Your dog's not big on guarding. Does he bark?"

"Not much." Melanie rubbed the dog's head. "That's one of many things I like about him."

"He looks like a good boy."

"He is." She held her hands out, palms up. "So, what is it you want?"

"Melanie, can I be honest with you? I'm not just passing by."

"How do you know my name?" She stood and said, "I'm calling the cops."

"Okay, I'll wait here." He folded his arms across his chest and stood still.

"Did someone put you up to this?" She looked at the yard behind her. "Is this a practical joke?"

"No." He flipped open his credential case with his badge and ID. "Don't freak out. I don't care about your weed."

Her face was frozen in fear.

"Melanie, did you hear me? I don't care about the herb." He hoped his words would sink in. "Can I come up on the porch?"

"Um, how is it you know who I am?"

"That's part of my job. May I?" He pointed to the gate.

"Do I have a choice?"

"Sort of." He took two steps up to stand level with the porch floor. "May I come in?"

"I guess so," Melanie said.

He opened the gate, passed through, turned, and closed it behind him. "Thanks. Do you mind if I have a seat?"

She waved her hand toward the chair. "Look, can I see your wallet thingy one more time?"

"You mean my ID?"

"Yeah."

Sam pulled a chair out and flipped open his identification and badge, laying them flat on the table for her inspection. "That's me when I was a little younger." He left the ID sitting in front of her, hoping it would serve as a reminder throughout their conversation.

She stared at the photo ID, then looked up and said, "Drug Enforcement Administration? Shit, this is great. This is just great."

"Melanie, for the last time, I don't care about your grass. I'm here to talk about a friend of yours, a little background information."

Her eyes narrowed. "Who? Who are you talking about?"

"I'd like to keep this confidential. Between us," he said. "You've got a friend, a blonde-haired woman in her twenties, who spends time on a nice boat in the Gulf. She has a male friend. Hispanic. Ring a bell?"

"Let's see." She tapped the tip of her finger on the table. "I'm not sure."

"Melanie, I don't have time for games. I laid my cards on the table and I've been nice. Why don't we both sit and chat, okay?"

She lowered herself to her chair. "Fine."

Sam took a seat too.

Melanie fiddled with her lighter and a small cigar box where Sam assumed she kept her stash. "I think you mean Beth."

He nodded. "Tell me about Beth."

"Look, I hardly know her. Can I ask why you want to know?"

"Yes, but if you did ask, I would tell you no in a nice way. Listen, I need your help. When we're finished, I'll walk away from here and forget about everything you've got going on at this table. There are people who might care about this stuff." He raised his eyebrows. "Your employer or the circuit court judges in Pinellas or Hillsborough Counties where you do your court reporting. As for me, I don't care, so let's get back to Beth."

She stared at him. "You know I'm a court reporter?"

"Yep."

The dog put his front paws on Sam's legs.

"Get down, Jiminy," Melanie said.

"Not a problem; I like dogs better than most people." He picked Jiminy up and placed him on his lap. "Please, you were getting ready to tell me everything you know about Beth."

She looked away from Sam toward the yard. "The truth is I don't know her that well. I've met her at clubs with a bunch of other people, and we hang out, but not just me and Beth."

"Keep going," he said.

"Beth likes to party, and she can get a little rowdy, but she's nice. The Hispanic guy you're talking about is, let's see, what does she call him? It's Mondo or, I don't know, something like that. Since you're DEA, I'm sure you know drugs are a big part of the scene."

"What's Beth's last name?" he said.

She turned to look at Sam. "I swear; I don't know."

He flipped one side of the leather wallet to close his credentials. "Melanie, you're not the only person I'm talking to about this. If I learn you weren't honest with me or held something back, I'll be disappointed."

She said, "I understand, and I'm telling you the truth. We're not that close."

"Where do she and her friend live?"

"Somewhere in Tampa, but that's all I know, because it's not a subject that's ever come up."

Sam scratched at the dog's ear. "What about the guy? Is Mondo, or whatever his name is, her boyfriend?"

"Yeah, I think so."

"Last name?"

"I don't know."

"What, besides partying, do they like to do?" Sam asked.

She sighed. "They talk about boats all the time. Beth invited me one time to go, but I didn't because I was busy that weekend, but I don't think I would've gone anyhow. It's fun to meet up and have drinks and dance a little, but they're part of a group that's into harder stuff than what I have here."

"Coke?"

"Yes," Melanie said. "And I won't touch that."

"Do you think they have a boat?"

"Yes, I think so because they're always talking about boating."

"You know anything about the boat?"

"No, but I'm guessing it must be big because it seems like they have lots of friends, so they all have to fit somewhere, right? But I've never seen it."

"Where do they dock it?"

"I don't know."

"Do you have plans to get together soon?"

"No."

"How do you make arrangements to meet up?"

She twisted her body to reposition herself in the chair. "It's a group thing where somebody calls."

Sam paused before speaking. "You can guess what I'm going to ask next, can't you?"

"I think so."

Sam slid his notebook and pen across the table. "Write her number for me, please."

"I feel like a rat."

"You're not a rat. You're a solid citizen who wants to do the right thing, and listen, believe me when I tell you that once I walk away from here today, no one will ever be the wiser I spoke with you."

"Oh, God." She chewed on her fingernail and looked toward a line of trees bordering the property.

"Melanie, you can count on it. Her number, please."

She returned her gaze to Sam. "I have to get it from inside."

"That's fine. Jiminy and I will be here waiting for your return."

She was inside for less than a minute.

Her hand shook as she wrote Beth's number.

Sam said, "We're going to keep this our little secret, right?"

"Yes, I'll keep it to myself."

"Thanks, and if this helps at all, you need to tighten up that joint a little because your paper is too loose. The trick is to let your thumbs do the work. Start rolling in the middle and go outward, and that'll make your joint firmer and not burn so fast." He placed Jiminy on the porch decking and stood. Smiling, he said, "You should at least get your money's worth." He leaned over and patted the dog on the head. "Take it easy, Jiminy."

He left the same way he came in, closed the gate behind him, and walked around the building to his car.

He stopped at the first pay phone.

"Bill Dunkirk speaking."

"Bill, I'm making progress, and I'm at a little gas station in the St. Pete area, hoping you can do queries for me."

"My day isn't complete without helping you. What do you need?"

"I've got a phone number and want to get an address for it. Might be in the name of Beth or Elizabeth. Any extra info you can give me on her would be a bonus. A person I spoke with confirmed Beth's boyfriend is Hispanic and goes by the name of Mondo or something like that."

"Okay, I'll check on Beth."

"Hey, Bill, I'm told she might live in the Tampa area, so I'm heading over that way now. If the number comes back to her, can you run her in NADDIS too?"

"I live to serve, and before we hang up, I have info to give you from the queries I made on the shoe store owner Victor Perez and the man involved in the car stop with an ounce of cocaine, Ronaldo Gomez."

"Yeah, I got blank screens or denied access."

"Right, I remember. Look, they're both known associates of subjects in an ongoing investigation by DEA Tampa. You don't need me on this; you need to talk to Tampa and start with Rafa or the case agent because you're bumping up against their active investigation."

"I'll see Rafa tomorrow and speak with him about it then, but meanwhile, let me give you the number, and I'll call you back when I get into Tampa."

CHAPTER SIXTEEN

Sam motored east along West Gandy Boulevard, crossing over Old Tampa Bay, then cruising into the city, five miles north of MacDill Air Force Base. It was six thirty, perhaps his best and only opportunity to grab something to eat.

He ate in a hurry, eager to speak to Bill and find Beth. When he was done, he threw the Burger King bag into a trash can but kept the cup filled with ice. He walked straight to the pay phone, and while he waited for an answer, he pinched at his belly, thinking of the need to get back to the gym.

"Bill Dunkirk speaking."

"Hey, Bill. It's me."

"Sam, get your pen and paper ready because the stars are beginning to align for you. Your Beth, aka Elizabeth Evans, lives in Tampa in a rental house; the owner info is inconsequential, but the good part is the telephone is in her name, but someone else named Ramón Monzon pays the electricity and water bills. You want to guess what nickname they sometimes use in place of Ramón?"

"That sounds fun, Bill, and under normal circumstances, I would love to play twenty questions with you, but—"

"Never mind," Bill said. "How about Moncho?"

"*Moncho* sounds a lot like *Mondo*."

"Especially to an English speaker, so it's possible Elizabeth Evans is doing the horizontal mambo with Ramón Monzon, aka Moncho."

"Damn, Bill. You're good."

"Sam, listen to me. I mean it. There's a heavy hitter cocaine family in Mexico and the boss's last name is Monzon. I'll keep checking, but remember, I told you to talk to your buddies in Tampa about their ongoing case. I'm betting they're related," Bill said. "Now there's more; Ramón Monzon is the registered owner of a 1986 Ocean Yachts Sunliner."

"That boat model and year fits with what I was told yesterday," Sam said.

"These Sunliners are nice boats. We're talking forty-six-footer with all the bells and whistles, and not many people can afford these bad boys."

"This Melanie lady said they're into boats."

"Ms. Melanie was right; now listen, Moncho registered this beauty to the same address where he pays the utilities for the girlfriend, but I promise you won't see this sitting in their front yard."

"Even I could have guessed that."

"I also have photos of Beth and Ramón aka Moncho. I'm sure I'm not the first to notice, but she's quite a looker. Anyway, you have fun while I do more research on your new friends. In the meantime, let me give you her address so you can swing by the place."

· · ·

He passed by the rental house, sitting one block off the water in the Ballast Point neighborhood, and parked a hundred feet away. It was time to sit and watch again—another day in the exciting life of a DEA agent.

He scanned the road in front and behind him. Overall, the neighborhood was appealing, except for Beth's house. He'd seen this kind of place before, the house with the untended yard, the faded paint, a loose shutter, the orphaned trash can at the curb, one car in the drive and two in the yard.

Lights were on in the house and there was a slight echo of music reverberating from within. He couldn't be sure if it was a television set or a radio; the main thing for Sam was, it meant someone was at home. He hoped his trip here wouldn't be a total waste of time, but there wouldn't be any way to tell by sitting in his car if Beth was home, or when she might come home, or if she came home at all. This was one of those times a partner was nice to have for simple conversation or to bounce ideas off each other.

Sam said to himself, "Oh, the hell with it." He exited his car and walked toward the house. The closer he drew to the door, the louder the music became. He rang the bell but wasn't sure if anyone could hear it over Bon Jovi's "Livin' on a Prayer." Through the window, he could see the TV tuned to a video channel with music blasting, so after several seconds, he knocked and said, "Hello?"

A woman in her mid-thirties, but with the looks of a life that hadn't been overly kind, came to the door. She looked pissed like he had interrupted her favorite song. One thing Sam knew for sure; it wasn't Beth.

He tried out his best smile. "Hi, I'm looking for Beth."

"She's not here."

"When will she be back?"

"Who wants to know?" She looked him up and down; her lips curled into a sneer.

"Um, I was talking to her the other night at a bar about a boat she said she had for sale, so I was coming by to look at it."

The lady scowled and said, "You got it wrong. There's no boat for sale here."

Sam tilted his head and backed up a step like he was checking to make sure he was at the correct address. "Weird, because this is the address she gave me. Or maybe there's someone else here with a boat for sale?"

A man of a similar age to Ms. Happiness appeared in the doorway. He raised his arm, resting his hand on the inside of the doorjamb, blocking out her face. Sam figured she must have realized he had dismissed her because she turned and walked away.

"What's the problem, man?" Mr. Happiness looked as pleasant as his friend.

Sam held his hand up. "No problem, like I was saying, I'm looking for Beth Evans, who told me she was trying to sell a boat, and I could swing by—"

"Listen, dude. No Beth. No boat. Got it?"

"I guess it would be a waste of time to come back another day?"

"Tremendous waste. This is when you walk back down those steps behind you and go back to wherever the hell you came from."

"Can I leave my name and number for Beth?" He had no intention of leaving either; he just wanted to piss the guy off.

"Take a hike."

"Gotcha and merry Christmas to you." Sam turned and walked up the street. He got into his car and drove about forty feet, turned right to park behind a ragged hedge. It was the perfect spot to hang without being seen from the house, but still allowed him to see the front porch through the thinning vegetation.

He thought he would give the place an hour and, if nothing happened, he would regroup until tomorrow, but he didn't have to wait that long. Ten minutes after he took a hike, two guys in their late twenties left the house together, but Mr. Happiness wasn't one of them. They didn't use any of the cars in the drive or yard. Instead, they walked right past him, taking no notice, heading toward the beach. Sam locked his car and followed, although he wasn't sure why, since he had no plan. When he reached the corner, he caught sight of the two men ducking into Corky's Beach Bar. He wondered if they might meet up with Beth.

CHAPTER SEVENTEEN

The bar had a tiki torch touristy feel but struck Sam as a hangout where the locals gathered. It was early, and the place wasn't crowded. Still, it was loud, with the bar's music, conversation, and laughter all competing for attention. He spotted the two men from the house standing beside a dark-haired young woman at the bar. It wasn't Beth, but the lady was gorgeous—long, lean, and exuding sexiness—and Sam was sure she was aware of that fact too.

The bigger of the two guys leaned over and kissed her on top of the head, convincing Sam they knew her. After the smooch, they walked around the bar and entered a door leading to the back.

Time to talk to the prettiest girl in the bar. He took the seat next to her, and when she looked at him, Sam said, "Excuse me, is this seat taken?"

She smiled and shook her head. "No."

He leaned in toward her. "Is this a good crowd for a Monday?"

"The usual, more or less. The place will be packed in an hour," she said. "Are you meeting someone?"

"Not anymore."

She stared at him in silence for a moment. "You're pretty confident in yourself."

"I just finished reading Dale Carnegie's *How to Win Friends and Influence People*, and tonight is my maiden voyage to practice his techniques."

"I've heard of that book. Do you think you learned anything?"

"We'll see. My name is Sam."

She extended a smooth, soft hand. "Pleased to meet you."

"And you are?" He kept hold of her hand.

"I'm Heather."

"Nice to meet you, Heather. Do you live around here?"

She raised an eyebrow. "You work fast."

"I don't mean it like that. I was wondering what it's like to live here," Sam said.

"You're not from Tampa?"

"No. I'm a transplant from Los Angeles."

"You're a long way from home. What brings you here?"

"When I was walking by the door outside, I saw you, and said to myself, I've got to meet her."

She smiled coolly. "Oh, I see; you're a professional bullshit artist."

"True, except for the professional part." He leaned his elbow on the bar. "No, I'm new here in town, and I was supposed to meet someone nearby to look at a boat, but they weren't at home, so I walked in this direction to check out the beach. I saw two guys talking with you, and when they foolishly walked away, I thought I would stop and say hello."

"You're funny; is that something you learned from your book?" She picked up her bottle of beer and drank the last swallow.

"Are you ready for another? I know a great bartender in this place," he said.

"Me too." She spun in her chair and waved the bottle. "Charlie?"

The bartender bent over and pulled a Coors Light from the cooler, then looked at Sam. "What'll you have?"

"What she's having. Thanks."

Sam turned back to Heather to continue a conversation that veered into thirty minutes about nothing.

When the bartender walked by, she said, "Charlie, do you have a pen I can borrow?"

"Sure." He reached under the bar and handed it to her.

She wrote something on a napkin, then slid it over in front of Sam. "Maybe you'll need help in your search for a boat?"

"I'm sure I will."

When the conversation turned to her work, Sam learned Heather was an elementary school teacher. He wondered if that might be information he could use at some point later. After several minutes of talking about the state of the education system in Florida, Sam decided to turn the conversation to the real reason he was there.

"I should have asked if you like boating?" he said.

"More than like, I love boating. Honestly, I don't know much about boats, but there's something about them I really enjoy. What kind of boat are you looking for?" Heather asked.

"Right now, a small bass boat to occupy my weekends."

"Sam, you need to understand something. There are two kinds of people in Florida: those who already have a boat and those still looking for one."

"When you're surrounded by water, I guess it comes with the territory. I was hoping I had a good lead on one because she sounded like she wanted to sell it fast."

"I know everybody in the neighborhood. What's her name?"

Sam hoped he had struck gold; she knew everybody, including those guys who walked out of Beth's house.

"Beth. Beth Evans. Lives a block from here."

Her eyes darted to the floor before she spoke. "Beth? No, I don't know any Beth."

It was too late; Sam saw the immediate recognition in Heather's eyes, and that told him everything he needed to know. She wasn't telling the truth, but why, he wondered? He said, "Anyway, that's what she told me, and her, I guess it was her boyfriend. Let's see, what was his name again, something like Moncho?"

He saw a different look than before; this time it was fear in her eyes.

"Nope. I can't help you," she said. "I have to use the bathroom."

Sam noticed the phony smile when she excused herself and figured maybe she was just covering for her friends. After she entered the same hallway as the two guys he had followed from Beth's house, he figured something was about to happen. He turned around in his chair with his back to the bar. A couple of minutes passed before the same two men he had followed walked in his direction.

The apparent leader moved in close to Sam, his pungent cologne making an advance assault. "Listen, pendejo, I don't know who you are, but I don't like you talking to Heather."

"It's a free country," Sam said.

The guy was fast with his hands, and powerful too. The punch landed squarely on Sam's jaw, knocking him off his stool and onto the floor. Lying on his side, dazed by the blow, he still had enough sense to realize that if he didn't do something fast, he'd be getting his ass beat and quick. With as much force as he could muster, he kicked sideways at the man's leg. As soon as his foot connected, Sam knew he had aimed well. The man's knee buckled outward and made Sam wonder if he had heard the snap of a bone. It was hard to tell with the music and other background noise.

Out of the corner of his eye, he saw tough guy number two reaching for something. At the last moment, he ducked behind the legs of the bar stool next to where he lay. A bottle crashed into wood, splintering into pieces, with one sliver hitting him in the upper cheek, close to his eye. But number two had left himself wide open, and Sam made him pay for his mistake with a solid punch to his Adam's apple. Now the second guy was clutching at his throat, struggling to breathe.

Sam scrambled to stand up. The leader was on the ground, but it appeared he still had some fight left in him. Despite the bum knee, he was also trying to stand. Sam didn't want to be his punching bag again, so he kicked the man in the face. Blood shot from his nose like water from a fire hydrant. He figured that would take care of the leader of the duo.

He turned to face the sidekick again, who was still clutching his throat. Before he had a chance to recover, Sam moved in close and kneed him between the legs. The blow to his groin took priority over his throat, and when he bent over in pain, Sam grabbed him by his shirt collar and launched him headfirst into the bar. Satisfied he was out of danger, Sam straightened up to come face-to-face with the bartender holding a small bat. "That'll be enough of that," Charlie said.

Sam leaned against the stool to catch his breath and held his hands up. "Yeah, that's enough for me. You better call the police, and listen, Charlie, when you call, ask for Lieutenant Carl Schneider, and tell him Sam is asking for him."

• • •

An hour later, Sam sat in his old high school buddy's car. "Sorry to be a pain in your ass, Carl, but I appreciate you coming out here."

Carl looked across at his friend and said, "Lucky for you, the bartender backed up your story that you were only defending yourself."

"That's the truth." Sam moved his lower jaw in a circular motion. "I got cold-cocked with a good right."

"Do you want to go to the hospital for an X-ray or have that cut looked at?"

"No, I'll be fine."

"I knew you'd say that, but I'm required to ask anyway," Carl said.

"Thank you for your compassion."

"Speaking of compassion, you may have broken that guy's leg."

"With all the excitement, I wasn't sure if that noise was bone snapping."

"How about his nose?" Carl asked. "Did you manage to hear that breaking?"

"No, I didn't, but that's a damned shame." He shifted his jaw back and forth.

Carl said, "I guess they weren't aware they were messing with the Tornadoes High School star middle linebacker, better known as The Wrecking Ball."

"I'm not sure that would've made a difference with these folks here. It's one thing for some guys to scare you away with a threat, but they wanted to make a point; stay away and for good, and they almost convinced me."

"You're pressing charges against them."

"Nah."

"Listen, tough guy, that wasn't a question. You *are* pressing charges. Civil liability-wise, the best defense is a good offense in case they try to concoct a bullshit story and have their friends in the bar back up what they're saying. I'll be expecting you early tomorrow morning at the station."

"Yes, sir." Sam couldn't argue with Carl's reasoning. "I'll be at your place at nine or so." Sam looked away for a moment, then turned back toward his friend. "Carl, can I bug you for any information the Tampa PD has on these two clowns, and anything on Elizabeth Evans and her boyfriend, Ramón Monzon aka Moncho?"

"You never sleep, do you?"

Sam said, "Sure, I do, just not that much. I didn't tell your officers this part, but the lady I was talking to at the bar before the fight may have set me up. She's an elementary school teacher, and I'll be talking to her tomorrow morning before she starts work."

"There won't be another crime scene, will there?"

Ignoring his question, Sam shifted in his seat, turning his body to face Carl. "That teacher knows this Beth person and Moncho, and I think he's part of a heavyweight drug trafficking organization."

"I'll have a detective do the research tomorrow and get back with you," Carl said. "Now, let's you, me, and Rafa get together before you head back to the West Coast."

Sam looked at his pager and saw that Bill was calling him from home. "Sure thing, that sounds good. Sorry, Carl, I'm getting paged by an intel guy back in LA, and I better call him." He rapped his knuckles on the dash and grunted.

"Is something the matter?"

"Man, I've got a bad feeling they might know something about the Jansens."

Carl frowned. "Sam, I hope this isn't quicksand you're stepping in."

"After tonight, I can't let it go." He extended his hand toward Carl to shake. "Thanks again. I'll see you tomorrow."

•　　•　　•

He walked to his car, happy to be in the fresh air, even if it was still humid.

He stopped at the first available pay phone, then punched in the numbers.

After they greeted each other, Bill said, "I'm glad you called because I've got useful info you'll want to know about. From what I've seen so far, this guy Moncho is the real deal in the drug world, and if I'm right, his father runs a huge drug trafficking organization operating out of Mérida, Mexico."

"Mérida?" Sam said. "In the Yucatán?"

"That's right, and I was certain I knew the name from before. Francisco Monzon, Moncho's father, likes to be daring and creative. Here's a quick history lesson for you: once upon a time, there were several independent drug trafficker types operating in western Mexico. They've been busy getting themselves organized as one cartel, but the information we have indicates they sometimes disagree and that leads to problems, and fighting, and dead people."

"Right, I've heard a bit about it, but that's strange he'd be over in the Yucatán?"

"Francisco is from the Sinaloa area like the rest of the cartel, but he tired of the bickering and packed up his bags and moved his operation to Mérida. That didn't make him real popular with the others," Bill said, "but so far, it's working for him. There's innuendo he's got connections to the top of the Mexican government, and other indications he dabbles in things related to activities by our own three-letter intelligence-gathering agencies."

"Makes you wonder whose team you're on sometimes," Sam said.

"I'm sure it can seem like it. There are also reports Monzon has a U.S. foothold for his cocaine distribution in Florida, and it looks like Moncho works that end for dear old dad out of Tampa."

"That's strange."

"Francisco Monzon's late wife, Stephanie Lewis, was a U.S. citizen from the Tampa area," Bill said. "Turns out she lived most of her life in Mexico, and although the reports don't say, I can guess Francisco kept her happy with occasional visits back to Florida, and that way, their son Moncho could enjoy the good life in both countries."

"I had a little run-in with folks tonight that are connected to Moncho, but I'll catch you up on that later. What this tells me is I'm on the right track."

"Sam, what that tells you is you're on *a* track. You'd best be careful."

"I will. Thanks again, Bill."

Sam hung up and dialed Natalie's number.

"Hello?" Her voice sounded tired.

"Natalie? I hope it's not too late to be calling."

"No, but I was worried." Her voice was quiet. "I thought you'd be here earlier."

"Yeah, I'm sorry," Sam said. "I've gotten busy with leads, but I wanted to see if you want company."

"Sure. Are you hungry?"

"Not at all; I just want to see you. I can be there in thirty minutes, if that's all right?"

"Yes," she said, then paused. "You sound different—is everything okay?"

"Yeah, I'm fine." Given how much his jaw hurt, it wasn't exactly the truth, but it wasn't exactly a lie. "I'll be at your place soon."

He hung up. Natalie's voice had sounded thin, lonely, and uncertain. He had heard that unmistakable melancholy in the past. The job, the hours, the unpredictability made it tough on relationships. He started the car and raced back across Old Tampa Bay. He was tired; it was late, and he had an early start in the morning.

CHAPTER EIGHTEEN

It was eleven when he arrived at Natalie's. The bounce in his step was gone; no taking two stairs at a time. He swallowed his pride and pushed the elevator call button.

Natalie was standing at the open door to her condo and extended her arms to hug Sam but stopped. "Dear God, what happened to you?"

"I got in a little tussle with two guys at a bar, but I'm sure it looks worse under this hallway lighting."

"You've been fighting?"

"Natalie, it's not a big deal. I sort of got jumped and—"

"Why would somebody jump you?"

"I'm following up on those guys with the boat and I guess somebody didn't like me asking questions. The good thing is I'm getting closer on several fronts. What I need now is a hug from you."

"You've got it." She hugged him around his waist. "Let me get ice for your face; it's swelling. Should we go to the hospital?"

"Yes, to the ice. No, to the hospital."

She touched her finger to his cheek and grazed her hand across his face, from his temple to the corner of his lips. He winced in pain. On the drive over, he'd wondered if his jaw was broken. It would have been a fair trade, he supposed, a knee for a jaw.

"You're hurting, Sam. What happened? Where were you? Why would someone do this?"

"That's a lot of questions, but the whole thing started when I got sucker-punched at this bar in Tampa."

"Did they catch the guys who did this?"

Sam gestured to the kitchen. "I'll take that ice if you've got a little baggie or a towel to wrap it in."

"Yeah, let me get that."

Sam stood at the counter while Natalie removed a bag of frozen peas from the freezer.

"Don't waste perfectly good—"

"Shush." She wrapped the bag in a dish towel and said, "Put this on your jaw, and I'll get antibiotic ointment too." She hustled to the bathroom; her voice carrying from the hallway. "Have you washed that cut with soap?"

"No, I didn't have a chance."

Waiting for her return, he walked closer to study several pictures in beach-themed frames hanging on the wall in the living room. "Is this you with your parents when you were little? What a cutie and look at that smile and those dimples."

"That's from a long time ago. Are you using the ice?"

"Oh, yeah, I am." He placed the bag on his jaw again. "How old were you?"

"I was six; now lie down on the couch and keep using the ice."

He was too tired to argue. Natalie returned with what appeared to be a drug store in her hands.

"What have you got—"

"Hush, no more talking. It's clear you can't take care of yourself. Are you allergic to ibuprofen?"

"You mean like Advil?" Sam said.

"Yes."

"Then no, I'm not; I don't think I'm allergic to anything."

"Stop talking. Here's water. Take two Advil, swallow and continue shushing," Natalie said, handing him the glass and pills.

Sam exhaled. "Okay."

"And keep the peas on your jaw while I wash this cut." She sat on the floor and set up her mobile medical unit beside the couch. "This might sting a little, but I'm sure it's nothing for a man who likes to get into bar fights."

"I didn't start—"

"Stop talking. And on a Monday night too." She opened a small bottle of antiseptic solution, then soaked a tissue with the fluid.

"You would prefer I do my fighting on a Saturday night?" Sam asked.

"I would prefer you to be quiet." She dabbed the wound on his cheek. "There's nothing wrong with your jaw the way you keep talking."

"Ow!"

"Don't be a baby." She wiped the cut several times, then pressed down once. "That should be clean now. I'll put antibiotic ointment on there." She set the cloth down, then squeezed a dab from the tube onto a white cotton ball. When she looked up again, Sam had removed the bag of peas from his jaw. "What do you think you're doing?" she asked.

"I don't know. What ... what am I doing?"

"I didn't say to move the peas; put them back on your jaw."

"It got too cold."

"Let me tell you something, Mister; you have no idea what cold is yet."

"Yeah, but I have a good idea what hot is." He reached to touch her side.

She swiped his hand away. "You're my patient now. Behave. Lift your head for a second, so I can sit on the couch." She moved to take the place where his head had been on the sofa. "Lay your head down on my leg, and no funny business."

He slid down a little, kicked off his shoes, curled his legs up to fit on the couch, and lowered his head onto Natalie's lap.

"Let's give that a minute, and I'll put a bandage on it, then we'll put the peas on there too. You should have done these things hours ago to keep the swelling down." She stroked his forehead, then ran her fingernails through his hair. "You like to keep your hair short, don't you?"

"It's so coarse, it's hard to control when it's longer." He closed his eyes. "God, that feels good. I'm putty in your hands."

"Sam, did they arrest those guys who beat you up?" she asked.

"Yeah, they got caught, and the police hauled them away."

"Thank goodness it wasn't any worse."

"Thank goodness," he said, feeling sleepiness overtaking him. "Natalie, thank you for letting me come over."

"You're welcome."

"How was your work today?" he asked.

"We had an alert today about a boater in trouble, but it was just an engine problem. I've got to be at work early tomorrow."

Sam's eyes opened. "Me too. What time are you leaving?"

"I need to be at the office before seven, so I'll leave at six thirty. You can stay here as long as you like."

He reached to set the alarm on his watch for six. "Thanks, but I'll go when you leave."

Natalie tore open a package of gauze dressing and applied small pieces of tape to both ends, then placed the bandage over the cut on his cheek. "Let's move the peas up here to your eye for a little while to help the swelling."

"Okay."

"Good. That's better," she said. "You're being more compliant now."

"I promise I'll be good from now on."

"Is the ibuprofen helping yet?" Natalie asked.

"Yes, I feel better just being here with you."

He felt her hand touch his forehead before his mind went blank.

• • •

When his watch alarm went off, he felt like a truck had run him over. "Oh, God help me." He heard the shower running and eased himself into a sitting position. When he stood, he had to wait until a wave of dizziness passed. He walked to the kitchen, searching a drawer for a pen and scrap paper and wrote Natalie a note, then slid out the door.

Traffic was a breeze so early in the morning. He would have time to make it to his motel, grab a quick shower and fresh clothes, and still reach the school before Heather arrived.

CHAPTER NINETEEN

The parking lot of Cortez Elementary School was empty except for a pickup truck that probably belonged to the janitor doing the early cleaning, Sam thought. He parked his car on an adjacent street with a clear view of the lot. School started in less than an hour.

Tampa was laid out in a grid-like pattern, a double-edged sword for surveillance agents. On the plus side, the long, straight roads allowed an agent to view a house or car from greater distances, but the downside was those same streets allowed subjects to see who was watching them as well.

Sam wasn't too concerned about Heather spotting him. He knew she wouldn't be looking for him on her way to school. From their conversation the previous evening, he had learned she drove a Toyota Celica.

He needed a first cup of coffee but couldn't risk missing the chance to speak with her before school began. When he spotted her car, she was heading north, coming in his direction on S. Lois Avenue. She appeared distracted, applying last-minute makeup in her rearview mirror. He started his car, made a U-turn, and followed her into the lot. When he pulled up next to her, she still hadn't seen him; her attention was fixed on the image in the mirror.

He came around the back of her car and tapped on the driver's side window. With a look of shock on her face, she jumped and dropped whatever was in her hand.

"Heather, we need to talk." He held his credential case open for her to see. "I know you have to get to school, so I'll be quick."

She looked straight ahead; her hands locked on the steering wheel.

"Heather, please."

Her head turned back toward him.

Sam said, "Can I sit with you in the car, or would you prefer to talk like this?"

"Come around the other side," she said as she moved her purse and a bag lunch from the passenger seat. She had a frightened look; her eyes flitted from side to side.

Sam felt so tired he almost fell into the passenger seat next to her. He hadn't yet closed the door when the words poured out. She said, "Listen, I swear I didn't know they were going to fight with you."

"I thought you were going to the bathroom?"

"I was—I mean, I did. When you mentioned Beth, then Moncho, I wasn't sure what to think, but the conversation scared me."

Sam said, "Is that how the dogs ended up getting sicced on me?"

She shook her head. "No. Look, when I came out of the bathroom, they surrounded me; their faces were inches from mine, and they asked me who you were, but they weren't asking, you know? They must have seen us talking, and I told them we had just met, and you were asking about buying a boat from Beth. One of them said something like, 'That's the same guy.' I didn't know what that meant, but I knew I didn't want to get mixed up in anything; and after they were done with me, I went out the back door when the trouble started. I didn't know you were a cop or a DEA agent, but there's something you don't understand. No one crosses these guys—Moncho's a big deal here."

"Heather, I was truthful with you last evening to some degree— but I left out the details about my work and my motivation. My name really is Sam, and I *am* from Los Angeles, and I do have an interest in boats. So, will you tell me how you know them?"

"From the bar, well, they don't work at the bar, but I think they work for one of the owners of the bar. Look, I'm not sure about the setup or what they do."

"Fine, let's set that aside. You be straight with me, and I'll do the same with you. You know Beth, right?"

"Yes."

"And Ramón Monzon?"

"Who?"

"Beth's boyfriend."

"I only know the name Moncho."

"But you know Moncho, right?"

"I don't want to be involved."

"Heather, I understand you're scared. I don't blame you. People like that resort to violence—it's their natural inclination. But I want you to understand this matter I'm looking into involves innocent people's lives. I know you're a good person." He turned in his seat and nodded to her. "You go into this building here every morning to teach and help kids grow up to be good people. I know you have a good heart. Am I right?"

Heather nodded. She teared up and sniffled. "I am a good person." She turned to face Sam. "I am, but you don't know what they'll do," she said. "They scare me." Her hands gripped the steering wheel.

"I understand, but do you know what I'll do? After we speak, I'll get into my car, and no one ever has to know you talked to me."

She sniffled again. "You promise?"

He raised his hand. "Scout's honor."

"I don't do drugs, not really," she said.

"Heather, I'm glad you don't do drugs. Listen, can we talk about Beth and Moncho?"

She nodded and folded her arms across her chest. "I hear things like Moncho is connected, because there's always a mountain of cocaine around at parties. Maybe you don't care, but I stay away from that stuff. It's just that it's everywhere now. The amount and availability of drugs has gotten crazy."

"I know it has. There's a fair amount of coke in Los Angeles, too." When Sam smiled, Heather laughed briefly and wiped at her nose with a tissue.

He had heard similar commentary all too often in the last few years, but right now, he didn't need to hear about Moncho's drug trafficking or anything about the Tampa party scene. He wanted to shift the course of the conversation. "Let's change the subject, okay? Have you ever been boating with them?"

She had a puzzled look. "Beth has invited me before."

"Did you go?"

"No, oh, God. Gross." She shuddered. "I almost did once."

"Tell me what happened."

"I followed Beth in her car to a house on Davis Islands one morning."

"When?"

"It was a while ago; I'm not sure, like a few months."

"All right. You went to Davis Islands."

"Yes, and if you know anything about that place, it's where the ultra-rich people live with the beautiful homes on the water and nice boats everywhere. That was the first time I saw for myself that Moncho or his family, or whoever it was, must have a ton of money. Beth told me once he was from Mexico someplace, but he lives at that house when he's in Tampa."

"Do you know the address?"

She turned to look out her side of the car before answering. "No, I don't, but I followed her to the place, and we had to wait at a gate before we could enter the driveway. She yelled for me to park on the street and jump into her car. I only remember this because Beth has this little white toy poodle that was barking like crazy at me, then I had to get into the car with it."

"What happened once you got inside the house?"

She turned back to face Sam. "I didn't know part of the deal with going out on the boat was me being set up on a blind date. Beth and Moncho, then me and somebody else, like a double date—overnight. I wasn't happy about that at all. I'm not a prostitute, and that's how it made me feel. And then, I met this crazy-looking guy. That was when Beth tried to talk me into it, but I don't like surprises, especially that kind."

"When you say he was crazy looking, how do you mean—in what way?"

"By looking like a wild animal," Heather said. "He had long hair, a beard, freaky eyes, and he was tall. I had no interest in being this guy's date or anything else. There was something creepy about him."

Sam thought of the driver's license photo of Ronaldo Gomez. He dug into his folder and removed a photo. "Is this him?"

She stared at the photo, then looked at Sam. "How did you know?"

"I didn't until just now. It's him, right?"

"Yes, that's him," she said. "My God, he acts even stranger than he looks, if you can believe it."

"What happened with going boating?"

"I didn't go. First, I had already decided I wasn't being set up on a date." She pointed to the photo. "Then Moncho and that guy started doing mushrooms, and I wanted nothing to do with that stuff, so I made an excuse to Beth in private that I wasn't feeling well, and I left. That's the truth."

"Did you see their boat?"

"Before I saw Moncho and his crazy friend that morning, Beth and I were already down at the dock looking at their boat. I like boats, but I don't know much about them or what kind it was, or what you call it, if it's a yacht, but I will tell you it was a nice boat."

"Where were Moncho and his buddy?"

"They were in their house, but while Beth and I were walking around, they came down to the dock area. I knew Moncho only a little from before, but not this other guy. They talked about their plan, like it was going to be the four of us going out. No way. Then they started on those mushrooms, and it didn't take long before they got all drugged out. They said something about going out to do a—what did they call it? A raiding party or something like that."

"What did that mean?"

"I asked Beth what they were talking about, and she said they like to mess with people, and it would be fun. Not for me. That's when I told her I didn't feel well and left."

"Have you seen Moncho and his friend since?"

"Not the friend at all," she said. "And I don't really want to see any of them. He frightened me, but I was also mad because Beth tried to use me; I could tell. The whole thing disgusted me."

"Do you know where the friend lives?"

"No, I don't. I've tried to forget him and that entire day."

Sam returned the photograph to his folder.

Heather said, "What happens to me? Am I in trouble? I had nothing to do with them picking a fight with you."

He saw a tear rolling down her cheek. "No, you're not in trouble, and I believe you," Sam said. "Hey, come on. Don't cry. You'll smudge your makeup, then your kids will wonder what happened to their pretty teacher." He smiled. "Everything will be fine."

She laughed again and wiped the tear away.

"Listen, Heather, I think you're a nice person, a genuinely good person. I mean that, and you deserve better friends than this bunch."

"Thank you."

"It's your business, but you can do way better than them. I'm asking you, please don't say anything to Beth about our conversation this morning."

"I won't; I promise—not to anyone, I won't," Heather said.

"Thank you. For now, the plan is for you to go be a schoolteacher and never hear from me again. Does that sound okay?"

"Yes, that sounds good."

Sam returned to his car and watched Heather walk toward the school, feeling good that he could trust her.

As he drove to see Carl at the Tampa Police, he thought of how different his life might have been had he remained a police officer. Would he still be a patrolman or a detective or even higher in the ranks? Then he dismissed the thoughts as useless distractions from his immediate goals. Today, he needed to weave together everything he had learned in the last week.

He'd been fortunate to find the Tuttle brothers in Venice. He'd also been lucky the Ardman couple had been so receptive to his visit and that Cindy Ardman remembered seeing Melanie, the court reporter, standing with Beth. As his father would say, he'd met some good folk, and he'd also met the no-matter-how-you-slice-it plain old bad people. Moncho, Ronaldo Gomez, and possibly Beth, fit that description.

The visit to Tampa had become personal, and he understood he could be wrong, but it now appeared quite possible that Moncho and his crew were connected to the disappearance of Chloe's parents. They were also part of a Mexican drug trafficking group, and the attack on him last night was a clear and simple message: stay away.

He felt a pang of guilt that he hadn't called Chloe in forty-eight hours. Between work and Natalie, there had been precious little time, but what did he know for sure that he could tell her? Nothing. Still, she was hurting, and he vowed to call her today.

And what about Natalie? Where was their new relationship going? They had just met, but he sensed a strong connection to her. Did the relationship have legs? He thought it did; he hoped it did. A new feeling crept into the core of his being; it wasn't guilt this time, it was loneliness. He had to return to Los Angeles soon, then what?

On a scale of probable outcomes, he knew long-distance relationships had almost no chance of surviving. This unfamiliar sensation was much more than a slight ache or twinge. It was a real pain, and it hurt when he thought about the inevitable goodbye to her.

He turned into the Tampa PD parking lot and looked for a visitor's spot.

CHAPTER TWENTY

Sam tapped on the door, edging it open. "Morning, Carl."

"There he is, The Wrecking Ball. Let's see the face."

Sam turned to give Carl a profile view.

"Not too bad. How's the jaw?"

"The guy has a good punch; it still hurts."

"It should," Carl said. "Turns out a Golden Gloves welterweight champion popped you, but that was his title several years ago, so you didn't take his best shot."

"That's nice. Thanks for sharing."

"The cut looks okay, but your jaw looks puffy," Carl said, still looking at Sam. He gestured with his hand. "Stand over there against the wall."

"Do you have to frisk me?"

Carl took a Polaroid camera from his desk. "Turn your face, so I can take a picture of the cut and the jaw."

"Is this necessary?"

"Turn your head," Carl said. "Stand still." A bright light flashed from the camera.

Sam took a step.

"Hang on, Slugger, stay there." After the second bright flash, Carl said, "Thank you." He pointed toward a piece of paper on his desk. "Fill out this part of the complaint form and sign, and I'll make sure the rest gets taken care of."

Minutes passed while Sam filled in the blocks highlighted by Carl, then he set the pen on the desk and asked, "What are the photos for?"

"One's for the police file, and one is for your scrapbook, in the off chance these guys decide to file charges against you."

"Yeah, okay."

"I spoke with Rafa a little while ago, and we agreed that we're all going out tonight."

"Carl, tonight I may be busy. I'm getting closer on this thing, and I plan to see it through."

"I understand, but that won't stop you from having a cold beer with us," Carl said. "Oh, in case you're keeping score, assailant number one has a fractured tibia *and* a broken nose, and assailant number two suffered a concussion and something I'd never heard of before called a laryngeal fracture."

"What's that?"

"In layman's terms, you broke cartilage around his larynx."

"Sorry, Dad. They hit me first."

"Yeah, and that's what kept them in handcuffs at the medical ward overnight. They'll make bail today."

Sam leaned against the chair in front of Carl's desk. "Did you learn anything about Elizabeth Evans or Ramón Monzon?"

"I've got a detective looking into it, and I'll get back to you later when we have something."

"If we're done, I'm headed over to the DEA to talk with Rafa."

"Hang on," he said, holding the Polaroid picture, "don't forget this."

Sam dropped the snapshot into his folder. "Thanks. Later, Carl."

•　　•　　•

Sam walked into Group Two to find it empty, except for the secretary sitting at her desk in front of a typewriter. He said, "I don't believe we've met before; I'm Sam from Los Angeles."

He found a friendly smile. "And I'm Tina, welcome to Tampa."

"Thanks. I was here last week, but I didn't see you."

"I was on vacation, but now I'm back. Yay." She smiled again. "What brings you here?"

"I'm on vacation myself, but stopping in to do a little work, use the phone and NADDIS."

"Make yourself at home," she said, and gestured with her hand. "As you can see, we have lots of empty desks to choose from."

"I spoke to Rafa and Joe Barber about their big case when I was here. Me and Rafa went through basic training together."

"That must mean you know where Rafa is now."

"I'm assuming he's behind that door right over there." Sam pointed to the Title III wiretap room.

"That's right, and I bet he'd love the interruption too. He always gets stuck listening to the wiretaps. He said before if he ever snaps, that'll be the reason."

"I'm sure. I'll knock on the door later, but I wanted to use the phone to make some calls, so I'll take a spot over there and enjoy the view while I'm on the phone." He went to a corner desk with Rafa's nameplate and dropped his folder in the middle. He lifted the receiver on the phone, pressed nine for an outside line, then tapped in the numbers.

"Hello?"

"Chloe? Sam here." He took a seat.

"Hi, Sam. How are you?" Her voice sounded excited.

"I'm good, thanks. I know I haven't called in a couple of days, but I wanted to let you know I'm still following up on stuff with your parents."

"You don't have to check in with me; I'm glad you called, but I figured you've been busy."

"I just wanted you to know I haven't forgotten, and as soon as I get something concrete, I'll share it with you." He spun his chair to face the window.

"Of course, and Sam if I can make you dinner, let me know. It'll be my way of saying thanks for everything you're doing."

"That's not necessary but thank you."

"Plus, I wanted you to meet Ryan," Chloe said. "He loves police shows, and I bet he'd have a ton of questions for you."

"I'll take you up on that sometime soon." He considered ending the conversation, instead he said, "How are you? Are you holding up okay?"

"Yes, it's still surreal to me. I keep expecting Mom and Dad will call me or come walking through the door, you know, all one big misunderstanding."

Sam could hear the tears behind the voice. What an awful thing to go through, wondering what had happened and knowing you may never learn why. He found himself getting mad and turned his anger toward Moncho, Gomez, and Beth. "Wouldn't that be wonderful?" he said.

There was silence for several seconds. He told himself to be patient and give her time.

"Sam?"

"Yes, Chloe."

"You don't believe that's going to happen, do you?"

This was the first time she had asked him what he thought. He didn't want to be in this position because it was beyond uncomfortable to tell Chloe what he thought she already knew.

"Chloe, I don't think it matters what I believe. If we keep the door open to the possibility that they're okay, then we're giving them a chance."

"Do you think so?"

"I do, Chloe, I do."

After another pause, she said, "Thank you, Sam."

"I'll be in touch; take care of yourself." He paused for a minute to collect his thoughts, then turned to face the desk and dialed Natalie's direct line.

"Lieutenant Timmons."

"Good morning," Sam said.

"Morning." Her voice was distant and cool.

"I'm sorry I ran out on you this morning, but I had to leave early. You were in the bathroom, and I needed to go to the motel for a shower and change."

"It surprised me you left without saying goodbye."

"I didn't want to interrupt your shower, but I left you a note. Did you see it?"

"I did. Thank you."

He detected a distance between them. "I'm sorry. I should have at least popped my head in to say goodbye, but I wanted to thank you for taking care of me last night. That was nice of you to do."

"You're welcome. How is your jaw and the cut on your face?" She spoke without emotion.

"I think it's better, mainly because of your excellent care."

"I'm sure. Sam, I have to go—"

"Natalie, is something wrong?"

"No," she said. "Everything's fine."

She answered too fast. There was something wrong; he was sure, and it wasn't hard to figure why. They had had a great weekend, but he was still someone largely unknown; then this relative stranger goes to her house late at night, beat up in a bar fight, and leaves early without saying anything.

Good move, Sam. He said, "Listen, I was thinking about taking a boat out to explore the coast around Davis Islands."

"I'm surprised you'd be interested in going boating."

"Yeah, it sounds crazy, doesn't it? Would you know of any outfits that do boat rentals?"

"Not specifically. Hold it; I have seen their sign from the road. The one I'm thinking of is near Davis Islands. It's called Bayshore Boats, or something like that."

"Okay, I'll look them up in the yellow pages. And again, I'm sorry about running out on you this morning." There was silence on the other end of the call until he spoke again. "Do you mind if I call you later on?"

"Yeah, that'll be fine. Look, I have to go."

The line went dead.

This one hurt. He knew he'd fallen for her and had sensed the same vibe in return. He spun in the chair again to look out the window and take a moment to digest the brief conversation. There before him, like a grand painting, was Tampa's skyline. Buildings, both commercial and residential, some famous, others not, stood at attention; vehicles on highways, their occupants going through the ritual of their daily lives. It was all there, but none of it mattered any longer. With an emptiness inside him, he thought about going to the airport, but discounted the idea. Then he thought about driving, but no place in particular.

"Dammit, I'm such a fucking idiot," he said aloud.

"Admitting you have a problem is the first step in the recovery process, Sam." A hand squeezed his shoulder.

He turned. "Oh, hey, Rafa, let me get out of your way."

Rafa waved him off. "Relax, I'm fine right here, but that's never a good sign when someone's talking about themselves the way you are." He sat at the adjacent desk. "What's going on?"

"I met this lady, a lieutenant with the Coast Guard in St. Pete. Her name is Natalie Timmons, and we had the best weekend, but I've already screwed it up."

"Coast Guard Lieutenant Natalie Timmons," Rafa said. "That has a nice ring to it. Is that who's helping you?"

"Yeah."

"Come on, man. You'll land on your feet."

Sam frowned.

"The word is you had a little trouble last night. Let's see." Rafa leaned forward in his chair. "Whoa, you took quite a shot. So, you're a bleeder, huh?"

Sam rubbed his hand close to his eye. "This was a shard of glass from a broken bottle."

"Oh, I thought that was from a nice right hook."

"No, the first punch landed on my jaw here." Sam pointed to the left side of his face. "Then I had the close call with a bottle that was smashed on a bar stool leg and when it shattered, a piece caught me here on the cheek. I guess you talked to Carl."

Rafa punched his right fist into the palm of his left hand. "Man, those Golden Gloves boys are bad asses, but damn, you showed those vatos. Carl said you put both dudes in the hospital."

"I was lucky to stay conscious after the first punch, then just as lucky that glass hit my cheek and not right in my eye."

"And you still put them both down."

Sam leaned his head back and yawned.

"Hey, don't get all quiet-macho-tough guy on me. If I did that, I'd take pictures and show them to everybody in the office, and everybody in the building. I might even walk down the street. Man, you did all right for yourself."

Sam couldn't help a small smile. "Yeah, I guess so."

"So, champ, you want to talk about our investigation?" Rafa said.

"Yes, listen, I'm bumping up against people who must be involved in one of your cases here."

"Man, it's not just one of our cases; it's *that*." Rafa pointed to the Title III room. "Your barroom brawl last night was with people who are suspects, or at least associates, in this case."

"What?" Sam took a moment to understand what Rafa was saying. "Come again."

"Yeah, man, that's what I'm saying. Those two assholes you took out are enforcers in the Monzon organization." Rafa nodded while he spoke. "They work right here in the Tampa part of the outfit. Look, this will be easier if I take you into the war room."

They walked toward a room marked NO ENTRY. Rafa pushed the door open, then turned to Sam and assumed a boxer's stance. "Did you know the guy who decked you was known as The Shark once upon a time? His signature move was he would circle his challenger, kind of dancing up on his toes, and when he saw an opening, he slipped in and knocked his opponent the fuck out. He was lightning fast, and strong too; we're talking about a real badass. Let me see," Rafa said, pressing his index and middle finger against Sam's jaw.

Sam yanked his head back.

"Hey, man, you should have your jaw X-rayed. It's looking swollen."

"Okay, I'll think about it."

Sam had lost interest in the fight conversation. His new focus was on the dozens of photographs posted on the wall, each with a name underneath, identifying the subject's role in the Monzon organization. Francisco Monzon was at the top, with a thick black marker line drawn down to Ramón aka Moncho. A row of photographs below Moncho included a picture of Ronaldo Gomez, and another row below him included the two guys Sam had fought at the bar. A dotted line connected the photograph of Moncho to an attractive woman, whose picture was positioned outside the main group of photographs; the name underneath identified her as Elizabeth Evans.

Sam pointed at her photo and said in a whisper, almost to himself, "This is Beth, and just like Bill described." He faced Rafa. "She's Moncho's—"

"You got that right, hombre; she's his main squeeze," Rafa said. "We don't think she knows much about their operation, but you'd better believe she's figured out he's a coke dealer."

"Where are you with the wiretap you're conducting," Sam said.

"Our wire is running on two phone lines at the Monzons' residence on Davis Islands, a compound that's tucked away on their own private inlet where they keep their marine toys." He pointed to one of the aerial photographs tacked to a corner of the wall. "Moncho is supposed to be running the drug operation here in Tampa," Rafa said. "He's being groomed by Daddy Francisco to take over everything, but right now, we're certain Francisco is still running things. And he runs a tight operation, and it's like he knows we're listening." Rafa pointed toward Francisco's photograph.

"We've been up for twenty-seven days, and we've gotten close to zilch. I don't think they'll approve us for more time—forget the judge who signed the wiretap order—the Justice Department doesn't believe in this any longer."

Sam stared at him. "You're kidding? So, Francisco, the dad of Moncho, is the kingpin, and he's here in Tampa?"

"No. Ninety-five percent of the time he's over in Mérida managing the overall organization; but he comes here sometimes. The word from our informant is he shows up to kick his son in the ass. It seems Moncho is a screwup, and if we can believe what we hear, Daddy's not too happy with him."

"Why do they have part of their operation here? That seems a little odd," Sam said.

"Great question. We think Francisco believes it somehow gives him an advantage over the other traffickers in Mexico. Also, according to the informant, Moncho didn't want to leave Tampa after his mother died."

"Hmm, that lines up with something I've heard before from an intel guy. Hey, before I forget, are you familiar with a shoe store called The Runner's Choice?" Sam reached into his folder. "The owner is a guy named—"

"Victor Alderete Perez in Apollo Beach," Rafa said.

"Oh, good, you know about him."

Rafa pointed toward his photo on the wall. "We know he's connected to this organization somehow, but how he fits in, we're not there yet."

"Hector Rojas had Perez's business card, The Runner's Choice, tucked into his wallet. Rojas is the money courier we took five hundred thousand dollars from over a week ago at LAX. Anyway, I went by the shoe store a few days ago, but it was closed," Sam said.

Rafa leaned against the wall. "We've had surveillance go by there every couple of days. There's no activity."

"I spoke with the owner of the baby furniture store next door to the shoe place. She's quite the character and won't be a reluctant witness; I couldn't stop her from talking. Bottom line, she said Perez is there once a week but never opens the store for business. She sees boxes of what she thinks are shoes being delivered, but they never go on display."

"Dammit," Rafa said. "I knew there was something to that place."

"You know what's in those boxes, right?"

"What do you think?" Rafa said.

"I think the store is a collection point for drug money that's being shipped out of the country and now I'm thinking to Mérida, Mexico. This was just one lead I was coming to tell you about, but I didn't know this was all connected to a wiretap investigation of the Monzons. I thought I'd be giving you a brand-new case to work on."

"How is it you can figure this out so fast, but our surveillance teams don't pick up on it?"

"I got lucky," Sam said. "I'm not telling you what to do, but if I were you, I'd put a full court press on the shoe store. If you can scrape together small teams to watch the place round the clock, it'll pay off, I'm sure. It's shady and my bet is money, a great deal of money."

"We have a status meeting tomorrow morning, so I'll bring it up."

"I have copies of stuff we took from the courier, and now it's become clear that Rojas was running money for the Monzon group."

"Man, you've put this whole thing together fast."

"I've been working with an intel officer in LA, a guy by the name of Bill Dunkirk," Sam said. "Every person or place I check out, he's been great about doing queries for me while I've been running around here." He walked over to inspect the photographs of the Monzon compound, then turned back toward Rafa. "It seems like the money courier, Moncho and company, and the Jansens are all pieces from the same gigantic puzzle."

"Mierda!" Rafa said.

"The connection to the boaters is just my conjecture," he said, "but listen to this. Rojas had a piece of paper in his wallet with an address, and it came back to a crappy-looking apartment building in Tampa. Bill got a NADDIS hit on the specific apartment unit, involving a vehicle stop where a guy had an ounce of coke in the glove box. The man in that car is here on your wall." Sam pointed to his picture. "Ronaldo Gomez."

"He's one freaky looking dude, isn't he?" Rafa said.

"Yes. Are you wondering how I got from him to the Jansens?"

"Tell me."

"I followed this one lead that may be serendipitous, and I won't bore you with all the details, but I learned about this couple who live in St. Pete near the Snell Isle Bridge area. They had a strange encounter with boaters not too long ago who pretended they were having boat trouble. For what reason, who can guess? Could be innocent, but I don't think so, or I wouldn't still be going at this."

Rafa rubbed his hands together. "All right."

"Who do you think those suspicious boaters were? And one clue is they're on your wall here." He waited while Rafa searched the photos. Sam answered his own question. "It was Moncho and Beth, but Gomez here is also a boat buddy of Moncho's. This lady who's a casual friend of Beth's told me a weird story where they talked about going on a raiding party; something where they mess with people, she said."

Sam paused for a moment to let Rafa digest all the information. "Look, I've broken rules to get where I am, but I'm following up on whether Moncho had anything to do with the Jansens. Looking at these photos of their compound makes me wonder."

"Wonder what?"

"This is on the Davis Islands, right?" Sam said.

"Correct."

"One person I spoke with was there. She described the place to me and saw Moncho's nice boat. I'm curious about what might be back there."

Rafa gazed at Sam. "I'll help you."

"No way, man," Sam said. "No sense in you getting into trouble, but I've got to think about this more." He bent over to get a closer look at a photo of the dock area. His voice quieted. "Anyway, this is what I have. I wish your wiretap were going better."

"Yeah, looks like this thing is going down the tubes. We think they may use code to communicate, but I'm thinking they're onto us, for sure," Rafa said. "Then again, every drug dealer thinks the police are waiting for them around the next corner."

There was a lull in the conversation until Sam said, "Hey, Rafa, you do some boating, right?"

"I've got a little sixteen-footer, but I never have time for it. Why?"

"I was toying with the idea of getting a little boat to do some coastal sightseeing while I'm here."

"You? In a boat? What's going on? What are you up to?"

Sam read the suspicion on Rafa's face. "You're right, it'd be nuts to think I would put myself on a boat."

Rafa slapped his hand on the back of Sam's back. "Don't get any crazy ideas, man." He stared into his friend's eyes for a moment. "Listen, I better get back into the wire room. What do you think? Me, you, and Carl meet up around seven this evening?"

"Yeah, sure, that sounds good."

"Keep your pager on, and I'll be in touch later. Hey, why don't you have your jaw checked too? I can see you're in pain from the way you're talking."

"There's no way I can sit in a hospital emergency room all afternoon waiting for an X-ray."

"Listen, if I guarantee you'll get right in without delay, will you go?" Rafa asked.

Sam looked at him. "How can you guarantee that?"

"Just answer the question; if I could guarantee it, would you?"

"I guess so, yeah."

"My friend is an emergency room doc. You're familiar with Tampa General?"

"Sure."

"When you get there, ask for Dr. Falcone. Henry Falcone. I'll call the hospital now to make sure he's around." He poked Sam, then said, "Unless you find someone in the emergency room with a knife sticking out of his chest, I guarantee you'll breeze right through."

CHAPTER TWENTY-ONE

The hospital visit was unexpected, but as the day wore on, Sam had to admit his jaw was aching more. But it wasn't all unwelcome news, because Tampa General sat at the entrance to Davis Islands, so he could swing by the Monzon compound afterward to look.

He drove across the short bridge to Davis Islands with the hospital to his immediate left. When he reached the emergency room, the number of people waiting gave him pause. He had read an article in the *LA Times* that people waited over four hours on average in Southern California area hospitals, and Sam figured things weren't much different in Tampa.

It seemed the people who were waiting looked much the same as patients at an ordinary doctor's office, except there were more of them. No one looked happy, but why would they? They were at a hospital. He thought about Rafa and his offer to help. The gesture was appreciated, but he couldn't go through with the waiting. Patience had never been his strong suit, but as he turned to leave, a voice behind him caught his attention.

"Rafa told me you'd come in here, look around, then attempt an escape."

Sam turned to see a middle-aged man—Rafa's friend no doubt—who appeared to be studying his face. "Could be broken, but it's hard to say just by looking." He extended his hand. "Hi, Sam, I'm Henry Falcone. Come with me and let's take a look."

"Do I need to check in?" Sam asked.

"Let's do a quick examination first, and if I think you need an X-ray, we'll log you into the system."

Sam followed the doctor. "I appreciate you seeing me right away. I'm working now and don't have much time."

Dr. Falcone had a warm smile. "That's something with which I'm well acquainted."

They entered an exam room. "Climb up here on the torture rack and let me have a look." The doctor's fingers probed his jaw. "Open your mouth," Dr. Falcone said. "Close. Again. Slow. Rafa said you took a good punch."

"Yes, it took me by surprise."

"If you have to get punched, and this is not an activity I recommend, maybe it was better it came as a surprise. When you're expecting it and your muscles tense up, you sometimes suffer a break that's worse."

"Does that mean you think it's broken?"

"If I had to bet, I'd say yes. Not a bad break, but an X-ray will tell us for sure."

Sam grimaced. "Listen, I appreciate your help, Doctor, but I'll have it checked as soon as I'm back in LA."

Dr. Falcone gave a short laugh. "Don't trust us here in the Florida swamps, do you?"

Sam said, "No, it's not that at all, but I'm working on something, and I need to get going—"

Dr. Falcone held his hand up. "You have a half hour, don't you? I'll call over to the Radiology Department, and they'll take you in right away, shoot me a picture, and I'll tell you how bad it is. We have a deal?"

"Thank you." Sam nodded, giving in. "I appreciate it."

"Not a problem. Once upon a time, my teenage son was going down the wrong path," the doctor said, answering Sam's unasked question. "Rafa helped big time."

•   •   •

An hour later, Sam was back in his car. Dr. Falcone called it a nearly indiscernible break and didn't think the injury required his jaw to be wired shut. He was told to stay away from eating hard or chewy foods for a minimum of two weeks, apply ice, avoid being punched again, and consult his own doctor for follow-up care at home. Sam folded up the unfilled prescription for Percocet, a mixture of acetaminophen and opioid pain medication, and dropped it into his folder.

He reached to turn the key, but something gave him pause; he remembered seeing a pay phone just inside the hospital entrance. Sam returned to the lobby area and dialed her number but was disappointed to hear the prerecorded greeting.

"You've reached Lieutenant Timmons. I'm not available at the moment; please leave a message, and I'll return your call as soon as possible."

Sam said, "Natalie, I wanted to say how sorry I am about earlier; that was insensitive, and I want to make it up to you. I have to, um, I have things to check on, but I'll call you later at home. I'm not sure when that'll be, and I know that doesn't sound so great after this morning, but I'll call you later." He hung up the receiver.

Dumb, dumb, dumb. He tapped his forehead to the handset in rhythm to the words inside his head. Opening the phone book, he perused the listings for a florist in Madeira Beach.

When he called, a man who introduced himself as Dan answered. Sam told him he'd like to order flowers for delivery. "What do you recommend when you, not you personally, but when you've been a jerk?" Sam heard a quiet laughter from the man.

"Nothing says I'm sorry for being a jerk like canna lilies in a nice pastel color."

Sam accepted the recommendation and gave Dan the address.

"We can have them there by early evening," Dan said.

Sam went back to his car, thinking if Natalie didn't want to see him again, at least the flowers would help soothe his bruised conscience.

He cruised on Davis Boulevard farther into the island, unable to stop gawking at the homes. Each was more impressive than the last; and Sam decided if these nearby neighboring houses were any indication, then Moncho and family were doing okay for themselves.

He turned right to enter the Monzons' street on the bayfront, but there was no house to see—at least not one visible from the car; instead, there was a massive wall that one could only assume, protected the estate from prying eyes. It was obvious security and privacy were paramount to the Monzon organization, and a great deal of planning would be required for the day Rafa and other DEA agents attempted to breach the property under the authority of government-sanctioned search and arrest warrants; if that day ever came, because Rafa had sounded pessimistic about their wiretap investigation.

He thought about the photographs taken by aircraft and boat surveillance of the Monzons' Davis Islands property that were posted in the war room. Those photos had revealed a twenty-thousand-square-foot home with covered porches, multi-leveled balconies, surrounded by a carefully landscaped jungle playground, an enormous kidney-shaped pool, and two enclosed marina berths. His memory of those photographs would have to suffice; the garish stone wall and lush landscaping prevented all inquisitive types from seeing much of anything from the street.

The thought he'd been toying with in his mind returned: approaching the property from the bay side—perhaps the weak link in their security setup—in a small boat to see what was going on back there. As ridiculous as it sounded inside his own mind to place himself in a boat, he wondered about the logistics of such an endeavor, and thought back to his conversation with Natalie, who had mentioned a rental place called Bayshore, something or other, on the main road leading to the island.

He flipped a U-turn and made his way back to Davis Boulevard, passed by the hospital, and left the island, then scanned both sides of the road. As Natalie had said, a sign for a business called Bayshore Boat Rentals was a stone's throw from Davis Islands. He stopped at the edge of the parking lot next to the street, thinking that if he gave himself the time to walk to the rental office, he might come to his senses and dismiss the crazy idea.

He didn't.

The lady behind the counter was the embodiment of Florida: the pretty face, blue eyes, straight light brown hair, and rich tan belonged on a billboard for the Sunshine State.

"Can I help you?" she said.

"Yeah, I was thinking about renting a small boat that's easy to operate; something to putter around Davis Islands for a little while."

"We hear that all the time," the lady said. "Always nice to check out how the other half lives, right? Is it just you?"

"Just me, yes."

After she explained the choice of boats that were available for tooling around the islands, Sam chose the model with a larger motor. The lady approved. "I don't guess people's weight; it's against my credo, but I think you'll be better off with a little more horsepower."

Sam chuckled. "I'm not a boating guy; is there anything special I need to know?"

"No special license, and I'll show you the basics for operating the boat. We keep the motors in tip-top condition, so no worries with a mechanical issue, but if something should happen, I'll walk you through how to deal with it," she said. "Don't worry, I promise we've been doing this a long time here."

Sam thanked her.

"How long do you want to use the boat?" she asked. "We close before it gets dark, so tonight we're looking at about seven-thirty."

"Seven-thirty, huh?" Sam checked his watch. "Um, let me ask you something. What if I needed it a little beyond darkness?"

"That's our policy. Safety drives our rules on that."

He debated whether he should try to convince her. There were several excellent reasons not to have a boat out past dark; he was sure. "Listen, this is a delicate issue. I saw you had a key drop at the front door—"

"That's for the rare times we're both gone. There are only two of us who work here, my husband and me."

"Yeah," Sam said, "I was just thinking if somebody had a problem and came back late—"

"One of us would have to stay here, and if the boater doesn't return within an hour of closing, we would notify the police or the Coast Guard."

It was something he hated to do because it made him feel like an asshole who thought the rules didn't apply to him. Plus, it didn't always work. He scratched at his chin, thinking. Time to be that asshole.

He removed his credentials from his jacket. "I'm an agent with the DEA, Drug Enforcement Administration, and I've got a little poking around to do after dark, but I swear I'll take good care of the boat. I promise if something happened, I'd be responsible—"

"You can stop right there."

Time for Plan B: Rafa's boat.

"My brother works for the Dunedin Police Department, and my husband and me are both team law enforcement, so when you get back here tonight, you'll need to lock the boat by chain. I'll show you how, then you can drop the key through the door, and we can settle up tomorrow on the final bill."

Sam placed his hands together in a prayer position in front of his chest and said, "Thank you so much; I appreciate it. By the way, I'm Sam from Los Angeles."

"I'm Sophie from right here in Florida. When do you think you'll be back?"

"I won't need it until six-thirty, so I'll wait for it to get a little darker first. I thought I might grab a bite to eat, then return, but I'll have the boat back here by nine, I'm guessing."

She asked for his driver's license and a credit card, then she brought him out to the dock behind the storefront to run through the safety points and show him how to operate the boat. "When you come back after dinner, you can take off without checking in."

Sam thanked her again. While he had been reviewing the boat's operation, his pager alerted him to a call from Rafa. He'd call later while he was enjoying another wonderful gourmet dinner out of a bag.

CHAPTER TWENTY-TWO

Sam punched the numbers in from memory. "You rang?"

"I have an update about a conversation we intercepted on the wire a little while ago," Rafa said. "But first tell me about your jaw. Did you see my friend?"

"Yes, I did. Nice guy. Thanks for arranging that. He spied me as I was making my escape from the emergency room."

"I told him you have zero patience and that when you saw all the people waiting, you'd leave. Is that a fair statement?"

Sam said, "It's like you were there with me."

"What did he say?"

"He had to study the X-ray for a long time to even see the tiniest crack. He said that there's almost no fracture; it's nothing at all."

"So, in other words, what you're saying is The Shark broke your jaw."

"Yeah, that's pretty much what I'm saying," Sam said.

"What did Henry recommend for you?"

"He said to rest, use ice, and take aspirin."

"Shit, that's what I do for a hangover."

"Me too. So, tell me, what's going on with the wire today?"

"Yeah, this was good stuff," Rafa said. "Someone at the house complained Moncho was doing his usual stupid shit and pissed off daddy Monzon again."

"You were saying something about that earlier."

"Right, I was, but check this out; there was a discussion about 'el jefe' coming to Tampa today. That's got to be Francisco Monzon; he might already be here by now. We're hoping we'll be able to pick up useful intelligence about what's going on. We could use all the help we can get to save this case."

"I'm sure." Sam felt bad about not letting his friend know he was about to check out the Monzons' compound on his own. "I'll let you go, but thanks again for the call and the doctor today."

"Hey, it's not a problem; like I was telling Carl earlier—somebody has to look after you. So, what are you up to now?"

Sam looked around. "Just kind of hanging out."

"I know you're not just sitting in a park reading a book," Rafa said.

"No, I'm not, but I am thinking about grabbing a quick bite to eat."

"All right, I'll see you in a couple of hours."

"Oh, I might be a little late," Sam said, "but I'll catch up with you guys." He ended the call and tried Natalie's direct line again. When she didn't answer, he guessed she had left the office already. He made one last stop at a pharmacy to buy anti-nausea medication, just in case. It was close to seven when he arrived back at the boat rental business.

He saw Sophie in the shop and waved at her from the parking lot, then walked around the back side to his boat at the dock. His pager went off again; it was Carl calling, and even though he'd be mad, his friend would have to wait a little while. A powerful force had drawn him to this place—there was no turning back now.

He looked around and said in a quiet voice, "Just don't mess up their little toy here." He slipped on his vest, took two steps down from the dock to position himself just above the boat, then he eased into the craft with exaggerated caution. Holding onto the dock for balance, he lowered himself to a seated position, but after sitting down, he realized he had committed a rookie mistake; the boat was still tied to the dock. Clinging to the wooden platform, he raised himself up and untied the rope.

Once he sat again, the boat sank into the water, motivating him to look over the side, the port side, he reminded himself, to check how close the water was to the top of the boat itself. He was surprised and happy to see there was at least a foot of space between the two.

The controls for everything were in front of him and manipulated by hand: the push-button start, the steering, and the acceleration. The engine cranked without hesitation, and he even felt a momentary bit of excitement as the boat surged forward.

Although the Monzons' estate would be easy to locate from the boat even in the dark, he wanted to see the backside of the property while there was still light. He stayed close to the shore as he'd been instructed, and after a short while, he admitted to himself that he was enjoying the trip.

He made a turn into their inlet, and as he approached the compound, the property's dense vegetation, combined with the evening sky and the estate's outdoor lighting, made it impossible to determine whether any lights were on inside the house. Then he skimmed by the enclosed berths; chains and padlocks secured both. Alongside the yard was a three-foot-tall fence separating a concrete walkway from the waterfront.

With solid darkness arriving soon, he steered out of the inlet and moved farther south around the island, biding his time. The water was smooth, and he found he could shut the engine off and feel no movement in the boat. The fading light coupled with the quiet made him think back to the Coast Guard cutter experience from years before; this evening's quick cruise, under his own command, was far more to his liking.

With a darkness surrounding him, he restarted the motor and headed north again. Twenty feet from the first berth, he killed the motor and allowed himself to drift toward the structure, using a penlight to illuminate the water directly in front. His tiny boat bumped against the side, and he used his hands to pull himself to the first padlocked door. Despite the lock, there was slack in the chain, but he knew if he manipulated that chain by his own hand even an inch and shined the light inside, he would be violating the law. It didn't matter; he had come too far to stop now.

The space inside the berth lit up enough to allow him to see the stern of a boat, but nothing more. He pushed himself in the direction of the adjacent berth area. This time there was less give in the chain, and he could only see the edge of something that appeared to be another boat. He shut off the light and leaned back to process what he had learned so far. Next to nothing, but to be fair, what had he expected to learn other than the Monzons had a spectacular estate?

Here he was again, he thought to himself, for the second time in the last twenty-four-hours: a man with no plan of action. Nonetheless, he was someone who needed to find a way to get a better look inside the covered berths. He knew what he was thinking would be more intrusive and more dangerous, but he couldn't stop himself. Not wanting to start the motor again, he pulled himself by hand toward the dockside. When he reached the property's edge, he sat still, pondering what he was about to do. Taking a deep breath, he tied his boat to a support pole and dragged himself up to the walkway. He waited a few seconds, crouching and listening for voices. This was madness. He had crossed the line when he stepped onto dry ground, and thus, entered the Monzons' private property. He heard nothing—no voices or noises from within—and crawled to the entrance of the covered space he hadn't been able to see inside.

His hand grasped the doorknob and turned; the door wasn't locked. Pulling it open, he shined his penlight to brighten the space. As he had suspected, there was a boat. He pushed the door open enough to slip inside, then he closed it behind him, and found himself standing on a wooden walkway around three sides of the boat.

A noise? Outside? What was it? He clicked off the penlight and ceased all movement, frozen like a statue. A full minute. Darkness. The only sound was his own heartbeat. He waited. It was nothing. He reminded himself to breathe. He switched on the penlight again and shined it into the interior of the boat. A shiver raced down his spine. Could it be? Had he found the Jansens' cabin cruiser? Even in poor lighting, he thought he could recognize the shape, the design, and the decking from the pictures Chloe had given him. He breathed in and out. *Think, Sam, think.*

He focused the light on the exterior of the cruiser, then aimed the beam at the registration number. *Good God!* He couldn't believe it. *This is the Jansens' boat. This is their fucking boat.* He thought about the sheer audacity of the people stashing the boat here. *Right here!* This Moncho guy and his friends—they must be out of their minds. They must have stolen it and brought it back at night. But why ... why steal the boat? They had everything money could buy already. And where were the Jansens? *God, no.* A sick feeling punched him in the gut.

He wondered how he could let the authorities know that the Jansens' boat was at the Monzons' estate. He couldn't just waltz into the nearest police station or FBI office and say he happened to be tooling around Davis Islands in Hillsborough Bay one evening under the cover of darkness, and despite a lock and chain, he looked inside the berth, then stumbled to the other side of the same berth, and accidentally opened a door, went inside and found their boat. But he damned well couldn't just ignore it. What about making an anonymous call to the police? What about ... dammit ... what should he do?

He decided it was best to meet with Rafa and Carl and run a hypothetical scenario past them, knowing he would essentially be admitting to an egregious violation of the law. His work back at LAX pushed its way ahead of so many thoughts crowding his mind; he missed the routine, the safety, and the mechanics of a job he knew so well that he could do it in his sleep.

He took another look at the registration number on the boat to double-check himself. No doubt about it, this was the Jansens' boat. He crept back around to the door. Time to get into his boat and leave. He reached for the doorknob.

A man's voice called from behind him. "Hey, cabrón. Hands in the air."

CHAPTER TWENTY-THREE

Sam sat alone on the afterdeck of the Jansens' boat, his hands tied behind his back and his mouth taped shut, congratulating himself that he had found the boat and screwed himself as well.

Now he understood why the door had been left unlocked. Besides top-notch security systems, wealthy estates employed private guards, especially an estate owned by a drug kingpin. He thought of the circumstances that led to his capture; of course, there would be security, but why in the hell would two guards be sitting in a darkened boat, and what was the chance of that happening right when he'd be here?

Sam figured the two Monzon security goons—in violation of their employer's rules—had been hanging out on the Jansens' boat, drinking and relaxing while taking a break from the job. He heard faint conversation outside the door, growing louder as people seemed to get closer.

The door to the berth opened, and a group of four entered. Two of the men were the guards who had captured him, and the other two were people he recognized from the photographs posted on the wall in the war room at the DEA office: Ramón "Moncho" Monzon and Ronaldo Gomez. They looked down at him from the walkway. "I like your badge," Moncho said. "This will come in handy." He flipped the credential case open for the others to see. "Police!" he said with exaggerated importance. "Freeze where you're standing."

When the others laughed, Sam cursed himself for being so stupid, for allowing himself to be caught, and for thinking he was so smart he could outwit everyone else.

"I like this too," Moncho said as he patted Sam's gun, which he now held in his own waistband. "This is a nice piece. You have a cool job, yes?" He pointed at Sam. "Too bad for you, pendejo. Your job and my job have major problems with each other. I think you might say they conflict. Am I right?"

Moncho was tall and thin, with stringy arm muscles, and wavy, medium length black hair, parted in the middle and frozen in place with a hold product. He crouched to sit on the walkway, his light brown eyes fixed on Sam. "I am so rude to not introduce us to you. My name is Ramón, but most people call me Moncho; and this is my friend Salvaje. His name in Spanish means something like 'the savage' or 'the wild one.' This is a fitting name for him, don't you think?"

Sam recalled the driver's license photograph he got from the Bradenton PD. He thought Salvaje looked even more menacing in person, and he could understand for himself why Heather had been terrified.

"And I will call you Agent Sam," Moncho said. "I don't think you'll need this gun anymore." He paused and looked upward, then returned his focus to Sam. "Yes, an idea has come to me. I have made a decision," he said, as if making a grave pronouncement. "I will make your handsome pistol a gift to Salvaje." Moncho removed the gun tucked into his pants and handed it over. "Is this okay with you?" He motioned with his arm. "Salvaje, our friend here cannot speak with the tape. Can you remove it?"

Salvaje grunted and jumped into the boat.

Sam looked up at the beast towering over him as a hand clawed at the side of his face, ripping the tape away in one rapid motion. His circumstances looked bleak, leading him to believe he would be killed and disposed of just like the Jansens—wherever they were.

Moncho said, "Hey, vato. I have a wonderful surprise for you."

Sam remained expressionless.

"Two friends of yours are here this evening, and I'm thinking you could have a friendly reunion with them." Moncho waved his hand toward a guard behind him, then pointed to the door.

His new *friends* entered. One hobbled forward on crutches; his nose looked like a faded red rose. The other was the second guy from the bar who swung a bottle at him.

"I bet you remember them; you know I had to pay their bail money today." Moncho wagged his finger at Sam and said, "You must be tough to walk away from a fight with my people. My friend with the crutches was a champion boxer. To be punched by him and still be able to fight back, you have my admiration."

Sam stared straight ahead.

"Before I let them take their revenge, would you tell me why you're here?"

If he was going to die anyway, he wanted to know the truth. He said, "What did you do to the couple who owned this boat? The Jansens."

"Ah, so that's your interest. Man, we had a bunch of fun with them that day. Old Mr. Jansen was being a pain in my ass, so I had to get rid of him."

"In other words, you murdered him?"

"Agent Sam, you are so good at interrogating; I find myself unable to resist your questioning," Moncho said. "I didn't like him, so I shot him with a speargun. You should have seen the look on his face; he was quite surprised, but he didn't seem to mind going for a swim. Now, la señora was much more pleasant, and quite an attractive woman. She was an older girl, but she had some fight in her. Didn't she, Salvaje?"

The beast smiled.

"My friend doesn't speak much," Moncho said, "but he liked her. Then he tired of her, and we dumped her too."

"And your girlfriend Beth was part of this?"

"Well done. You've done your homework. Beth is an exceptional actress. She convinced Señora Jansen that she was in desperate trouble. I think if you had seen it, you would have believed in her performance."

"All of you are murderers."

"Agent Sam, you're so good at this game. Yes, we are murderers. You have solved your great mystery. Are you satisfied?"

Sam felt sorrow for the Jansens. And Chloe. She would never know what happened. Nor would Natalie. Nor would anyone. He said, "You're nothing but a punk hiding behind your drug money and a private army. I'm sure your mother must be proud."

Moncho's eyes turned dark. "A la gran puta! Never talk about my mother, cabrón," he said. "I'm finished with you." He waved a dismissive hand at Sam and turned to the ex-boxer. "You can beat him to death now."

Sam took a last shot. "Not very sporting, are you, Ramón Monzon Lewis?"

Moncho's face showed surprise at the mention of his mother's last name.

"Yeah, you're good at killing innocent people who are weaker than you, but where's the sport in that? I beat this chump's ass once; I bet I can do it again. Why not untie me, and we can see how tough your boxer friend is?"

Moncho said, "I like how you think, Agent Sam. This sounds fun, but how fair is it for him to fight you with a broken leg?"

"He's the champion fighter, not me."

"You're right." Moncho turned toward the boxer. "You would like to fight him?"

The man's lips curled into thin lines. "Yes, but this time I will kill him."

Salvaje helped the boxer into the boat.

"Wait." Moncho held up his hand. "This is still not fair, and I'm thinking we could make things more even, so let's give Agent Sam a good whack on the leg."

Salvaje signaled the two guards. One guard put his foot over Sam's neck while the other grabbed a leg and straightened it out. He tried to break free, but it was pointless. The giant kicked his leg. Hard, again, then a third time.

For several moments, Sam held his breath, then said, "You motherfucking piece of—"

"Hey, don't get so salty, ese," Salvaje said, and kicked Sam's leg again.

After they removed the rope from his wrists, Sam clutched at his leg, writhing in pain.

"Come on, vamos, muchachos, let the party begin," Moncho said. "Stand Agent Sam up, and we'll witness these two warriors in action."

Sam clung to a grab rail, unable to put much weight on his leg, while trying to think of something he might do to free himself from captivity.

"Hey, pendejo, you better defend yourself," Moncho said.

The boxer allowed his crutches to fall away and limped toward Sam. When he closed to within three feet, Sam launched a big swing with his right fist and missed, almost falling down face-first. The boxer punished Sam for his mistake; he delivered several sharp blows to Sam's abdomen and rib cage, then punctuated the vicious attack with a left hook. Sam dropped to the boat decking, gasping for air. The only positive, if there was one, was that the last punch had landed on the unbroken side of his jaw.

The boxer looked toward Moncho and flexed the muscles in his arms.

"Agent Sam, I'm disappointed that wasn't much of a fight. I expected more after what they told me about you." Moncho waved his hand toward the boxer. "End it."

But Sam fought back. With his good leg, he kicked sideways into the cast, protecting the boxer's broken leg. Like a wild animal attacked by a larger predator, the boxer screamed as he fell onto the deck. Sam reached for his opponent's face and gouged at his eyes with his thumbs, but the boxer wasn't done either. They rolled back and forth, hands intertwined, but wrestling on the floor played to Sam's advantage where he could leverage his greater weight and strength to expose the boxer's vulnerabilities. Once he got the smaller man in a headlock, he knew it would be simply a matter of time before he choked his adversary into submission.

The door opened again, and three men entered. Sam thought he recognized one of them, but he kept a firm grip around the boxer's neck. The others, including Moncho and Salvaje, stood at attention.

"What is going on?" an older man said, then pointed at Moncho. "I want this stopped immediately."

Salvaje and others pulled Sam and the boxer apart.

"I've only just arrived, and this is what I find. Ramón, I want all of you inside the house now."

Moncho's eyes widened. "I didn't know, I mean, no one told me you were coming here today."

"Because I didn't want you to know of my travel," the man said, firing back.

Sam studied the faces of the new arrivals. It became clear the one man who had been speaking was Francisco Monzon, head of the Monzon crime family.

"Look at what we've done," Moncho said. "We captured a DEA agent sneaking around, and we were having a little fun with him."

"Is this not the case? Playing games; always having fun," Francisco said. He opened the door and said something in Spanish. Sam watched as Moncho walked outside. Francisco turned to the two men who had accompanied him, then spoke in Spanish again. One bodyguard jumped into the boat and stood next to Sam. He figured they had to be Francisco's personal bodyguards and knew they would be proficient with a variety of weapons, hand-to-hand combat, and prepared to die to protect their boss.

Francisco went outside and closed the door behind him. Sam could hear the back-and-forth conversation in Spanish, between father and son. Despite speaking fair Spanish, Sam couldn't gather the meaning. Still, he knew what a disagreement sounded like. After a few minutes, the conversation outside quieted and Francisco returned alone, holding Sam's badge and credential case. He passed it to the bodyguard who remained standing on the platform beside the boat, then spoke rapidly in Spanish while his eyes moved from person to person standing nearby. Salvaje reached into the waistband of his trousers and lumbered toward the same bodyguard. He handed over Sam's pistol. His head hung low as he dropped into the boat again, then he picked up the crutches and helped the boxer to his feet. Sam watched Moncho's minions depart, each with a distinct hangdog expression; a scene reminiscent of disobedient children who found themselves in trouble after the parents arrived home. Francisco and his two bodyguards remained.

Sam studied the man, who stood in silence and appeared to be deep in thought while he held his hands behind his back. Francisco was a handsome figure, tall and lean, with meticulously styled hair and beard. His fine clothes were neatly pressed. He guessed the leather shoes alone cost more than his own entire wardrobe. The gold chain necklace, bracelet, and multiple rings all added up to someone who cared a great deal about appearances.

Francisco stared down at his shoes. "My son has been a disappointment to me." Then his gaze turned toward Sam. "His mother, my late wife, coddled him; always excusing his deficiencies and lack of effort."

Sam chose silence as the better response to Francisco's comments, wondering where this conversation and encounter might lead. His leg throbbed from Salvaje's kicks, his ribs ached from body punches, and his jaw hurt on both sides of his face, and yet, he remained untied.

Francisco snapped his fingers and said something in Spanish. The bodyguard handed over Sam's DEA credentials. Francisco looked inside the wallet. "Special Agent Samuel H. Dahl with the Drug Enforcement Administration. What does the *H* stand for?"

Sam saw no reason to play tough guy or remain silent. "Henry," he said.

"This name has family significance?"

"Henry was my grandfather on my mother's side."

"I see." Francisco handed the credential case back to the bodyguard.

Dressed in suits and ties, the two bodyguards, now standing once again side by side, looked like twin mountain peaks. Six feet, six inches, with broad shoulders, they were impressive in appearance. Sam understood why he had been left unrestrained—Francisco felt no need to do so while the mountains stood nearby.

Francisco ran his fingers through his graying hair and asked, "May I address you by your given name?"

Sam shrugged.

"I presume because of your work, Samuel, you know who I am." He raised his eyebrows. "And the ugliness that I represent to you?"

Sam shrugged a second time. The throbbing in his leg had subsided to a modest degree, giving him hope the bone wasn't broken.

"I'm certain it matters little what I say, but I'm not such a terrible person."

Sam gave no reaction to the statement.

"Would it shock you to learn your own intelligence agencies have climbed into bed on occasion with a horrible drug trafficker like myself?"

"Not so much," Sam said. Especially after what Bill had told him the night before, he could believe some agencies within the American government weren't always following the same playbook. He was sure they had their reasons: some good, some bad, some perverse.

Francisco said, "At times, I've assisted my government and that of the United States."

Sam rubbed his jaw and stared straight ahead.

"This is true. I've provided information to root out rebel forces and other elements that would like to make changes, or even overthrow the Mexican government. At first, their contact surprised me. Once I asked one of your government operatives why they would choose to work with me, knowing I'm responsible for so many thousands of kilograms of cocaine in Americans' homes and schools."

Sam rocked forward for a moment, then leaned back.

"He said it was for the greater good. Samuel, do you ever wonder if the people who pontificate endlessly about eradicating drugs mean what they say? This so-called war on drugs is profitable for us both. While we reap billions of dollars from the drug trade, your government spends billions to stop it. But let's not pretend any longer. Neither side is going anywhere; thus, we both profit and the game continues."

Francisco waved his hands downward, as if he were dismissing the subject. He stroked his beard and said, "Is it not unfortunate I must protect my interests by spying on my own son?" He sighed and ran his hand along the gunwale. "I realize this boat doesn't belong to us, because I have my people here watching and I know its story. I don't condone my son's activities, but I cannot change the outcome." He stared at Sam before speaking again. "A matter of curiosity. Would you tell me why a DEA agent would be interested in this boat?"

Sam noted Francisco spoke English with an accent, but his command of the language was impeccable. He thought about the question and saw no reason he shouldn't answer. "A childhood friend of mine used to have parents she loved. They were Ben and Carol Jansen. This was their boat until your son and his friends killed them."

"I see," Francisco said.

"Now my friend can't sleep at night. They've destroyed her life, and she's going out of her mind, agonizing over her parents. She asked me to help find them, or at least find out what happened."

"This work isn't part of your job, but I can see you're a good and loyal friend who only wanted to help." Francisco paced to the left, then to the right, stopping where he had started. He clasped his hands in front of his waist. "I believe you, but this isn't the only reason you're here. Am I correct?"

Sam stared at Francisco.

"I'll take your silence to mean no. My son is a simpleton. He would never think to consider the other reasons you might be here. He would prefer to entertain himself by watching grown men beat each other to death rather than be curious and ask questions."

Sam said, "All right, I'll tell you why. Your son and his friends' good times led me to your drug trafficking, and I couldn't look at the one without seeing the other."

"Yes, I see. Did you know I'm aware of the actions and efforts by your airport office in Los Angeles?"

Sam's face remained impassive; he tried to hide his surprise.

"Samuel, when one of my employees returns from a business trip and instead of bringing me my money, he gives us a paper receipt saying the special agents of the Drug Enforcement Administration took it, of course, we have our lawyers check. I thought I recognized your name when I read it on your credentials earlier."

"I'm doing my job," Sam said.

"Of course ... of course you are. I would be less than honest if I said your efforts didn't affect me, but I understand it's the cost of doing business. You take a little here and a little there, and if I'm being honest—and I am—it amounts to a nuisance, nothing more."

Sam thought about the audacity of that statement. He had seized over five hundred thousand dollars twelve days ago, yet Monzon considered it to be only a *nuisance*. He knew it was true, but for someone to say it aloud was something else.

Francisco said, "Not that I'm happy about it or that I don't care; I do, but I can look past it. In fact, I appreciate you're a professional in what you do; I too am a professional, but we're on different sides of the same coin, yes?"

"Something like that."

"Far more important to me now is I believe we're under investigation by your office here in Tampa. I will share a secret with you. In spite of my childish son, I have excellent people who work for me here. They have seen the—how do you say—surveillance activities with the van and cars and the helicopter. The extent of your investigation, I can't say, but I can imagine, and that puts us at odds."

Sam rubbed at the soreness in his rib cage.

"You must understand your activities in Los Angeles are one thing, but this business here in Tampa concerns me more. This effort could damage—perhaps even destroy my livelihood, and that, I cannot abide," Francisco said.

The man does his homework, Sam thought. The money, the resources, the network he commands. He knew the DEA would always be outgunned, given the insatiable appetite for drugs that existed across the United States. Sam turned his palms up. "Look, I'm a visitor here in Tampa. I can't help you."

Francisco laughed. "I could use someone like you in my organization. We could do quite well together."

"I'll pass."

"I didn't believe you would ever consider such an offer," Francisco said. "So be it."

He began pacing again until stopping to face Sam.

"I came here to deal with the usual problems. My son is close to the top of the list. This boat you are sitting in is an example of his stupidity, and I'm unsure what he was thinking, if there was any thought at all. One night soon, we'll have to take it out several miles into the Gulf of Mexico and sink it."

"It would be a shame to sink this boat," Sam said. "Why not abandon it someplace? Then someone could find it and return it to the family."

"What a lovely thought. In a perfect world, it would be a wonderful gesture, but I'm afraid that won't happen in this case. I'm certain you're intelligent enough to realize we cannot let you walk away. Samuel, you'll have to be on this boat too."

"Don't guess I could change your mind on that subject?"

"No, I think not." He slapped the back of one hand into the palm of the other. "Before we do that, however, I need you to tell me the details of your agency's investigation into my business."

"The truth is, I don't work here."

"Do you take me for a fool? What's your American expression? You're a smart guy. I know you work in Los Angeles, but I believe you have information about these activities here as well. With the proper motivation, I think you'll share that knowledge with me. Here's what will happen; my assistants are going to restrain you again."

Francisco nodded to his bodyguards. The mountains moved in his direction. One flipped Sam over like he was nothing more than a rag doll and retied his arms and legs.

"Now you're going to beat the information out of me?" Sam asked.

Francisco spoke in an undertone in Spanish, and one guard left.

"Nothing so crude," Francisco said, turning back to Sam. "My assistant is alerting individuals I employ who make people talk for a living. I brought them here to confirm suspicions that someone within my organization, someone with whom I've placed my trust, has been providing information to your government. I believe you use the term *snitch* to describe such a person, but before they can deal with our snitch problem, they will have to work on you first. Samuel, I can say with certainty they're quite talented at inflicting immense pain without ever striking the subject. And a doctor will be present to ensure you don't die before we're ready for you to do so."

"Well, this is shaping up to be a red-letter day."

"I've not heard this expression before. Yes, I suppose it is indeed," Francisco said. "Samuel, I would like to give you one more chance to talk. From one professional to another, I can promise you a quick and painless death if you do."

Sam flared his nostrils. "I've got nothing to tell you."

"We shall see. You'll find that once the procedure begins, you'll beg to talk."

Francisco turned and left, leaving one mountain behind.

CHAPTER TWENTY-FOUR

The mountain stared straight ahead. He didn't seem like much of a conversationalist, so Sam figured there was no reason to talk things through with him.

His thoughts centered on his predicament, and it appeared he had two options. Three, if he included the unrealistic option of joining Francisco's organization. The latter choice meant he would continue working as a DEA agent but would be required to feed information to his new master. Although rare, there was a precedent for this type of arrangement, as Sam knew a few bad apples sat rotting in every profession. The downside to this option, besides being a total scumbag, lay in the public disgrace such alliances often ended, not to mention the serious jail time that would ensue, and ultimately, a shank in the back from a fellow prisoner.

Of the other two options, one was ugly and the other shitty.

The ugly option was Sam telling Francisco what he knew, then he would be killed. Even if he divulged everything he knew, would Francisco ever believe the investigation was going down the tubes? No, there was no way he would ever believe the Department of Justice intended to terminate the wiretap, as this would amount to a violation of the first rule of drug traffickers: trust nothing and no one.

The shitty option involved fighting through whatever torture Francisco and his men had planned with every ounce of strength. Following the struggle, they would kill him.

He tried not to think about the torture. Instead, he told himself to focus on pleasant thoughts like Natalie. He hoped she liked the flowers. It would have been nice to see her again, but that wasn't happening. It was a good thing she hadn't invested too much in the relationship, he thought. Maybe Chloe and Natalie would become friends, as they both would have had people in their lives who had disappeared without a trace.

The second mountain returned with a folded-up table of sorts, something like a massage table. He stepped down into the boat, said something in Spanish to his partner, then disappeared behind Sam.

An enormous hand wrapped around Sam's neck while another grabbed at the seat of his pants. The mountain carried Sam into the galley of the boat and plopped him on the table—it was definitely not one that a masseuse used. They worked without speaking, leaving Sam with the impression they'd done this before. They removed his shoes and clothing and tossed them to the floor next to the life preserver that he had used with his rental boat. How ironic, he thought, seeing his clothes piled up beside the preserver, an object that served the singular purpose of saving lives.

He felt like a fish about to be filleted. As he lay naked and humiliated, the two men used leather straps attached from underneath the table to bind his arms, legs, torso, and head. Then they stuffed a rag into his mouth and applied heavy tape to seal his lips shut.

After both mountains left, he assumed he was alone once the door closed. He tried to move his limbs, figuring that not trying was silly. His efforts were useless.

He breathed softly through his nose and closed his eyes. One never knows how it's going to end, he thought. In a perfect world, he would live a long and happy life, retire one day, and drink cold beer while he hauled in large bass from his own little corner of a lake somewhere. He wondered why he wasn't more upset; he knew he should be.

Minutes passed until a noise stirred him from his thoughts. A new face appeared: a younger man with dark hair and eyes to match. He had extraordinary eyebrows, so thick they resembled black carpet runners. Because he couldn't turn his head, Sam had only a limited range of vision, but he caught a quick glimpse of an IV bottle in the man's hand. He felt a tapping in the crease of his left elbow pit, then a stinging sensation.

Sam gathered there would be no introductions. In his day-to-day work, identifying the people with whom he interacted was important, so he took the initiative and assigned the name *Eyebrows* to the new guy.

Eyebrows left the room, returning a minute later, holding a box to his chest. Sam heard the man humming to himself while he apparently unpacked things and set them on the table behind him. His face came into full view as he stood beside the table and leaned over Sam. He pressed a sticky object onto the right center of Sam's chest above his nipple and another one below the nipple on the left side of his rib cage.

"The pads I attached to your chest are part of a device called a defibrillator." Eyebrows had finally spoken. "If your heart stops beating, the doctor can press the shock button, sending an electrical jolt through you. Most of the voltage passes between the electrodes through your heart, resulting in a strong contraction in that muscle, with the goal being to restart your heart."

Eyebrows tore the tape from Sam's face and inserted a wooden block between his back teeth on the right side to keep his mouth open. Then Eyebrows thrust a cylindrical metallic device into Sam's mouth. The drilling began immediately. As the bit bore through enamel deep into the pulp chambers containing some of the human body's most sensitive nerves, Sam's hands clenched and every muscle in his body tightened. The onslaught from the drill's whirring noise in his ears, the intense vibration in his aching jaw, and the flat, dry odor from two of his molars being perforated created an absolute madness in his mind.

Eyebrows inserted wires into the molars, then removed the rag stuffed in his throat. In its place, he shoved a large ball of plastic wrap deep into Sam's throat, before removing the wood block. "Those wires in your teeth are the first of several that I'll place at certain parts of your body. The ends are silver because we find this metal to be an excellent conductor of electricity."

His body was already soaked in sweat, and as the process wore on, Sam questioned his decision to endure whatever it was they had planned for him. But Eyebrows wasn't finished. He stabbed the sharp ends of wires under the nails of Sam's fingers, then repeating the process, pressing them under his toenails. A minute passed until Eyebrows pushed something into Sam's right ear canal, followed by another object going into his left. Finally, the man inserted a last wire, pushing it slowly, carefully, and deeply into his urethra.

"The doctor will be here soon." Eyebrows began to turn away but stopped. "You should have talked. I've done this before; look man, everyone gives in." Patting Sam on the arm, he said, "You'll wish you were dead, but the doc won't let you die."

What have I done to myself? Sam wondered.

CHAPTER TWENTY-FIVE

The door opened, and the sound of footfalls moved in his direction.

"Hey, Doc," Eyebrows said.

The doctor spoke with a raspy voice like he'd been smoking at least one lifetime. "Let's get started. He's a big fella. I think you can turn up the juice on him from the start."

"You're the doctor," Eyebrows said.

Sam kept his eyes closed until the doctor spoke. "Open your eyes, or we'll tape them that way."

He complied, thinking it would be better to blink rather than being forced to always keep his eyes open.

"Mr. Monzon instructed me to allow you one more opportunity to cooperate. Blink your eyes if you're prepared to talk."

Sam had already decided on the shitty option; he refused to blink.

"Your choice," the doctor said in a cold, businesslike manner. "The IV will provide a drip of methamphetamine to keep you conscious and alert. I'll use it as I see fit. The wires fitted in various places in your body will be used to conduct an electric current and will produce enormous pain but not enough to kill you, but if I'm wrong and your heart stops, I'll attempt a restart with the defibrillator, or I can administer an injection of adrenaline into the heart muscle." The doctor's eyes shifted in the general direction of Eyebrows. "Let's begin."

From behind him, the start-up of a device produced a humming noise. Sam was sure the machine was related to the electric current the doctor talked about.

The next moment, Eyebrows said, "Doc, would you mind cranking up the tunes on the box next to you?"

Military marching band music began playing. Sam could only guess the sound would cover his muffled attempts to scream; now he thought he understood why Eyebrows stuffed the plastic into his throat.

Without warning, the first shocks pierced his ears. They seemed to meet in the center of his brain, producing an explosion of pain. His legs and arms convulsed, and his torso bucked against the thick straps keeping him immobile. He'd felt pain before when he broke his collarbone playing high school football, or when he fell off a ladder and chipped a bone in his elbow, or when he got shot in the arm. Those instances were pain. There was no word to describe this. A guttural sound came up from his throat, then the current stopped.

The second time, again without warning, a shock tore through his right foot and up his leg. Then his left hand. The guttural sounds rose in his throat again until a new current shot through his back teeth. He began losing consciousness and felt a perverse sense of gladness.

Within moments, a jolt rocked Sam's heart, and in a remote corner of his brain that was still functioning, he realized the doctor must have started the methamphetamine drip.

A new shock hit him inside his penis; the stabbing pain extended deeply into his gut. For a moment, he thought he might be strong enough to rip away the straps that bound him.

The current kept coming, shifting between parts of his body. There was no pattern; he couldn't predict where the next shock would hit. There was no means to prepare himself, and each time he felt like he might lose consciousness, the drip dragged him back.

The torture went on without end, and when he could think for a second, he wanted to tell his captors everything. *Everything.* He didn't care about his job, the oath, right or wrong, who died, who didn't. Nothing mattered.

And still the shocks continued. His heart was beating like a jackhammer—yet the amphetamine drip wouldn't allow him to slip away. Not an inch. He was stuck in an eternal hell.

When would they stop and allow him to confess everything he knew and everything he'd ever known? He would do anything for his new master. Inform, steal, kill. *Anything.*

How could his body take this? Why wouldn't he die? Why couldn't he die?

The shocks ceased, and the music stopped too. He didn't know how long the torture session had lasted. His sense of time had been obliterated. The doctor leaned over him and said, "If you're ready to talk, blink twice."

Sam blinked over and over, more than twice, more than twenty times. He couldn't stop himself, having lost control. He lay in the wetness of his own urine and sensed the sweat and mucus on his face.

"Open your mouth," the doctor said. He reached in with forceps and removed the plastic from his throat.

Sam took the first of several long breaths.

"You'd like to talk?"

He tried to nod but realized he couldn't. He said, "Yes. Yes. Yes, I will. Anything you, you want."

When he opened his eyes again, Francisco stood over him. "Samuel, I'm delighted you will cooperate."

"Yes, I, yes, I cooperate. I, I—" His speech was out of control.

"Fine, I understand." Francisco held his hand up. "Now, I want you to tell me about the investigation your agency is conducting in Tampa."

"The, the, the investigation," Sam heard himself say, "the investigation is, is, is—"

The doctor said, "We've been at it for about forty minutes. He's quite strong, but it's common for anyone to babble after this amount of time. He may lose consciousness as his central nervous system tries to recover."

Sam said, "Talk, I talk, I talk ... investigation ... investigation ... it's the, the, the—"

"Do what you have to do to stop this nonsense, Doctor," Francisco said.

The amphetamine drip reached his heart within seconds, then a jolt rocked him to the present.

"What's going on with the investigation?"

His heart was racing, his brain was functioning at a minimal level.

Francisco slapped his face. "I want to know everything about the investigation."

Sam's awareness was heightened; he felt a knot deep inside his core, ready to burst, like he might explode at any second. "The, the investigation, the investigation—" Irrepressible crying halted his speech. "Is, it's about. No, no, you piece of shit—" His own words were interrupted with a mixture of uncontrollable laughter and crying, then he said, "You're shit, you're—"

Francisco shook his head, then waved his hand at Sam. The doctor stuffed the plastic wrap into his throat. Seconds later, a door closed, and once again, the military marchers had returned, moving in step to the cadence of drums, while sonorous brass instruments trumpeted memories of past battlefield victories.

The first shock hit, followed by an animal growl erupting from deep within him.

He returned to the fiery pits of hell.

CHAPTER TWENTY-SIX

No reality existed anymore except the searing pain from the tips of his fingers to the end of his soul. There was nothing else, except the feeling he was being eaten from the inside out, like rats gnawing at his organs, one fiber, one cell, at a time. It was a deep, cavernous abyss from which there was no escape.

The doctor's voice sounded. "He's becoming immune to this level—up the current twenty-five percent."

His brain whimpered no, but when the next wave of electricity shot through his teeth and ears at the same moment, the *no* was vaporized inside his mind, leaving only an acrid smell of burning tissue.

The rhythm of his heart became highly irregular; the upper chambers pounding out of sync at two hundred beats per minute, scurrying around the corners of his consciousness like a mouse. Cardiac arrest was imminent, and when another deep, involuntary sound escaped from his throat, his limbs shook with fury, then slowed to something akin to a death rattle.

Sam's mind formed words that bounced off the inside of his skull: *I'm ... at ... end.*

There was an unfamiliar noise, and it wasn't the doctor or Eyebrows, nor did it come from inside himself; rather, it was a voice from somewhere else. Sam's eyes followed a shadowy form racing in his direction.

I'm here, Death. Please take me now.

The electricity shooting through his body had ceased, and Sam closed his eyes, allowing a deep yearning of acceptance and gratitude to wash over him. He used every precious molecule of remaining strength to push toward his only friend: Death.

A glorious peace embraced him until a voice inside his head said, "Sam." His mind floated toward the sound of his name. *Yes, Death. I'm here.*

Something shook him, and again, he heard his name. "Sam!"

His eyes opened to see the outline of a new figure standing over him. "Sam, can you hear me?" He closed his eyes again to block out the interruption on his journey with destiny.

"Come on, Sam!"

His crippled mind fashioned a single thought. *Don't mock me, Death.* He tried to resist, but he couldn't stop his eyes from opening. A strange sight confronted him. The same figure from before remained standing over him, holding a gun to someone else's head.

"Listen, you son of a bitch, take that IV out now. And you, get your ass over here. Take every one of these things out of him or you're getting a bullet in your brain."

Stabbing pain shot through various parts of his body: feet, hands, penis, mouth, and ears.

"And get that shit out of his mouth too."

A sensation of air moving through his throat into his lungs brought a new awareness.

"Now undo those straps."

His legs were freed first, then his arms, followed by his torso and head.

His voice was weak. "Weren't you Rafa?"

"Sam, it *is* me. I *am* Rafa. Hang on, while I deal with these assholes."

A deep calm swept over him. From where, he didn't know, but he drew the strength to raise his nude body to a sitting position and touch his feet to the decking. He extended his arms, turning the palms of his hands toward himself in fascination. A peculiar feeling coursed through the billions of restless neurons pulsing throughout his body, and with it, incredible power and strength. In an instant, the heightened electrical signals transmitted messages from one part of his body to another, from his arms to his legs, from his fingers to his toes, from his gut to his skull, creating a new state of being that simulated an overall invincibility and a numbness to pain.

He was a mighty oak tree, protected from all the dangers surrounding him. His feet rooted into the ground; he was one with the Earth, in sync, moving in a slow circle. His arms were the branches, his fingers its leaves, emitting stinging impulses to ward off peril. From high above, he witnessed the man he remembered as Rafa tying rope around other humans' arms and legs, then wrapping heavy tape around their mouths, and covering their heads with pillowcases.

Their puny movements and feeble voices amounted to wisps of frail wind passing nearby, nothing more. For a time, he lorded over those beneath him until the experience of detachment from human interaction was interrupted by crackling jolts of energy puncturing small holes, then pathways into his brain. New thoughts and sentiments poured into his mind like water flooding into a valley through a breached dam.

The insensitivity yielded; his perception of feeling returned. In the passage of a minute, his mind refocused on himself. His arms were no longer branches, his fingers were no longer leaves; he was a man, not a tree. Flexing the muscles in his legs, he wondered whether they could support him enough to take a first step. He gripped the side of the table and edged one of his feet forward.

Rafa came to his side. "Easy does it, buddy. Hang here for a second. I think we can lower the volume on this music."

He returned to Sam's side, holding his clothes. "Come on, let's get you dressed."

His equilibrium was off, and when dizziness seized control, he almost toppled over.

"I've got you, Sam, I've got you," Rafa said.

He pushed Rafa away and dropped to his knees, spewing vomit onto his captors lying on the floor.

"Good. Get rid of all that poison inside you," Rafa said, steadying him until he was done.

Sam grabbed the edge of the table and dragged himself to his feet. A minute passed as a sense of normalcy, at first spotty and uneven, returned. After he dressed and pulled his shoes on, Sam felt like he had regained some control, but his voice was still ragged and halting. "How did, how did you know?"

"How did I know you were here?" Rafa asked.

Sam nodded.

"When you didn't answer your pages, I remembered what you said before about wanting to come here. I also checked with the guys in the wiretap room, and they said the phones here had gotten quiet—way too quiet. Anyway, I wanted to check on whether you were trying to patch things up with the lady you were talking about earlier."

"Natalie?"

"I remembered the name, Lieutenant Natalie Timmons. Took some doing, but I got her unlisted home number and called."

"You spoke to Natalie?" Sam said, tears streamed from his eyes.

Rafa rested his hand on Sam's shoulder. "She said you weren't there and told me about the last conversation you had with her, that you were thinking about renting a boat to go sightseeing around Davis Islands. I knew then for sure you were coming here, so I got a friend's boat close by, then I cruised around, and on my second pass, I saw the little rental boat. I knew it had to be you."

He couldn't stop himself from crying. Sam put his head between his hands, attempting to regain control of his emotions. "Listen, Mon, Moncho told me, he told me they, they took the boat and killed them," he said. "They killed the Jansens. Francisco—he was here with me. He, he—" Sam tried to control his stuttering. "Francisco's the one who did this—did this to me." He clutched at the table to hold himself upright as chills shot through his body.

"Sam, take it easy."

He leaned over the table to center himself.

"I saw people moving around in the house," Rafa said. "That's why it took time to get in here because I had to wait. Now we need to move, and fast, before someone comes out here to check on you." He glanced in the door's direction. "Is this the missing boat you were looking for?"

Sam stared at the decking. "Yes, it is."

"I've got an idea," Rafa said, removing a portable radio from his pocket. "Operations base from Tampa 203."

A voice from the radio answered, "Go ahead, 203."

"This is an emergency. I need you to patch me through to a landline."

"Standby, 203."

Sam closed his eyes and took a deep breath to steady his voice. "What are you doing?"

"I told Carl earlier when you didn't answer your calls to stay close to his phone. Think about it; they kidnapped you. We've got a stolen boat here. They admitted to you they killed the owners. So, not too long from now, we'll have Carl and a fucking army coming through their front door."

Desperate to process his lethargic thoughts, Sam nodded and said, "What can we do?"

"When the police arrive, we'll be waiting outside the back door, ready to squeeze their nuts in a vise."

Sam remained motionless; sluggish thoughts trapped inside his brain.

Rafa said, "I'm sure there's still water stored in the bathroom. You'll feel better if you splash water on your face while I talk to Carl."

The voice crackled from the radio. "203, what's the landline number?"

Rafa pointed toward the bathroom. "Go, Sam, I've got this."

CHAPTER TWENTY-SEVEN

Furious and embarrassed, Sam didn't have time to clean himself as he would have wanted. He splashed water onto his face and neck; then he toweled off. Each moment that passed, his mental clarity improved. All the while, an anger churned inside him, and as he returned from the bathroom, his rage boiled out of control. He stole quick glimpses of everything in the galley. Opening a drawer, he found what he wanted, what he needed. He gripped the serrated butcher knife in his hand, running a finger along the blade, finding it sharp enough to slice through a neck or two.

He went to the main deck, then poked his head around the corner to peer at Rafa. His friend was busy watching the house through the narrow opening of the covered berth doorway.

With a smile, Sam turned back to the galley. A malicious joy filled his heart, certain that the good doctor and Eyebrows were unaware at this moment that a rational, clearheaded, perfectly sane man stood in their midst and was hell-bent on killing. He edged toward his former captors, thinking first, he would deal with the doctor. He knelt over the body, his face inches from the man's head, shrouded in a pillowcase.

Speaking in a quiet voice—one he forced himself to control—he said, "You can't hide from me." Sam could taste the fear, savoring the dread and terror from the doctor. Enticing, enslaving, and seductive, the desire for revenge was irresistible.

Rafa's voice interrupted his thoughts. "Sam, what are you doing?"

He heard his friend's footsteps coming toward him.

"What time ... what time is it, Rafa?"

"It's almost eleven. Why?"

He stood, keeping his back to Rafa. "Do you know? Do you understand? Can you comprehend what they did to me?" His body shook as he wept, and when Rafa embraced him, he almost collapsed. "They broke me, Rafa, they, they completely broke me."

Rafa gripped Sam's shoulders, turning him around. "Sam, they didn't break you. You're here now, standing on your own two feet. You're strong, and you're a better man than they are."

Sam breathed out and placed the knife on the table, then closed his eyes and patted the handle before pushing it away.

Rafa said, "Let's crawl up close behind the house, and as soon as the cavalry shows, we'll be ready."

• • •

Distant sirens provided the first clue to the coming storm. Soon the nighttime sky near the Monzon compound was a scene of flashing blue lights and noisy sirens. Carl's voice came over a loudspeaker: "This is the Tampa Police Department. Open the gate or our truck will break through. I repeat, open your front gate, or we're coming through by force."

The once quiet street on Davis Islands had become a war zone. Thirty seconds hadn't yet passed. No matter, a loud crashing sound masked everything else; the truck rammed its way through.

They hid in the heavy shrubbery near the main entrance to the back of the house. Sam found it impossible to stay still, unsure whether it was the electric current still running rampant in his nerves or the remnants of amphetamine that lingered in his veins? When he raised himself from a crouching position, Rafa grabbed his leg.

"We've got to stay down. The police will come back here too, and they won't know who you are. Get down here with me and be ready if Moncho and his cockroaches scurry out the back door."

Sam crouched next to Rafa. He knew he needed to stay out of sight, but he wanted to do something. He wanted revenge—he wanted to wrap his hands around Francisco's neck and choke the life out of him.

Peering through the shrubbery, Sam saw two figures move inside the darkened house; their faces were visible for only a second as they passed through a sliver of light. Moncho and Salvaje scrambled from one side of the living room to the other, then Moncho darted up a hallway, only to return seconds later. Sam caught a split-second view of a young blonde-haired woman in the same room, poking her head out from the inside of a hollow, oversized ottoman in front of a large sectional sofa. *Beth Evans?*

When he heard the police entering the house, Sam prayed Moncho and Salvaje would come running out the back door. They didn't. Instead, they cowered beside the sofa until a dozen police officers, with guns drawn, swarmed the room.

Two officers approached the rear door, peering out into the darkness. When the floodlights were activated, Rafa and Sam sat on the ground with their hands held in the air. "We're DEA agents!" Rafa screamed. He pointed a finger toward the badge hanging from his windbreaker.

An officer said, "Hands up! Don't move!" He approached, taking short, careful steps, and kept his gun trained on them.

Carl stepped out back and said, "Officers, it's okay, they're DEA, and they're with us."

Sam's mind was still playing catch up with his thoughts trailing too slowly behind what needed to be said and done. "There's two ... two men tied up on the boat that belonged to the Jansens. It was stolen ... and they were killed."

Carl directed several officers to the boat, then pointed at Rafa and Sam. "Stay close to me. We don't want an accident here."

After they entered the house, a shout from another room sounded. "Gun! Lieutenant, we have a gun. Also, a DEA agent's badge, a pager, and keys."

"We're on our way," Carl said.

They went into the room from where the officer had shouted. Sam's belongings sat on top of a liquor cabinet.

"I'll hang on to all of it for now," Rafa said.

"Yeah, okay." Sam nodded, then said, "Those two on the floor are, are—" Sam had to catch his breath first. "They're Ramón Monzon and Ronaldo Gomez." He walked over to stand beside the sofa. "This one told me," he said, pointing to Moncho, "he, Gomez, and his girlfriend killed the Jansens. They stole their boat and murdered them." His hand shook badly as he lifted the lid of the ottoman. A young woman peered up at the police officers surrounding her. Sam said, "Moncho's girlfriend, Beth. Elizabeth Evans."

The police found Francisco's bodyguards in the garage, smoking cigarettes while they relaxed in lawn chairs, as if they didn't have a care in the world.

Officers searched the entire house, but Francisco was nowhere to be found. A police officer on the perimeter detail reported he'd seen no one on the street except an older gentleman walking a small dog. He said the concerned but very polite man had approached him to ask about the sirens and police activity.

Sam's heart sank. "That bastard walked away in plain sight using the dog, Beth's dog, as his cover. He's gone; I'm sure he's already headed back to Mexico."

Sam slumped on the couch; his eyelids drooped. It was passed midnight. The horror he had endured, and the lack of sleep, had taken their toll.

Rafa sat next to him. In a muted tone, he said, "Let's get you to the hospital now."

Sam locked his arms across his chest. "No. No hospital."

"You've got to have a checkup—"

"Not tonight. I know I should, Rafa, but please, not now. I just want to sleep."

Rafa said, "I understand." He turned to Carl. "I'll take Sam home with me. We'll deal with the doctor tomorrow."

Sam opened his eyes. "The little boat out back. I'm supposed to return it and lock it up with a chain at—"

Carl said, "Don't worry about it. I'll have someone take it over later."

"Rafa has the keys. She told me to drop them through the door—"

"We've got this. Grab some sleep." Carl put his hand on Sam's arm. "We have enough to hold these guys until we hear from you later today."

Rafa said, "Carl, I'll swing by tomorrow to pick up my friend's boat. It's also tied up at the dock in back. Can you have an officer take us to my car?"

•   •   •

Later, on the drive to Rafa's house, Sam dozed off for several long seconds at a time, only to be roused from his sleep by phantom electric currents shooting through his body.

As Rafa coasted into his garage, he asked, "Do you want anything to eat?"

During the drive, Sam's speech had slowed; now entering Rafa's house, he slurred his words. "Can't think about food. Sleep only."

"Elena made up a room for you."

Sam dragged himself behind Rafa, who pointed to the bedside table. "She left sweatpants and a shirt for you to wear and clean towels in the bathroom."

Sam turned to Rafa and put his hand on his friend's arm. Barely audible, he said, "Thank you, Rafa."

CHAPTER TWENTY-EIGHT

He had dozed fitfully, his sleep riddled with nightmares. Awakened in a panic, uncertain where he was until the memories flooded in, he finally realized he was at Rafa's house. He dragged himself out of bed and staggered down the hallway, waiting for his heart to slow.

Rafa's wife, Elena, sat in the kitchen, watching a small television set on the counter next to the refrigerator.

When Sam appeared, she hurried over to him. "How—oh, Sam—how are you?" she asked.

"Elena," Sam said in a hushed tone. Then he tried to produce a smile, any semblance of one, but he couldn't. He felt like he was still waiting to hit the ground after being thrown off a building.

They embraced for a quick moment. Elena said, "I'm so sorry. How are you?"

"I'm not sure yet. Tired, I think." He closed his eyes for a moment. "Yeah, that's what I am—I'm tired." He reopened his eyes and shook his head.

Elena set her hand on his arm. "Would you like coffee or something to eat?"

"No thanks. No appetite right now," he said. "Not even coffee."

"Rafa got called into work, but he asked me to call him when you woke up."

"I owe Rafa my life."

"He told me a little about what happened and said I should take you to the hospital. We can go whenever you'd like."

Shaking his head, he said, "I'm not up for going to the hospital. I can't imagine going there now."

"I'm sure we could get you in to see our doctor right away, if you'd prefer."

He ignored the question, instead he said, "Could I ask a favor of you?"

"Anything," Elena said.

"Could you take me to where I left my car yesterday? There's something I have to do right away."

"Sure. Can I find something for you to wear?" she asked.

Sam ran hands over his shirt and sweatpants. "If I could borrow these for a little while, that should take care of me until I get to my motel."

"Rafa said he wanted you to stay with us," Elena said, holding Sam's hands. "He was adamant."

"I'm sure."

The drive to the boat rental was quiet. Sam knew he was not up for being around people or socializing. Once they arrived at the Bayshore Boat Rentals, he thanked Elena and promised to check in soon with Rafa.

An hour later, he reached his motel room and turned on the television to run in the background. The midday news spoke to a police raid that had taken place overnight at Davis Islands; thankfully, they hadn't connected the story to the Jansens' boat yet.

$$\bullet \quad \bullet \quad \bullet$$

Sam tapped on the front door. The two broken figures stood, staring at each other, like hollow husks of corn in a fallow field ... nothing left to give.

Chloe shook herself. "I'm sorry, Sam, please, come in." She went into the living room and sat for a moment, then stood again. "Something to drink? I just made a fresh pot of coffee, but I don't know why." She picked at the lint on her sweatshirt. "Something told me to make it, and now you're here."

"Coffee sounds good," Sam said.

"Let's see." She turned, then turned again. "I've forgotten where my kitchen is."

"I should have called before coming over."

"These last weeks, it's been so crazy. It's a blessing I'm allowed to work from home these days." She ran her hands over her jeans. "I don't have to dress for anyone or anything."

They went into the kitchen. "Cream or sugar?"

"Black is fine."

"Do you mind if we sit in here and talk?" she asked.

"This is, this is fine, Chloe."

"It's so strange, but every room in the house is cold to me now except the kitchen."

Sam gathered his thoughts, thinking about how he would tell Chloe the truth.

She brought two cups of coffee to the table. They sat in silence, staring into the backyard. Sam was content to sit in silence and let the quiet wash over him.

Minutes passed until Chloe said, "I've got to get out there and cut the yard, and don't get me started on those weeds. Ryan said he wants to start mowing the lawn, but I don't know if eleven's old enough. He said we should buy a riding mower." Her empty laughter filled the room. "I told him our yard is too small, but he's so funny and clever too. He said he could cut other people's yards and start earning money for college. He knows the right buttons to push, doesn't he?" There was another long silence until Chloe said, "I need to run to the store today. Ryan said he's out of cereal and—"

"Chloe—"

"And I can't ever keep up with the milk he drinks." She stood, taking her coffee mug with her to the sliding glass door that led to the deck. "Sam, how old were you when you started cutting the yard?"

"Chloe—"

"I think he's still too young because lawnmowers can be so dangerous. Don't you think—"

"Chloe, we need to talk—"

"I think eleven is too young—"

"Listen to me—"

"Maybe next year—"

"Your parents aren't coming home."

Her body jerked. "Maybe not today, but they're—"

"Your parents are gone."

She gave a short laugh. "They're just on their boat."

"They're never coming home. Never."

She turned to face Sam. Her eyes burned through him.

"I'm sorry, they're not, Chloe. They're not coming home. Ever."

"Do I want to know?" She set her coffee mug on the table and asked, "Is it connected to the police raid I saw on television this morning—the one on Davis Islands?"

Sam nodded.

"When I saw it on the TV, I knew, I just knew somehow you were there ... and my parents weren't." She sat at the table. Her moist eyes rested on Sam.

He swallowed and found the strength to look into Chloe's eyes. "I had been following leads that took me to a group of people, not nice people, Chloe, I'm afraid." His heart skipped a beat; it had been doing that since he'd woken up. He restarted. "I found your parents' boat last night, and a man admitted to me they had stolen it. He ... he also told me he and others killed your parents while they were out at sea."

Chloe put her head between her hands.

"The police will talk to you about this, but I thought it would be better to hear it from me first."

She raised her head to face him. "Why do you think whoever this man is would say this? Maybe he's not being truthful? He might be lying. People like that, they lie, they do, they lie."

Sam leaned forward, dropping his gaze to the floor. "He was telling the truth, Chloe. I found the boat hidden inside a covered berth at that house on Davis Islands. I confirmed the registration number. These people who live there are known drug traffickers, and they had a history of doing bad things. One person I talked to a couple of days ago said they would go out on their boat, pretending to have a mechanical problem, and mess with people. They must have gotten a bizarre kick out of doing this. The police will do a complete forensic examination of the boat and find the hard evidence."

"Then you believe it?"

Sam raised his head, his gaze meeting Chloe's stare. "I do. Yes, I do."

"Do you know how they died?"

"You don't want to—"

Her angry eyes bore into him until she screamed, "I want to know!"

His voice was barely above a whisper. "The man said he shot your father with a speargun and pushed him into the water. I don't know about your mother other than he just said they got rid of her. I have a friend with the Tampa Police. Before I came over, I called him and asked if I could give you his name and direct number. You might remember Carl Schneider?"

Chloe said, "He was your best friend in high school. You played football together."

"Yes, he was, and we're still close friends. When you're ready, he's expecting your call." He removed a folded piece of paper with a phone number from his pocket and left it on the table.

"I'll call him, Sam," she said. "I'm sorry I yelled. You're only trying to help, and after everything you've done, this is how I repay you? Please forgive me."

"You've been through a lot." His voice was flat, with little emotion.

She hugged herself as tears flooded her eyes. "I knew, but I still hoped."

"Chloe, may I use your bathroom?"

"Of course. It's down the hall and on your left."

He closed the door and leaned over the sink. His body trembled and there was no color to his skin. He ran the water in the sink, then splashed his face and neck. He was under attack again. Taking deep breaths, he waited for his heart to slow. Nevertheless, his hands shook no matter what he tried to do; and they wouldn't stop.

He opened the bathroom door and shoved his hands into his jacket pockets. When he returned to the kitchen, Chloe stood by the sliding door, looking out into the yard.

She turned back toward the kitchen and startled when she saw him. "I didn't hear you come back in."

"Sorry, I wanted to give you a moment."

She wiped away the tears but couldn't keep pace with the deluge. "It's all so useless. I feel so alone. My parents, they were—they were everything to me. My mom, my dad, they didn't deserve this."

He took a step forward and hugged her. "I understand, Chloe, believe me, I do." She held on like she might not let go. "I'm sorry I couldn't bring you better news." He rubbed her shoulder. When he stepped back, he realized he wasn't immune to the raw emotions, either. "May I use your phone?"

"Yes. I'll be outside."

After the door slid closed, Sam dialed the number. He closed his eyes while the phone rang.

"Hello?"

"I need your help, Annie. I need your help now."

CHAPTER TWENTY-NINE

He was home. The couch in his apartment became his refuge. With the days running together, his emotions festered in a vat of doubt, humiliation, and brooding self-scrutiny. The one constant was his insatiable need to be isolated. He violated his self-imposed confinement only once when he orchestrated back-to-back doctor and dentist appointments.

The nights were the worst. The space behind his eyes became a battleground where sanity and lunacy fought for control. To compensate for the lack of sleep, he dozed throughout the day, but when his mind gave way to sleep, the faces of Francisco, the doctor, and Eyebrows haunted him. He woke up soaked in sweat from the nightmares that plagued him, shaking in fear, waiting for the electric current to start again.

Slowly, he allowed himself glancing blows with reality: a predawn run or a quick conversation by phone. Still, he was a hunted animal, hiding in its den, preferring the cover of darkness.

But time passed, and like a fish snagged on a line, he felt the gradual pull to normality, whatever that might be. To the outside world, he tried to project strength and fortitude, but within the safety of his apartment, he stared into space, losing himself in time, only to emerge into a morass of fear and helplessness.

Before he left Tampa, Carl said he would have to return if there was a trial for Moncho and his associates. Sam wondered about the prospects of a prosecution that had the Jansens' boat, Moncho's own admissions to him, but no bodies. The police found Carol Jansen's bloody clothing balled up in the trash on the boat; blood had also been found on the decking. Carl had said they were awaiting test results, but he felt certain the blood would match one or both Jansens' genetic makeup. Using DNA to identify victims was a new technique, but it seemed foolproof, as far as Sam could tell.

The three murder suspects each hired their own attorneys, but for the time being, they presented a joint defense. A public statement from the group's spokesperson told a story of how the trio came upon the empty boat, floating listlessly in the Gulf, but they offered no explanation for why the Jansens' boat had remained on their property, other than they were too busy to follow up with the police. Moncho's attorney said in a separate statement the admissions made by his client to a DEA agent had been drug-fueled nonsense and asked that they be given no weight.

The judge deemed Moncho and Salvaje to be strong flight risks and ordered them to be held without bail. Beth was another story. Because she was the daughter of a wealthy family with strong ties to the community, the judge set a one-million-dollar bail for her. In less than an hour, her father posted bond. Carl said it wouldn't be long before Beth's attorney severed the joint defense agreement and, to save her own skin, she would become an adversarial witness against Monzon and Gomez.

Rafa told Sam the wiretap had ended with nothing to show for it, and despite around-the-clock surveillance of The Runner's Choice, no one saw Victor Alderete Perez, the owner again; the store with the odd assortment of shoes on display had been abandoned.

Chatter from informants claimed Francisco was back in Mérida. Rafa had been his usual optimistic self, proclaiming, "What goes around, comes around. One day, karma will catch up with that asshole."

After a period of isolation, Sam felt he was on the mend and ready to return to work at LAX. His doctor had said his physical state was fine. There would be no long-term damage from the abuse he had suffered. However, he recommended Sam seek treatment from a counselor specializing in helping patients who had experienced mental and emotional trauma.

From his bastion on the couch, he called his partner, Blue. Trying to sound upbeat, Sam said, "We're close to the end of September. How are we doing with getting Roy his record?"

"No closer than we were before you left. We've been in a big-time drought."

"Roy must be going crazy."

"You wouldn't believe it," Blue said. "Every few hours, he pops his head around the corner, looking disappointed when he sees me at my desk and not in the terminals."

"How would you like help Monday?"

"Are you ready to come back?"

"No, but I have to pay the rent."

"Brother, I feel you. Are you doing all right?"

Sam bit into his lower lip, then said, "Yeah, fine, I guess. It's time for me to move on."

"I'm always here for you, man, whenever you need me or want to talk." Blue paused. "Hey, listen, have you met with the therapist you told me about? You know it's a good thing to get all that stuff out."

Without enthusiasm, Sam said, "I know it is. I, look, I'll be back on Monday. Would you mind telling Roy?"

"You got it."

Sam hung up and laid his head back against the arm of the sofa. His mind returned to his new habit of reflecting on everything that had happened in Florida, an activity he considered a critical part of his self-prescribed treatment plan to aid him on his road to recovery. Like a race car driver careening out of control, the raw memories of the physical torture he endured and the tattered emotions from the brief but intense relationship he'd had with Natalie still dominated his thinking.

After an hour with no resolution to anything, he decided to accomplish something, even if only an insignificant task. He dragged himself from the couch and shuffled off to the dirty clothes hamper in the bedroom. Dumping the contents out, he wondered if he had the courage to walk to the laundry room on the first floor. He might run into a tenant at the building; the thought sent a shiver down his spine. When he kicked the pile of clothes into the corner of the room, the bathing suit he bought in Florida caught his attention. A tiny smile crossed his face when Natalie's humorous threats to throw the suit away flooded his thoughts.

His mind turned to Madeira Beach. He lay next to Natalie, looking at her beautiful face while her eyes squinted in the sunlight. Her laughter at his stupid swimsuit seemed so real in the moment. At first, a glow of hopefulness permeated his soul, then the pain deep in his core returned. It was time he came to grips with reality; the relationship with Natalie was over. He stepped over the swim trunks and crept back to the safety of his couch.

He thought about his last conversation with her before he left Florida. She had agreed to meet for coffee at a shop near her condo. Had she been crying? It looked like it, but he couldn't be sure. No matter, she had remained resolute, and her words, though true, still stung.

"Sam, I can't hang around every night wondering when you'll come through the door. And then, if you don't, I can't sit here worried sick wondering where you are, thinking, is this when Agent Guerrero calls me again to ask if I've seen you? Are you hurt? Are you dead? I'm sorry, but I can't do that."

He raised himself off the sofa and stumbled through the apartment. He knew in his heart she was right. Facing the mirror over the dresser, he stared at himself. He and the problem were the same. There was only one person he could think of whom he trusted enough to talk about something so personal.

•   •   •

He stared out the back window that afforded him a peekaboo view of a small, wooded park across the street. It would be difficult to ask Bill about his late wife, but he felt compelled to do so. After his friend answered, he asked, "When did you realize Claire was your one and only?" He gripped the portable phone, afraid it might fly away, and he'd never unlock the secret.

"You don't mince words; you come right out with guns blazing, don't you?" Bill said.

"I know you were always happy with Claire, so I was just wondering when you knew she was the one."

"When did I know? I don't know if it was one thing. She was a kind person—the kindest. I'll never forget the time I was so damn busy at work I couldn't see straight. I found out I had to fly to New York for a trial, and I only had a few hours to get home, pack, and catch the flight. Claire and I had been seeing each other for a while. By then, we'd been living together for, let's see, three months. I came running in the door, back when I could do that sort of thing, ready to throw stuff together, but Claire had left her office early to come home and pack for me. I tell you she had everything I needed for my trip, including a book I'd been reading. It may seem small, but it's the little things that add up to something bigger than the both of you sometimes. She was always interested in other people more than herself, right up to the day she died. I'll never stop loving her."

"That makes sense."

"I take it you met someone?"

"I did in Tampa. I think ... I thought she could be the one." He swallowed hard. "I should get back to it. Thanks for your time, Bill."

CHAPTER THIRTY

Sam wanted to be the first in the office. He was sure a mountain of bureaucratic bullshit awaited his return, and it would be nice to get things done without constant interruptions. He cut the car engine and took a long look around. The double-wide trailer sat right where Sam had left it three weeks ago: next to the parking lot between sleek-windowed terminal buildings, oblivious to those who might ridicule it. For Sam, it was a welcome sight, even if it looked like it had been swiped from a distant farm in Kansas and absentmindedly dropped by a tornado.

It felt like a year had passed since he had last stepped into the office. He took the three steps up the backside of the trailer and slid the key into the familiar lock. The door opened with a quick scraping noise coming from the floor. Lights were already on, and someone had disabled the alarm. *So much for alone time.* He passed by years of junk pushed into a corner, a water cooler, and the two side-by-side interview rooms.

Roy stood anchored to the doorway of his office and beckoned Sam inside. "Goddamn, I don't know if I can say anything to help, but I'm glad you're back."

"I'm ... I'm here," Sam said.

Roy glanced sideways toward his chalkboard. Sam knew it wouldn't take long for him to get to it—he was nothing, if not consistent.

He used his pointer stick. "Sam, we're so close."

"Roy, I can see another certificate of commendation in your future."

"I've got the space and a nail for it on the wall already. We've got three days left in September. Do you think we can break the record?"

Sam studied the figures written on the board. "Yeah, if we find someone stupid enough to be carrying, let's see, three hundred and eighty-one, no, eighty-two thousand dollars of drug money, and his cover story is something like he's using the cash to open a grasshopper farm in Colombia."

Roy said, "It would mean the world to me if we could do it."

"I know it would. All right, I better get caught up before the mob shows itself, and I can't hear myself think."

"Have you heard?" Roy said. "I've put in my paperwork to retire the thirty-first of October."

"That's nice. Congratulations," Sam said flatly.

"Have you ever thought about management?"

"Sometimes, I guess."

"Think about it more because the DEA is aging, and there's going to be several vacancies coming up. Speaking of which, a group supervisor in Tampa is pulling the plug too. You're from Florida; I'm sure you can get any job you want. Maybe it's time to take advantage and go home."

Sam wasn't ready to contemplate career moves, at least not moments after he showed up for work for the first time in weeks. "I should do my time sheet first, so I can get paid." He walked through the silent bullpen to his desk, seeing how the empty throwaway coffee cups had gravitated to his corner of the office. He swiped them into the trash can and kicked the one that fell onto the floor under someone else's desk.

Thirty minutes later, the only other person in the office was Rose, the task force's secretary, hidden behind a wall of file cabinets. The typing noise rising from behind her bulwark was the only evidence of her presence.

A tiredness had overtaken him, and it wasn't even eight o'clock. His pager vibrated; Annie had called. He had neither the time nor the inclination to return the page, but he called her number, anyway.

"My sweet little brother, thank you for the roses. At the risk of sounding ungrateful, I'm not sure why you sent them; all I did was make dinner one evening and a pot of coffee in the morning."

"Annie, I didn't send flowers. It's a nice thought, it is, but it wasn't me."

Sam heard Annie speaking to someone else who must have been in the room with her: "Sam said he didn't send the flowers."

"Are you talking with David?" Sam said.

Annie returned to the conversation on the phone. "No, it's my neighbor, Tammy. You met her at Trevor's party. She's the one that was fawning over you constantly, making sure you had enough to eat and drink."

Tammy's voice sounded in the background. "Annie, I can't believe you just said that. Hi there, Sam. Gorgeous roses."

"Hi, Tammy. Listen, Annie. I'm guessing David sent them."

"The card says they're from you. Besides, hubby doesn't even send flowers on our anniversary."

"I'm at a loss to explain, but I'd remember sending flowers."

"I was going to give you a hard time about the spelling. The card says to Annie, Trevor, and David, but someone spelled Trevor's name with two E's, like T-r-e-v-e-r."

"Sorry, it wasn't me."

Annie said, "I'll call the flower shop that delivered them."

"I'm sure it's a mix-up."

"Tammy just left," Annie said, her voice taking a serious turn. "How are you doing?"

"I'm getting back into the flow of things here at work. It'll take time, I imagine."

"Sam, please tell me you've at least called to make an appointment with someone about what happened, you know, like a professional?"

"I did," he lied. "My doctor gave me a name, and I've already got an appointment set up. Listen, Annie, I'm getting signaled from the guys. I need to get back to work."

"Fine, get back to your *guys*. We'll talk soon. Bye."

Sam dove back into a pile of DEA-6 reports he had written weeks before. He had to review and sign each one, indicating they were correct in their final form. Not yet finished with the first paragraph of the first report, he heard the office door open. The shouting began immediately. "Where is he? Where's my buddy?"

Sam knew catching up on reports would have to wait.

"Well, look at what the cat dragged in," Blue said.

Sam looked up. "Hey, Blue."

He placed his hand on Sam's shoulder. "Next time you go on vacation, I'm going with you as backup." Blue wheeled a chair over to Sam, stopping with only a foot of space between them. "How are you?"

"I'm present and accounted for."

"Man, I've missed your ragged ass. Did you miss me?"

"Yeah, every single minute," Sam said.

Blue howled in laughter, perhaps a bit too loud for Sam.

"I'm glad you made it back. You're damned lucky; I guess unlucky first, then lucky next."

"Yeah, that about sums it up."

"I guess you can work a missing person case."

"It's a small world," Sam said. "Who could have ever guessed the money we took off Rojas here at LAX would tie into a Title III wiretap investigation in Tampa, and those same people would be responsible for the Jansens' deaths?"

"Crazy, right? I never asked you, how'd their daughter take the news?"

"She was crushed, but she was also ready to deal with the truth. And it was hard to break it to her, but better to hear it from a friend instead of a stranger at the police department, or worse, having to find out about it watching the evening news."

Blue stared at Sam. "That must have been tough to tell her."

"Not fun, anyway, here I am. Roy already talked to me about making another seizure, so we can break the record."

"I've been hearing it every day since you left. We've been on a cold streak. Maybe you can change our luck. You've heard he's retiring?"

"End of October," Sam said, rapping his knuckles on his desk. "Thanks for the welcome back, but I need to finish reading these reports. Then, for Roy's sake, we better head out into the terminals."

"Sounds good." With a push, Blue rolled in his chair back to his own desk.

Sam had just started reading when he saw the blinking light on his phone. He unhooked the receiver and spoke without enthusiasm. "Sam Dahl speaking."

"Good morning, Samuel. You have returned to work, I see."

He knew the voice. It was one he could never forget.

"Samuel, are you there? You don't wish to speak with an old friend?"

"You're no friend of mine," Sam said.

"Perhaps I've used the term in a sarcastic manner. You are like the great American cowboy who gets back in the saddle to ride again. Good for you. I wish you the best of luck in detecting your money couriers at the LAX."

"What do you want, Francisco?"

"To hear your voice and for you to hear mine."

"You've succeeded in both your goals. Congratulations."

Sam recognized the rich laughter.

"You're so quick-witted. Can I be frank with you?" Francisco said.

His heart pounded. His limbs felt paralyzed. Was it fear? He wasn't certain. "You can be as frank as you want. I don't care."

"My son is a stupid boy, but he's my son, and I want him back."

"Maybe a jury of his peers will find him not guilty, then Moncho the murderer can go home to daddy."

"I would prefer not to leave his chances for freedom up to twelve strangers."

"You're a fucking maniac."

"Samuel, I sense you're still holding on to hostility because of what happened, but you may be right; perhaps I am a maniac, as you say."

"Is there a point to this call?"

"Yes, I must insist that you aid in my son's release. He's being held without bail, and that must change. Whatever dollar amount the judge imposes on Ramón holds no importance to me but being locked up with no chance for freedom is unacceptable."

"So, you'll foot the bill no matter what, then Moncho can disappear forever."

"Either that or you must assist in another way," Francisco said.

"You don't have a say in the matter, and you can't torture everyone in the world."

"True, this is true. I do, however, have a say in what happens to people who are important to you. Just as I cannot torture everyone, you cannot protect everyone. Not your sister, Annie, nor her husband, David, nor, let's see, yes, you cannot protect your young nephew, Trevor, or any of your other friends who invaded my home."

Hearing the names, Annie, David, and Trevor sent shock waves through his body. He thought about his conversation with his sister a short while ago. Could this lunatic have sent those flowers? But why? "Francisco, I'll hunt you all the way to hell if you hurt anyone—"

"The situation with the Jansens is regrettable. It shouldn't have happened, and to show you I have a heart, as compensation, I can ensure their grandson, Ryan, can afford the best university when the time arrives. No one else needs to suffer anymore. Consider my offer with care. I'm a patient man, but I have my limits. A new hearing for Ramón's bail is next Monday, so I expect action by then, or, if this is easier, you can tell the police you were confused about what my son said. Your mind was quite unclear at the time; it was a difficult night for everyone, you would agree, yes? If you do as I say, I'll send you a bouquet of lovely flowers to seal our agreement. Good day, Samuel."

Unbelievable. When would the nightmare end? The threat was obvious; if Moncho's bail wasn't reduced or if Sam didn't help in another way, people he loved would be harmed or killed, like his sister, Annie, and Trevor, who was only eleven years old. Francisco had proven he had a long reach and an ability to collect intelligence; he could find out things about his family, his friends, and his co-workers. No one was safe.

Sam dropped the handset onto his desk and raced from the office. Blue called after him, but he couldn't stop; he wouldn't stop. He ran across the parking lot, almost getting hit by a car, then sprinted to the nearest terminal. Once inside, he found a pay phone. He realized he had become like the paranoid drug dealer, no longer trusting the phone system in his own office. He called Carl on his private line.

"Answer, dammit," Sam said to himself. "Answer, answer."

"Schneider."

"Carl, it's not over. He's still out there." Sam was breathless from running.

"Sam? What?" Carl's voice seemed taken aback. "What's happening? Slow down. Who's out where? What's going on?"

"Francisco called me at my office. He wants Moncho out. He wants him free—"

"You spoke to him?"

"Yes, that's what I'm saying." Leaning against the wall, Sam was still trying to catch his breath. "He said if Moncho isn't freed on bail, he'd go after people close to me."

"Sam, people like that make threats. They can't back them up; this isn't Mexico."

Sam ran a hand through his hair. "Carl, you don't know this guy. He's the devil. He has the power, and he knows the names of my family and where they live. Right before his call, Annie called to thank me for flowers."

"I don't understand. What's wrong with that?"

"Carl, I didn't order any flowers. There was a card with their names on it. Annie, David, and Trevor are my only family. The last thing he said to me on the phone was if I did what he wanted, he would send me flowers too. Don't you see?"

"Hang on, Sam, just a second."

He could hear Carl speaking with someone else for a few seconds. There was a lapse in conversation, then nothing.

"Carl, are you there? Hello, Carl? Carl?"

"Sam, I'm here. Hold on." There was another interval while Carl spoke again to someone. "Excuse me, can you pull the door shut? Thank you."

Sam's heart was pounding. He could only think of how many people might be hurt or worse because of him.

"Dammit, you're right," Carl said. "I just received flowers."

"You see now? He's sending a message to me. No one is out of his reach. I bet Rafa gets flowers today, and maybe others too. This is his way of saying everything is under his control. He knows about my sister and my nephew. Carl, my nephew is eleven years old."

"You might want to make phone calls, starting with Rafa, and find out if the same thing is happening," Carl said.

"What does your card say?"

"My first and last name and that they're from Samuel."

"I'll start calling now. If they haven't received any, I'll tell them to call me if flowers show up."

"Yeah, okay," Carl said, "but other than Rafa, I wouldn't tell anyone outside law enforcement, like your sister, the entire story." Sam heard him draw a deep breath. "Look, you're concerned, of course, you are, and I am too, but I don't think they're in immediate danger now."

"How can you be sure?"

"He's giving you time. From what you said, this Francisco said as much. The bail hearing for Moncho isn't until next Monday, so we've still got time."

"Time for what?"

"Time to think of a plan. Call Rafa and brief him on what's happening."

"I will."

After disconnecting with Carl, he dialed another number.

"Group Two."

"Hi, is this Tina?"

"Yes."

"Tina, this is Sam Dahl. We met a couple of weeks ago."

"How are you? Everyone's been talking about what happened."

"Listen, Tina, this is important. Is Rafa there?"

"He's here, but not at his desk. He loved the flowers you sent him," she said. "That was—"

"Tina, you've got to find him for me. *Fast.* It's an emergency."

"Okay."

"I'll wait. I'm on a pay phone, but I'll wait."

Minutes passed. A man came up to him and said, "Hey, are you going to be long?"

Sam turned his head away.

The man pressed. "You're not the only one around here that needs a phone—I have a call to make too."

Sam spoke without looking at the man. "I'm using the phone now."

"Yeah, but that's your second call and you're not talking to anyone—"

Sam wheeled on the man and exploded. "Go somewhere else but get the fuck away from me."

"Fine," the man said, holding his hands out and backing up. "Easy does it. Jeez."

"Sam?" Rafa said, his voice sounding uncertain.

"Good, you're there; I received a call at the office from Francisco."

"You're kidding?" Rafa asked.

"No, he threatened me that if Moncho's no bail setting isn't adjusted, he's going to come after you and Carl and my family. His message was clear. He wants his son out on bail, so he can skip out to Mexico, I'm sure."

"The judge sets bail. You don't have control over that," Rafa said.

"I know that, but he doesn't. Anyway, if I recanted what I said about Moncho, they might have no choice but to cut him loose. But his goal is to get a bail set at any amount of money. That son of a bitch doesn't care how much; he'll pay it and his son will disappear. This guy can do anything."

"Sam, he's blowing smoke."

"No. I believe him," Sam said. "He's buying flowers for people to prove he knows where everyone lives or works. And Tina told me you got flowers. He wanted to prove his point to me by mentioning my sister and nephew's name, and he also talked about Chloe's son, about paying for his college to show his appreciation for helping him."

"Jesus, this is crazy. I was wondering why you'd send flowers and use the name Samuel?"

"Now different people are getting flowers, like Carl and Annie. I'm going to check with Chloe, maybe Natalie too. He didn't mention Natalie, but who knows?"

"There are rules in this drug war," Rafa said. "Then there are the unwritten rules. This asshole has gone over the line."

"Carl said I shouldn't tell anyone outside LE about the story behind the flowers. Look, I'm in a jam, but I don't want something to happen, even though Carl thinks we have time because the bail hearing isn't until next Monday."

"I agree with Carl," Rafa said.

"Didn't you say someone saw Francisco in Mérida again?"

"Yes, and by more than one source."

"What do you think about contacting our office in Mexico?" Sam asked.

"Our closest office is Mexico City. We don't have any agents stationed in Mérida, except for some police types on the payroll. We have a few days. My advice is to sit tight."

"I understand, but by the end of this week at the latest, I'm going to have to tell the truth, and people will have to go into hiding. Rafa, I'm worried if you aren't safe, then Elena isn't either."

"We'll work this thing out," Rafa said.

Sam hung up. The two calls had helped, and his heart rate had slowed. He had settled into being pissed off. Lost in a million thoughts, he leaned his head against the cabinet enclosure. He needed to speak with his mentor.

CHAPTER THIRTY-ONE

Sam held a hand over his ear to block out the sound of loud conversation behind him in the terminal.

"Bill Dunkirk speaking."

"You won't believe this; Francisco called me."

Two minutes passed while Sam explained what had happened. When Bill didn't speak a word, Sam asked, "Are you still there?"

"This is a surprising turn of events," Bill said with an eerie composure.

"Bill, are you hearing me? This guy's a nut. He's making threats against people all around me if I don't do what he says."

"It *is* strange. Usually, his type hides out somewhere, licks their wounds, then gets back to business. Making this into a personal vendetta is unusual."

Sam was frantic. "Bill, I've got to do something."

"This problem could resolve itself."

Bill's calmness was driving him crazy. "What? How so?"

There was what seemed like an interminable silence until Bill spoke again. "I can see—" Bill cleared his throat and restarted. "Yes, I can see where the other major traffickers in Mexico might view Francisco's threat against an American agent's family in a negative light. Making good on a threat to hurt or kill people close to one of our agents would no doubt bring a massive amount of unwanted attention to Mexican smuggling operations. That would be unacceptable to them, and they would feel compelled to eat one of their own."

"That assumes something would have to happen first to someone."

"I disagree; it wouldn't have to go that far," Bill said. "In my opinion, Francisco has put a huge target on his back, my friend. Let me process this, and we'll talk again later."

Sam walked to the office, willing himself to put one foot in front of the other and somehow keep moving forward. Bill's reaction to the threat from Francisco surprised him, but after a few minutes, he reached a different conclusion. *That's how the man is wired; he never gets rattled.*

Seated once again at his desk, Sam felt his partner's eyes on him.

"Sounds like your trouble has found you again," Blue said.

"He's a son of a bitch that needs to—"

His pager beeped—it was from Natalie. *Oh, God, not her too.*

She answered after the first ring. "Lieutenant Timmons."

Despite the circumstances, he tried to sound chipper. "Hello, Lieutenant Timmons."

"Hi, Sam. I was thinking about you this morning."

Sam held his breath for a second; it was so good to hear her voice.

Natalie said, "I wanted to tell you that senior staff met yesterday afternoon concerning the Jansens' situation. We've made adjustments in how we'll handle cases like this in the future, when we don't make a rescue in the first forty-eight hours."

She sounded officious, so he had to accept the call was professional in nature. He was ninety percent resigned to the fact that she was over him. He almost wished he could say the same about his feelings for her.

"Our new course of action will involve more coordination and detailed follow-up with the smaller local and harbor police outfits. We were lacking in that area, and you showed us a weakness in our procedures."

"As I recall, that was your idea checking with the small law enforcement stations along the coast; I just carried it out. By the way, I never shared that information with the DEA, seeing as I was acting on my own."

"Not to worry," Natalie said. "The idea was submitted through the chain of command, with no reference to you. Anyhow, I thought you'd appreciate hearing it."

"It was a great idea; you should be proud of yourself."

"How are you?"

He didn't want to address that question directly. "Today is my first day back at work." He wondered if Francisco could know about Natalie but convinced himself in seconds that there was no way he could have connected Sam to her already. Besides, he knew Natalie would say something about receiving flowers. "How are you doing?" Sam asked.

"I'm not going to pretend. I miss you, and I wanted to hear your voice."

The lump in his throat made him think he might choke. "I've ... I've missed you too," he said. "I thought about you when I was looking at my bathing suit the other day."

He heard the laughter—her wonderful laughter. He couldn't help but smile, and for a minute, everything was right with the world.

She said, "I should have thrown it away when I had the chance. You're never going to wear it again, are you?"

"I'll make it my super-duper emergency backup bathing suit."

"I guess that'll work." She drew a breath. "I better get back to work. It was nice to talk to you. I'm glad you're doing okay."

But he wasn't doing okay; he was lonely and depressed, and he felt rotten and angry as hell at a madman who had reared his ugly head again. He wanted to tell her all those things, but he didn't—because he couldn't.

"Thanks for calling. It was great to talk with you. Maybe I can ring you sometime to chat?"

"Sure, Sam, that would be fine. Bye-bye."

He hung onto the receiver for several seconds, not wanting to give up whatever remained between them, even if it were only a chance to see whether a long-distance relationship could have worked.

He knew Blue was watching him. "What?" Sam said, not able to hide the bitterness in his voice.

"Oh, nothing. I was wondering if you were up for hitting the terminals," Blue said.

"You can act all you want. Did you enjoy listening in?"

"Very much so," Blue said. "Damn, you were busy in Florida. I was reading this past weekend about the concept of a 'staycation.' You vacation at home where you can relax, save money, and, best of all, stay out of trouble."

"Blue, you know you're a pain in my ass, right?"

"That's why you love me so much and want me in your life."

"Alright, let's go into the terminals, but you might have to listen to me complaining a little."

Blue drew closer and rested his hand on Sam's back. "No problem, partner."

•   •   •

Once they reached the Eastern Airlines ticketing area, they hung back and watched the passengers standing in line. Monitoring a flight was the last thing Sam wanted to do. He did it anyway.

"Looks like the psychopath in Florida isn't done with me yet." He caught Blue up with what was going on.

"He doesn't understand you have no control over bail and that kind of stuff. If he calls back, tell him to call the prosecutor or the judge," Blue said.

"I think he'd like me to recant my statement, but that's not happening." He waved his hand back and forth. "No way."

"You didn't have to say that," Blue said. "Hey, would you look at the guy in line with the yellow sports jacket? That should be a criminal offense to dress like a damn banana in public."

Sam couldn't help but smile a little. It was good to have Blue by his side again. "Hang on; it looks like Mason wants to chat. Maybe he has something for us. I'll be right back." He walked to the Eastern Airlines counter where Mason, a ticketing supervisor, was waiting.

"How's it going?" Sam asked.

"Fine, I haven't seen you around for a while," Mason said.

"I took time off; it's my first day back. Looks like another busy day for you."

"It's going to be a long one. I just wanted to say hello. Give me a holler if I can do anything for you. I'll be on the floor until we process the Miami flight."

"Thanks, Mason. We'll be hanging in our usual spot."

He turned back toward where Blue had been standing, but his partner had moved to the door leading to the curbside passenger drop-off area. "Hey, what's up?"

"This is interesting." Blue said, nodding toward the long line of passengers in ticketing. "That guy there, in the black windbreaker, standing in line at the back. He came in with nothing in his hands minutes ago. You see him?"

"Yeah."

"He was standing where I am right now, looking out to the sidewalk. I didn't think anything about it until he walked out to a taxi that pulled up. Then this dude in a nice suit got out, took an envelope from his jacket, and handed it to him. At the same time, the driver of the taxi took a suitcase out of the trunk and left it on the curb."

"I understand why it caught your attention."

"The strange thing was they never spoke as far as I could see. The suit handed him the envelope. Then, *bam*, he was done and out of here. Could be nothing, but I thought the black windbreaker might be worth watching. When he gets closer to the front, we'll have Mason check him in."

Minutes passed while they watched in silence.

Blue said, "Look how he keeps fiddling with the suitcase. It's locked, buddy, stop worrying already. Here we go. He's reaching for that envelope Daddy handed him out on the sidewalk before they parted ways. I bet you five bucks he's itching to look inside."

"Not taking that bet."

"That's it. Come on, kid, open it. You know you want to look inside and run your greedy fingers through it."

The young man unsealed the envelope, peered inside, and thumbed the bills.

"Let's watch how he pays for his ticket and what name he puts on the ID tag," Blue said. "I'll ask Mason if he can take over the line and check him in for us."

A minute later, Blue returned. "We're all set with Mason. If you'll follow our boy to the gate, I'll hang back for the details on our traveler."

"You got it."

A few minutes passed as the line moved forward.

"Your guy's looking good," Sam said. "Paid for the ticket with those nice, clean bills."

"That's a good sign. Okay, he's off. I'll catch you at the gate."

Sam fell in behind, ten feet from the subject. As he walked along in silence, his mind kept retreating to his own problems, the worry over his friends and family, especially his nephew.

His mind ceased wandering when the man wearing the windbreaker stopped at a bank of phones, looked around, and unhooked a receiver. Sam made a note of the phone being used and the time of the call. He was sure Blue would want to subpoena the telephone company for phone toll information. When he looked up from his notebook, he saw someone familiar walking past. Francisco? *Holy shit.*

Sam spun around to take in the entire area, not believing what was happening, then turned back toward the subject still standing at the phone. He decided to ditch him, so he could catch up to Francisco. What would that psychopath be doing here? Right here at LAX! And now? They had just talked on the phone. He closed the gap between them in seconds and grabbed at Francisco's shoulder. When the figure turned around, it wasn't Francisco.

"Hey, man, what's your problem?" the stranger said, glaring at Sam.

"Sorry. I'm sorry; I thought you were someone else."

The man pulled free from Sam's grasp, shook his head, and walked away.

Sam wondered if he were losing his mind; he looked back in the black windbreaker's direction. He had finished his call and was on the move. Blue had also caught up and was trailing behind. Sam fell in step with his partner, hoping Blue hadn't witnessed his complete breakdown with the Francisco look-alike. When he said nothing, Sam felt instant relief. Thank God no one noticed him cracking up in the airport, surrounded by hundreds of people.

•   •   •

Hours later at the DEA airport office, Sam said, "Blue, we've finished the count. Here's a receipt to give to the courier—a total of $436,110."

"Looks like Roy gets his record," Blue said.

"Sam, you've got a call from HQ on line one," Rose said, her voice sounding from the secretary's station behind the cabinets.

"Okay, thanks." He patted Blue on the back before walking to his desk. "Nice work today, partner."

He brought the phone to his ear. "This is Sam."

"Special Agent Samuel Dahl?"

"Yes, that's me."

"Agent Dahl, I'm Antonio Estrella, a doctor on call with your agency headquarters. Do you have time to chat?"

CHAPTER THIRTY-TWO

Dr. Estrella, the shrink on call to DEA, seemed like a nice enough guy; and within minutes of Sam having answered the phone, they were on a first-name basis. Sam knew the doctor wanted to come across as comforting, trying not to make his call a big deal. It made sense, though, that headquarters had contacted him. Sam was surprised they hadn't already called him at home; after all, anyone carrying a gun was a serious issue—but a crazy man with a gun was a recipe for disaster.

He provided Dr. Estrella with the name of the therapist his personal physician had recommended.

"Have you made an appointment with the counselor, Sam?"

"Not yet, but I'm going to call her real soon."

"People are concerned about you. We care about you and want what's best for you and your well-being. Please tell me you're calling the counselor the moment we hang up. Can I count on you to do that, Sam?"

"Yes, I will—I promise. I'll do it right now."

Later, Sam stood alone in Terminal Two under the guise of working. He needed alone time.

As promised, he called the therapist before he left the office. Her name was Gloria, something-or-other. She said she was a friend of his personal physician and had been expecting a call. His first session was scheduled for Thursday the following week. Now his thoughts were laden with who he was and who he could be. His confidence was at an all-time low, not a good thing for a DEA agent who often relied on instinct and a peculiar intuition. Bill told him that building confidence in oneself took time and experience, but rebuilding confidence came from not living in fear of being wrong. In his present state, idle curiosity and wonder felt like a risk.

He leaned against a wall, tapping his head against it as people with busy lives streamed past him, oblivious to his frustration over his inability to do anything about the threats Francisco had made.

•   •   •

Two days had passed with no further communication from the madman. That part was fine, but Sam couldn't think of any solution to the predicament in which he found himself.

It was Wednesday. He wondered when he should tell his sister, and what about Natalie? She hadn't been mentioned, but anything was possible. And what about briefing the threat to other law enforcement authorities? He knew he couldn't walk in at the last minute and dump the monkey on someone else's back, leaving them no time to prepare. Bill was preaching patience, still professing they had time.

He wandered without purpose, except to escape and contemplate, then doing the only thing he could think to do. With a newspaper in hand, he dragged himself to a dark, empty gate, where he sat for an hour, turning pages, staring at headlines, and imagining a life in a different job, a different place, and in a different time.

He folded the newspaper, stood, and wandered back to the office. Several people shouted, "Sam!" when he walked in. He had forgotten about the party. It was the thirtieth of September, the last day of fiscal year 1987, and Roy had bought two dozen doughnuts to celebrate the fact that under his supervision, his office now held the record for the most money seized at LAX in a single year.

"Here he is, the man of the hour," Roy said. "You led the way." He bear-hugged Sam, slapping him twice on the back. "And thank you to everyone for making it happen."

Shouts of joy and hearty whooping sounded, facilitated by the sugar high from the doughnuts. Blue sat at his desk, looking like a little boy merrily munching on a chocolate-glazed cruller.

Screw it, thought Sam. He selected a simple glazed doughnut and took a seat next to his partner.

Blue said, "No one except Roy cares about the record. We're all just happy to have doughnuts in the afternoon. I'm going in for another. What about you?"

Sam held up his hand. "No, thanks." His mind drifted to Natalie. It was going on seven in the evening in Madeira Beach, and he wondered what she was having for dinner.

He lifted the phone receiver and entered a number.

"Bill Dunkirk speaking."

"Hey."

"Hey, yourself," Bill said.

"I'm going crazy with this waiting and nothingness."

Another round of his colleagues' shouting ensued. Sam turned his chair toward the wall.

"Sounds like a party. Was my invitation lost in the mail?" Bill said.

"You know cops and doughnuts; everybody's happy for a little while."

"Doughnuts? What's the cause for celebration?"

"Roy got his record for money seizures at LAX. Now he'll have something to reminisce about when he's sitting in his rocking chair back in Jersey."

"Since it's thirty September, I've been putting together an end-of-year report for the bosses," Bill said. "All our statistics: arrests, convictions, drugs, and money seized. You're an intelligent guy, Sam. Why is it our stats get better every year, yet the price of a kilo of coke keeps dropping?"

"Because we're on the Titanic, bailing water one tiny bucket at a time."

"Man, we're two cynics, aren't we? Let's focus on the good news for your group. LAX led the country in money seizures, except for Miami's airport."

"We'll never top those guys," Sam said.

"Don't feel bad; Miami is the funnel where the money goes before most of it heads south to Colombia. Makes it easier when you play all home games like the Miami office."

"An agent there told me that some days they don't go out into the terminals at all because they can't keep up with the paperwork," Sam said.

"That's pretty sad."

"What about Mérida, Mexico? There are bucks going in that direction, right?"

"They've got dollars going there too, but Mexico's not Colombia. At least not yet, but mark my words," Bill said, "all of our enforcement efforts and attention focused on the Caribbean Sea and South America will have unintended consequences."

"Such as?"

"As long as the enormous demand for coke from the U.S. exists, that stuff will find its way here, and my bet is, with the pressure on in Colombia, Mexican traffickers will take over control of the cocaine trade. The problem is, instead of being a continent away, they'll be right at our own back door. Those are unintended negative consequences."

There was a silence for a few seconds.

"I'll have to do something soon; start telling people about this thing with Francisco and his threats. You keep telling me to wait but—"

"Have patience, my boy. Things have a way of working out how they're supposed to. Do you remember when you were young, and you could go to a movie and forget about everything for the afternoon?" Bill said.

"Are you saying I should go to the movie theater to forget my troubles?" He heard Bill's merry laughter.

"I was around ten and can remember if I worked it right when the movie ended, I could hide in the corner behind a short row of seats, then pop back up when new paying customers started filing in. My record for most times without paying was four. They never caught me. The world is changing, though, because you don't have to go to the theater; there are stores popping up where you can rent movies to watch at home, and you don't have to hide to see them a second or third time."

"That's the only thing in life that's simpler."

There was another silence until Bill said, "I'm telling you to give this another day, and yes, go watch a movie. Maybe we'll have more to talk about tomorrow."

"I hope you're right," Sam said, and hung up. He spun around in his chair. The boxes of doughnuts were empty except for the remnants of glazed shards of sugar. The party was over and so was his workday. He stood, put his jacket on, and tapped his pocket to make sure he had his keys.

"Are you done for the day?" Blue asked.

"Yeah, I'm getting in the wind."

"Hang on. I'll walk out with you."

CHAPTER THIRTY-THREE

After a fitful night's sleep, Sam felt neither rested nor relaxed when he awoke for the last time that morning. The sky outside his bedroom window was still dark as he thought about the phone call he planned to make to his sister later in the day. Their conversation would create a difficult situation. Annie and her husband David didn't have the freedom to run away and hide; both worked, and they had a son in school too.

It was no use; his good friend sleep had become a stranger, and he knew it wouldn't be returning, at least not today. He raised himself out of bed. If he couldn't sleep, he wanted to do something productive.

He slid on shorts and a T-shirt, grabbed his keys, and jogged to the gym. The facility opened at five, so people who had to work early, or the insomniacs, could get in a good workout. Loading cast iron-plates onto the barbell, he performed repetition after repetition of various free weight exercises until he could do no more, then he turned his attention to the punching bag, which in his restless mind, took the form of Francisco. He pounded the heavy bag with rights and lefts, taking great satisfaction with every blow he delivered. When he could no longer lift his arms, he ran home.

Later, as he was pulling into the parking lot at work, his pager beeped—it was Chloe. He debated going to a pay phone for privacy's sake but opted to make the call from the office. Perhaps she wanted to say thanks again? It wasn't necessary. He scratched at his chin and remembered he hadn't shaved before coming to work. Without a doubt, this had been the longest work week of his life.

"Hello?"

"Hi, Chloe, it's Sam."

"Thanks for calling me back. I guess you're at work. Am I disturbing you?"

"Not at all," Sam said. "How are you?"

"I'm good; I mean, I'm getting better. It could be the anger I feel toward those people is helping me. Isn't that strange? The anger replaces the uncertainty, and somehow it keeps me focused," Chloe said. "Never mind. I'm just babbling."

"No, not at all. Your voice sounds stronger. That's good."

"Thanks. I was calling to say thank you for the lovely roses you sent. It was so kind of you to do that."

Sam's heart felt like it had fallen to the floor.

"They're so nice. I've never received blue roses before. I've been told that every color means something. When I called the florist, I asked what they meant. Do you know what the blue color signifies?"

He was stunned. When would the guy stop? It must be another of Francisco's reminders that no one was safe. Not even Chloe—and her parents were killed by his monstrous son.

"Sam? Hello?"

"Yes, Chloe, I'm here," Sam said. *At least, physically,* he thought, *I'm here, but I'd like to be standing over Francisco's body, emptying my pistol into his fucking brain.*

"I thought I had lost you for a second."

"No, I'm right here. You were talking about the color of the roses."

"Yes, they're so unusual. I was curious if you knew their meaning?" Chloe said.

When Blue entered the office, Sam looked away, so he wouldn't be interrupted, but his partner charged toward his desk, grabbed a notebook, and began writing as if he were attacking the pad with his pen.

"No, I, I can't, I can't say that I do."

"I'll bet you do. According to the florist, they signify mystery and intrigue. Only a secret government agent like you would send that color."

Blue shook the notebook at Sam.

"Chloe, can you hold on for one second?"

"Sure."

He read Blue's note while cupping his hand over the handset's microphone; and looked at Blue like a wild animal. "You're sure? This isn't funny if you're messing with—"

"I wouldn't do that to you," Blue said.

Sam held up his hand to his partner. "I'm sorry, Chloe. I'll be right with you. Can you hang on?" He didn't wait for an answer.

He barked at Blue. "Where did you hear this?"

"I was at the airport police station and saw it on their TV," Blue said. "This was the story running."

"Then, this is true? For sure?" Sam said.

"Sounds like it, my man. The news said the Mexican Federales verified his identity just hours ago."

"Yes, yes, yes!" He leaped toward Blue, hugging him. The handset's cord tugged on the phone, yanking it to the floor.

"Hey, Sam, you're on a call, brother," Blue said.

"Oh, yeah." He retrieved the phone and put the receiver back to his ear. "Chloe, I'm sorry; we got a bit of news."

"Whatever's going on there sounds exciting."

"They're saying Francisco Monzon, the father of Moncho, is dead. I'm not sure how yet, but that's the news."

"I guess that's justice," Chloe said.

"That's justice, all right. I'll let you go, but you were saying the flowers mean mystery, right?"

"That's what the florist said. I'm sorry I didn't call you sooner. I'm sure you were thinking what an ingrate I was."

"Why would I think that?" Sam said.

"I wasn't here on Monday for the delivery, so my neighbor accepted them for me. She forgot about them when she went out of town. She got back this morning and brought them over, so I called you as soon as I received them."

He couldn't stand still. Energy was pulsing through his body. "It's fine, Chloe. I didn't think a thing about it. You're so welcome. Thank you for calling."

"Sam, thank you. Bye-bye."

After hanging up the phone, Sam said, "Woo-fucking-hoo! Unbelievable!" He pounded his fist on the desk. "This is a great day. I want to see the story on TV." He looked at Blue. "Not that I don't believe you; I just want to see it for myself."

Blue turned to a sheriff's deputy nearby and said, "That's code for he doesn't believe me."

"No, I do, I do." The light on his phone flashed. He said, "I can't talk to anyone right now."

Rose emerged from her fortress behind the file cabinets. "That's Bill Dunkirk waiting for you. He wants to talk."

"Okay, Rose," Sam said. "I'll talk to Bill. Thank you."

"I guess you've heard the news." Sam stood behind his desk. "It's true, right?"

"Evidently." Bill's voice sounded reticent.

"You don't sound excited; this is great news."

"I'm sorry, it is great news," Bill said.

Sam sat. "Do you know how it happened?"

"As the story goes, there's been an on-again, off-again battle between Francisco and another drug organization in Mexico, and it appears it was on again late last night while he was having a sleepover at a lady friend's place. I gather he didn't cover his tracks well enough."

"The son of a bitch had it coming," Sam said.

"I'd say so."

He couldn't see Bill, but he could tell something was amiss. "What's the matter? You sound, I don't know, quiet."

"I would like to hear an official verification from someone other than the Mexican Feds," Bill said. "Whoever did it wanted him dead for sure. The reports are his body has more holes in it than Swiss cheese, and that includes his face."

Sam remained quiet, trying to process everything. The pieces of an intricate puzzle were begging to be fitted together. "They can always check his dental records because I can tell you he was one dapper dude, and he had beautiful teeth. Maybe they were God given, and he's never been to a dentist his entire life, but I'm betting he's got dental records somewhere."

"There's a thought," Bill said. "Listen, Sam, don't worry about this anymore. Your guy is done for. You can sleep tonight."

Sam weighed his next words with careful thought. "The night I was being held captive, Francisco told me he had been in contact with U.S. intelligence agencies. He said he helped the Mexican and U.S. governments battle rebel forces attempting to overthrow the Mexican government. Do you believe him?"

"Who can know?" Bill said. "There are many layers to the various efforts governments take to survive. Sometimes the lines can blur."

"But do you believe that?"

"Why not ask me if the Rams have a shot at the Super Bowl this year? I would say, of course, they have a shot. But a great shot? That's anyone's guess," Bill said.

Sam smirked. "You're not going to answer me, are you?"

"I already did."

"Maybe like Rafa was saying to me the other day, Francisco was breaking an unwritten rule by making threats against family and friends."

"Could be."

"Do you think an imaginary unwritten rule like that exists?"

"Don't be naïve."

"You don't think it's true?"

"It's like you're asking me if there's honor among thieves," Bill said, then sighed. "Listen to me, Sam. Are you relieved Francisco is dead? Are you happy your sister never has to know the story behind the flowers? And are you pleased she won't have to worry about her son? If your answers to those questions are yes, accept it and move on."

"I'll put it out to the universe that I appreciate whoever helped." Before he could say goodbye, the call ended. He put his jacket on.

"Are you going someplace?" Blue asked.

"Yes. Would you like to go back to the police station to watch the news?"

"Sure."

• • • •

Travelers packed the terminal, everyone hurrying to get to their destinations. Someplace new or old. Work or home. Sam wondered if the view from a mile above would look like a giant anthill that had just been disturbed.

The news had since moved on from Francisco to other stories. "Can I buy you a coffee instead?"

"No thanks," Blue said. "Doctor's orders. I'm limited to one cup a day, and it's the hardest thing I've ever had to do, except for listening to Roy talk about breaking the record for the last month."

"Bill told me to let it go and move on with my life," Sam said without explanation.

"But you can't."

"No, I can, I can." Sam stared off into space for a moment. "Do you ever think about who works for who in our own government?"

"Why?" Blue said.

"Well, have you ever wondered if there are people who work at one government agency but also work for another—like one of our spy agencies?"

"Not a lot, but my guess is since they have ordinary citizens in private industry on their payroll, they probably also have people at other government agencies tracking things too." Blue scratched at the side of his head. "Think about it: those kinds of agencies need eyes and ears, so what better way to spy than to have other government agencies do it for them."

"That's what I'm thinking too." Sam nodded. "Man, I don't know; I have the feeling this thing in Mexico didn't just happen. Of course, I'm happy and relieved, but—"

"But?" Blue asked.

"But I still wonder if this was happenstance or if someone pulled strings on this. Bill said reports are that a rival drug trafficker got to Francisco. I can't help but think someone out there whispered in somebody's ear and said you'd be doing us a huge favor if you took this guy out."

"Could be."

Sam could feel Blue studying him.

"Listen, I've been wanting to talk to you about something," Blue said. "Maybe it's time you should think about going home. Why don't you look at putting in for the supervisor job in Tampa?"

He turned to look at Blue, his mouth open in surprise. "That came out of nowhere. Are you trying to get rid of me?"

Blue chuckled. "No, not at all. But everyone needs change. Sometimes. At least think about it." He tugged on his jacket and smiled. "Something else I need to tell you. I've made it official; I submitted papers to retire in December."

Sam looked at him. "Damn, you kept that secret. I'm happy for you."

Blue said, "What this means is I won't be around to carry your ass at work anymore."

"When you put it like that, I guess not."

Blue put his arm around Sam's shoulder. "Come on. Let's head back to the office before Roy gets worried about us."

CHAPTER THIRTY-FOUR

His old life began to reemerge. Days had passed since the news about Francisco. The court hearing for Moncho played out as expected; the judge denied bail again, citing the flight risk and the seriousness of the charges. Then, if it wasn't Carl or Rafa telling him everything that had happened in Moncho's criminal case, it was someone else. Every update also served as a reminder of how much he missed Natalie. Past relationships had always been easy for Sam to forget. Things were different this time.

Determined to move on with his life, he had started an intense physical fitness regimen: running, lifting weights, punching on the heavy bag, and watching what he ate. After a hard workout at the gym, he prepared a healthy green salad with baked chicken on the side.

He turned on the television, looking to catch the playoff game between the Twins and the Tigers. Leaning back on the couch, he brought the first bite of chicken to his lips when the telephone rang. He debated whether to answer or let it go to the machine. After three rings, a sense of duty compelled him.

"Hello?"

"Good evening, Samuel."

He dropped his fork onto the floor. A wave of electricity raced through his chest.

"I hope my call hasn't disturbed a quiet evening for you at home."

"But you're supposed to be—"

"Dead? You mustn't believe everything you hear. I've been thinking about you. If we had been playing chess, I would have complimented your move. You almost checkmated me. Magnificent work. Absolutely magnificent."

"As much as I'd like to see you dead, that wasn't me who got those people to come after you."

"Don't fool yourself. No doubt you spoke to people about our last conversation, and it reached someone who can move mountains." Francisco paused, then gave a dry laugh. "I must apologize we cannot speak longer, but there are people here in Mexico who would use any means, legal or otherwise, to track me down."

"Look, Francisco, your beef is with me. Leave the innocent people out—"

"I want you to listen to me. Although the judge refused to reduce bail, I have spoken with an outstanding team of attorneys who represent my son, and they believe he has an excellent chance for an acquittal."

Sam said, "I wouldn't know."

"I would also like to remind you, Special Agent Dahl, the laws in your country apply to you as well. You cannot run around—what's your expression—willy-nilly, doing whatever you wish. What were you thinking when you broke into our residence? In your country, even lowly drug dealers have a reasonable expectation of privacy."

"Your son is a despicable person, a murderer, and you're no better—"

"I must go. If it puts your mind at ease, we shall call a truce. Someday, though, I promise you, we *will* become reacquainted."

He heard the click disconnecting the call. In an instant, the bastard had reinserted himself back into Sam's life. Francisco would never go away and there would never be peace in his life while that madman walked the face of the earth. He held the phone in his hand, gripping it so tightly, he thought he might crush it. His head rolled back onto the couch as he stared at the ceiling. He was no longer hungry, and he had no interest in the baseball game. A puzzling stillness surrounded him. Sam wondered what needed to be done, or more precisely, what *he* needed to do.

•   •   •

It was nine in the morning when he rolled into the World Trade Center garage. He parked his car, then walked by the bank of elevators on the first floor toward the Splendid Travel Agency at the south end of the building.

"Sam Dahl!" Melissa, the owner and operator of Splendid, said after he stepped inside. "Where have you been keeping yourself?"

"Hey, Melissa. Sorry I haven't been by in a while, I've been busy at LAX. How are you?"

She held her hands out. "I'm splendid, of course." Her huge smile forecast the next question. "What can I help you with?"

"I'd like to book some travel."

She raised her eyebrows. "Business or pleasure?"

"This is going to be a little of each, I think."

"Sounds intriguing. Where are you going?"

"Mérida, Mexico. I'd like to book a flight departing tomorrow."

"How exciting for you. Mérida is the cultural heart of the Yucatán Peninsula. Would you like me to arrange lodging?"

"Yes. I want to be in the San Pedro Uxmal area."

"You don't kid around. I like a no-nonsense traveler who knows what he wants." She typed information into the computer on her desk, then studied the screen for a moment. "I can put you on a great flight at ten in the morning with a connection through Mexico City."

Sam looked over his upcoming schedule on a pocket-sized calendar he kept in his jacket pocket. He was reminded of his first counseling session the following day; that would have to be ditched. "My schedule's clear," he said evenly.

"Wonderful, and what about a return ticket?" Melissa asked.

"Best if we leave it open-ended. I'll be in contact when I'm finished."

•   •   •

Sam slid the travel agency envelope into his jacket pocket and walked through the World Trade Center's first floor to find an unoccupied pay phone.

"Bill Dunkirk speaking."

"I got your page a while ago," Sam said. "I've been busy. What's up?"

"I've got news for you, but not the good kind."

"Oh?"

"Yeah," Bill said. "I've heard through unofficial channels that the man killed in Mérida wasn't Francisco. His face may be gone, but the dental records never lie. This dead man had no fixed dental prosthesis on the left lower jaw."

"What does that mean?"

"The real Francisco had bridge work. This guy didn't," Bill said.

"I see."

"You're not surprised?"

Sam said, "I'm down here on the first floor; we could talk in person. If you think you can sneak away from the office, I'll buy you breakfast at the Bonaventure."

"The Bonaventure Hotel? What's the special occasion?"

"Does there have to be a special occasion because I want to break bread with my friend?" he said. "Come on. I'll wait for you at the sky bridge."

They sat across from each other at the table. Neither wanted to be the one to speak first, but after ordering their breakfast and making small talk, Bill broke the ice. "I take it from your reaction, you already heard the news."

Sam waited until the server finished pouring their coffee. "I received a call at home last night from Francisco." He took a sip of coffee and looked across the table at Bill. "I have an unlisted number."

When Bill said nothing, it was Sam's turn to comment. "You're not surprised either."

Bill gave a slight shake of his head. "I'll give him this. The man has a long reach. What did he say?"

"That depends on whom I'm speaking with this morning—my friend Bill or a secret government agency?"

He smiled. "Let's say you're talking to plain old Bill this morning."

"Okay, plain old Bill, Francisco said he wants a truce for now. The way it sounded, he had a close call. He complimented me, saying I made a nice chess move. I told him I wanted him dead, but I couldn't take credit for it. It appears for now he's getting out of the flower delivery business."

"That's good news," Bill said. "I'll share something with you. Did you know Francisco Monzon is called the Gato by his friends? And his enemies too."

"Let me guess, they call him that because he has nine lives, like a cat."

"Yes, but there's another reason too."

"What's that?"

"Just like a cat, he likes to play with his prey before killing it," Bill said. "A friend told me he may seem like an elegant, sophisticated fellow, but that's surface stuff. Underneath, he's ruthless and possesses no conscience. This same friend told me this morning, quote, 'The world will be a better place without him.'"

"You can tell your friend I don't disagree," Sam said.

"I imagine we'll cross paths with Francisco again. One day, he's a useful tool for our government, the next day, he's just a tool. Who knows what may happen to the Gato?"

Their conversation paused when the server brought their meals.

Sam said, "Yeah. Who knows? He promised me someday we'd get reacquainted. Maybe we will." Sam removed the travel agency envelope from his pocket and placed it on the table.

Bill tilted his head to look. "I see somebody's been busy this morning."

"How's your bagel?" Sam said. "Did they give you enough butter and cream cheese?"

"I've got enough to work with here."

"The thing is, Bill, I can't live my life according to someone else's whims and fancies, and I'm damned tired of reacting to his every move. The Gato wants to play. That's fine; I'll grant him his wish, but next time, it'll be on my terms."

Bill eyed him for a moment before speaking. "Your mind made up?"

"Yes."

"Mérida?"

Sam nodded.

"Soon?"

"Tomorrow."

"And no chance I can talk you out of this?"

Sam shook his head.

"We never had this conversation." Bill removed a pen and pocket-sized notebook from his jacket. "Mérida's a lovely city. There's so much to see and do there. My friend who told me the Gato story is well acquainted with that part of Mexico. He can answer questions and help you with anything you require while you're there. Think of him as a very special tour guide in Mérida." Bill wrote something on a slip of paper and slid it across the table. "Goes by the name of Chaac. That's the number where you can reach him day or night."

Sam eyed the note. "He's reliable?"

"Like a Diehard battery. I'll let him know, so he'll be expecting your call."

"Got it," Sam said. "I wanted to speak with you about something else."

Bill spread butter on his bagel. "Okay."

"I'm thinking about putting in for the group supervisor job in Tampa. I think it'd be a good move."

"You told me you met someone there. So, what's driving this decision? Is it personal or professional?" Bill asked.

"Mostly personal, and that's the part I haven't resolved." He set his fork on his plate. "I've been wondering if she'd be interested in a man who had regular work hours. A man she could count on to be home for dinner. You know, a man she didn't have to worry about every time the phone rang."

"Those are all good questions for her," Bill said.

"Right, I need to talk to her." He stared down at the table.

"Hey."

Sam lifted his head and fixed his gaze on Bill.

"Before you talk to her, you need to ask your own self a question."

"What's that?" Sam said.

"Do you think you can be that kind of man?"

ABOUT THE AUTHOR

Although it was nothing like he remembered from the television shows he watched as a kid, Christopher Amato worked an entire career in federal law enforcement.

He wrote his first novel, *A Letter from Sicily*, a family saga inspired by his grandfather who was born in Sicily but relocated to the United States when he was a young child. He drew on his law enforcement background to write his second book, *Shadow Investigation*, a crime thriller set in the year 1987.

Christopher and his wife, both avid travelers, have trouble calling any one place home. Someday they hope to grow up and settle down.

You can check out his website at www.christopheramato.org.

NOTE FROM THE AUTHOR

Word-of-mouth is crucial for any author to succeed. If you enjoyed *Shadow Investigation*, please leave a review online—anywhere you are able. Even if it's just a sentence or two. It would make all the difference and would be very much appreciated.

Thanks!
Christopher Amato

We hope you enjoyed reading this title from:

www.blackrosewriting.com

Subscribe to our mailing list – *The Rosevine* – and receive **FREE** books, daily
deals, and stay current with news about upcoming
releases and our hottest authors.
Scan the QR code below to sign up.

Already a subscriber? Please accept a sincere thank you for being a fan of
Black Rose Writing authors.

View other Black Rose Writing titles at
www.blackrosewriting.com/books and use promo code
PRINT to receive a **20% discount** when purchasing.